Tiger Spring

Tiger Spring

Huu Uoc

Translated by Phan Thanh Hao
Adapted by our Veteran Friends

Deeds Publishing | Athens

Copyright © 2023 — Huu Uoc

ALL RIGHTS RESERVED—No part of this book may be reproduced in any form or by any electronic or mechanical means, including information storage and retrieval systems, without permission in writing from the authors, except by a reviewer who may quote brief passages in a review.

Published by Deeds Publishing in Athens, GA
www.deedspublishing.com

Printed in The United States of America

Cover and interior design by Deeds Publishing

ISBN 978-1-961505-07-0

Books are available in quantity for promotional or premium use. For information, email info@deedspublishing.com.

First Edition, 2023

10 9 8 7 6 5 4 3 2 1

To the memories of my faithful wife, my beloved comrades, and the mothers of Vietnam.

... For the Love of my Life.
The Late Madam Nguyen Thi Ly
An incense for thy wifey soul

How! You haven't arrived for Tet.
The times have passed of countless springs
I glance to the small garden where darling stood
The Galangal plant has shed its leaves ever since
The bed is wide, and the night is long
Darkness is thick, but your voice is silent
How! I now understood..."The day's
long as a hundred years."

… For my Comrades.
The "Souls" of Fallen Soldiers
The scent of fire

The scent of fire's not alike as burning corpse
… Foul, fishy, fragrant, ecstatic
The scent of fire is not of the flowers' perfume
… Infatuated with glamour
The scent of fire is not the smell of
suffocating burning grass
… The scent of fire has the breath of man
The scent of desirous life…

... For Mothers of Vietnam
My Mother
Lullaby of Flourish Grass

Evening dusk! Mother's come by her son
A green grave as round as a cradle
My son lies here, my son lies here,
Your comrade lies here ...
Gentle wind blows on summer noon,
Burden and grief weighty on one's shoulder
Lullaby, Lullaby, my son's sleeping ...

Foreword

When asked by Anh Nguyen to edit, publish, and endorse this novel by a former North Vietnam Army (NVA) soldier, I hesitated. As a 1966–1967 Infantry lieutenant serving with the United States 4th Infantry Division in the central highlands west of Pleiku, along the Cambodian border and in the jungles astride the Ho Chi Minh trail, I saw all NVA soldiers as my enemies. They were there to eliminate my fellow Soldiers and me, and we were there to eliminate them.

As in all wars, the tendency is to dehumanize your enemy and revert to a "kill or be killed" mentality. I was able to do that…until we captured one of them. At that time, my heart went out to him. I pictured myself as being one who had been captured and how scared I would be. As we took his weapons and inspected his personal belongings to see if he had any information we could benefit from, we found letters from home, pictures of loved ones, and other personal items, just as they would have found on us if our roles were reversed. These were young soldiers doing what their country told them to do, just as we were doing the same for our country and the people of South Vietnam.

With my curiosity aroused at this unique opportunity to look into the life of an NVA soldier and his comrades, I started reading. The more I read, the more I was drawn into the story. Their lives were very similar in some ways to us, and vastly different in other ways. They were committed for the duration of the war. Their families and friends were subject to bombing attacks by American planes in North Vietnam. We were in Vietnam for about a year and returned to our safe homeland to resume our lives.

I encourage my fellow Vietnam veterans, their family and friends, and all others who read this to keep an open mind and realize these NVA soldiers were much like we were…doing the job their country sent them to do.

Lt. Gen. Hal Moore, who commanded the first major battle in the Vietnam War, met with the NVA commander on the battlefield in the Ia Drang Valley in 1993 to relive that battle from November, 1965. That effort started the thawing of hostilities between the veterans of the two armies. While memories will never go away, hopefully *Tiger Spring* will give American veterans a better understanding of those from North Vietnam we once met on numerous battlefields in Vietnam in the days when we were all young Soldiers.

Deeds Not Words,
Bob Babcock
CEO/Founder Deeds Publishing
Infantry Officer in Vietnam—1966–1967

Preface

Sad And Beautiful Love Songs
Nguyen Quang Thieu
Chairman of Vietnam Writer's Association

During the war and after the reunification of Vietnam, there have been thousands of novels written about the US-Vietnam war. Therefore, it is that those who continue to write about this war face a huge challenge in trying to find a unique way to write about the war. If they can't, then their books leave no new impressions on their readers and just sink and disappear into a huge vat of war literature.

Huu Uoc approaches the war in a way many contemporary writers have either wanted to do or were uncertain how to do. In *Tiger Spring*, Huu Uoc has found his own way. It is what I ricall 'a war within a war'. In all previous literary works, the US-Vietnam war was depicted as fierce, a war that took extraordinary will to wage, a war of infinite sacrifices for peace and for reunification. Besides recounting all the hardships of war: hunger, bomb raids, deaths, and tragedies like all the other wars on earth, Huu Uoc has created a space, a space in between those bomb raids, bullets, and death in which he has inserted another kind of war—a war destructive of human nature.

The Vietnamese soldiers left their warm homes and came to the front carrying an unbreakable ideal; they fought selflessly for peace of the country. But they still carried an eternal human beauty which no weapons could grind down. They were not robots for destruction, they were human beings. And it is only when human beings orientate to the most human characteristics that humanity exists.

Tiger Spring is the first war novel that I have read which accurately depicts love, the strong sexual desires experienced by those who were close to death. Love and sex in fact occupy a large part of the entire novel. The soldiers in *Tiger Spring* have to fight two wars at the same time: a war against the enemy aggressors, and a war against their own humanity. The enemy of humanity is that which tries to deny or oppose human nature. An armed aggressive war can last for tens or hundreds of years. But the war to protect one's humanity never ends.

Does depicting the "most human" issues of love between men and women and the instinctive sexual desire that nature has given to human beings in an epic war story a betrayal of the ideals of that war? Does it eliminate the heroic qualities of the liberation soldiers? This is a very important question that Huu Uoc had to ask and answer for himself.

We can say that depicting the love of a man and a woman, especially under the climax of sexual desires that can occur in the face of death on the battlefield, can lead us to one of two choices: either the writing shines an honest light on the soldiers' true and valued humanity, or it drowns it in a swamp of cowardly sensuality. This is an extremely challenging issue for writers. When the writer deals with it and pushes it to the climax, it's as if the writer has to walk between the fragile line of beauty, love, and sensuality like walking on a tightrope between two tall buildings. Reading through these situations honestly made me feel both scared and nervous. But I feel Huu Uoc succeeds fully in his task.

Please read this novel and come to your own conclusions. I would take one example from the story: when the Political Commissar Mao catches Hoan and Lan red-handed when they were making love in the forest, the moonlight shining on their naked bodies, on the beauty of their human joining. That beauty stunned Political Commissar Mao and the others accompanying him, so much so that he burst into tears. A most terrible "spiritual battle" was taking place in the Political Commissar's mind. Is it a sinful act of soldiers during wartime or is it a beauty of human love? And fortunately for readers, it is a very human beauty we see: the love between men and women. That beauty has turned all these seemingly mundane external acts into holiness.

Due to military discipline imposed on the armed forces on the battlefield, Political Commissar Mao has to punish these "two soldiers". But he did not punish that "couple" who were in love. And in his soul, the beauty of a man and a woman making love to each other under the splendid moonlight in the very place where death always lurks forever shines in his memory. That image proves the undying nature of love. And it, I think, is a great secret of humanity as evidenced by all the vicissitudes of its history. It was because of that "secrecy" that could not be extinguished in the soldiers' souls that brought them to total victory.

And also because of that "secrecy" that the liberation soldiers took care of, with a true empathy and great selflessness, a captured American soldier, the then No. 1 enemy in the battlefield. The detail about the captured American soldier is a minor section of the book, but it helps clarify the other stories of the soldiers' humanity. Even during the war and especially afterwards, Americans keep sincerely trying to discover how Vietnamese soldiers could win over an army whose troops were equipped with the most sophisticated and advanced weaponry in the world.

American military scientists, historians, and writers who have read captured diaries from Vietnamese soldiers have come to realize that in all that writing, what was always expressed was the love of their homeland, the love between young girls and young men, and their dream of ending the war so that they could go back home to marry, have children, and till their land. Even when carrying a gun to fight against the enemy, their dream of living a true human life was their strongest emotion.

The main message in *TIGER SPRING* by Huu Uoc is to reveal the greatest quality of humanity. The Vietnamese soldiers who appear in this novel were not destructive machines, but men and women who fought for that beautiful dream.

Tiger Spring

The war is over, victories and defeats, hatred, and pain will disappear over time. But the whispers of love, the kisses, the love-making under the moonlight, the peaceful dreams in the dark forests covered by the shadow of Death will never die. All echoed as sad and beautiful love songs. That's the clearest sound that stayed in my ears when I left the last pages of *TIGER SPRING*.

Ha Dong, the days of social distance.
NQT

Reflections from a Friend

Today, I remember Huu Uoc as a retired Lt. General who honors the living. I remember his sorrows and comradeship for the memories of the countless souls of fallen soldiers. The strength of his character and his appreciation for life became the wisdom for his existence.

He may have won a few battles on the Truong Son Mountain range, but he lost the justice war at home on the Red River of Hanoi. His unjust days in the penitentiary have educated him on how fragile life and love are. Three years later, he was presumed innocent by the Reformists. They restored his glory days and let him become the voice for justice of his beloved Country.

In many ways, he has lived his life for his belief, his family, his comrades, and the people of Vietnam. He is a great warrior and a true patriot that can be perceived through the spirits of his poems and music to whom he is dedicated…

…In The Memories of his Faithful Wife, his Beloved Comrades, and Mothers of Vietnam.

Anh Nguyen
Peachtree City, Georgia. USA

1

Finally, the 26th Reconnaissance Company arrived at the headwaters of Tiger Spring, the starting point of the Ho Chi Minh Trails in the Truong Son Mountains, close to where Route 9 bisected Quang Tri Province from east to west. It was morning, the sun glimmering through the leaves and glistening on the dusted faces of the young soldiers.

The company, little more than 100 soldiers, spread out along the rock-strewn stream bank. Leaving their rucksacks, weapons, and sacks of rice on the rocks, the soldiers rolled up their pants and waded into the stream, scooping up water with both hands and splashing it on their faces. As they waded out, they could see dozens of white fish streaming down the current in the middle of the stream; the sight made them cheer. One soldier quickly stripped naked and jumped into the deeper water in the center of the stream. In moments, the rest of the men had shed their uniforms and followed, going after the fish.

They'd only managed to seize a few when a cobra the length of a chogi pole appeared, undulating through the water. The snake raised its hooded head out of the water and opened its mouth as wide as a spreading hand. "Snake...snake!", some of the terrified soldiers yelled as all the men swam frantically back to the bank.

Worried that the poisonous snake would attack his soldiers, Company Commander Tuan, called "The Beard," by his men, quickly pulled his belt off and without taking the time to further undress, jumped into the stream, swimming after the cobra. When he was within reach, he repeatedly struck the snake's head with the belt, raining blows on it nonstop. As the snake's head lowered, Tuan leaned forward and grabbed it just below the head with one hand, then swam back. As he stood up on the bank, the young soldiers, still naked, shaking their heads, stared at him and the biceps-sized snake that had wrapped itself around his belly.

Tuan waved at Huu, his liaison to the next company in the column. "Get me the rice wine canteen, the mess-tin in the back pocket of my rucksack, and a dagger."

As soon as Huu returned, Tuan unwrapped the snake from his belly, still clutching just below its head with one hand, and, with the other hand, stabbed it. As its blood began to flow out, he ordered Huu to collect the snake blood in his mess-tin, and then poured in a third of a bottle of the wine. When it was full enough, he put it on a rock. And grinned. "Drinking wine mixed with snake bile will relieve bone ache, detoxify and stop malaria," he explained to the watching soldiers. He slid the tip of the knife around the snake's neck and then peeled the skins off the snake until its body gleamed bare and white as a new, young, banana stalk.

He passed it to Huu. "Cut it into pieces, salt it and put it in the mess-tin. It'll make us a nice dinner."

Huu held the body of the cobra by its tail. For the first time, Tuan had a chance to appreciate the size of the bicep-thick creature. Even though the snake had been beheaded, its long, skin-stripped body kept writhing. Tuan looked at Huu, noticing for the first time how fragile-looking and baby faced the boy was; his body, even around his pubis, was nearly hairless. He chuckled. "You just starting to grow a bush, boy? How old are you?"

The other soldiers around them giggled.

"I'm seventeen years old," Huu mumbled, flushing.

"Why did you join the army so early?"

"My father is a District Chairman; it was what he wanted. When I went for my recruitment physical, I weighed only 42 kilograms. My mom didn't want to let me go, but my dad pressured the Recruitment Board to take me. I'm my mom's favorite, since I'm the youngest. She was terrified that I'd be killed; she wouldn't stop crying. But my dad said I am too thin, she was afraid that I might be killed in the battlefield, and she cried a lot. My father told her: "If he dies, it will be an honorable death for our family and the whole clan: for the Fatherland, for the Party, for the Nation. Our family is a revolutionary family, so we can't be afraid to make any sacrifice.""

Tuan laughed. "Say, are you afraid of death?

"I don't think about death, so I don't fear it."

Tuan patted Huu's shoulder. "Then you truly are from a strong Communist family. Come on, pass me the snake blood and bile…"

He shook the mess-tin of snake wine. The Beard took a sip. His eyes dilated and his face took on a glow. The snake blood wine stuck on his mustache and the unshaven stubble on his chin. When he wiped his mouth with his hand, it also came away covered with snake blood.

He turned to the soldiers: "Anyone want to have a drink with me?"

The soldiers all stared at him fearfully and shook their heads. He spotted Mao, the Political Commissar, and waved him over. "Mao, Mao…come here!" He tried to pass the mess-tin to Mao, but Mao smiled and waved it away.

"You're truly a hero to gulp this down, it stinks—get it away from me. Listen, get your clothes changed, we have to get out of here. This is a key target for American aircraft…" He passed Tuan a new uniform.

"Attention, about face," Tuan commanded as he took the garments. Everyone, including the political commissar, turned around. Tuan took his wet clothes off, dressed hurriedly in dry ones, and then shouted orders: "Get your gear ready, quick time, march in one line. Platoons One and Two take the point. The 4th Battalion is locked in behind us."

It seemed to the young soldiers, the feeling of marching toward the battlefield made them very excited. Burning and olding guns to fight against invaders. To liberate he South become a reality that made song: *"Soldiers of Vietnam, we go forward, with the one will to save our country. Our hurried steps are sounding on the long and arduous road… we swear to tear apart the enemy and drink their blood. Hastening to the battlefield. Forward! All together advancing! Our Vietnam is Strong's eternal."*

And *"To liberate the South, we determine to advance, to exterminate the American imperialists, and destroy the coun-*

try's sellers. Oh, bones have broken, blood has spilled, the hatred is rising high, our river and mountain have been separated for so long. Here, the sacred Mekong River..., here, the glorious Truong Son Mountain are urging us to advance to kill the enemy. Shoulder to shoulder, under a common flag! Arise, oh...brave people of the South!" As a seasoned warrior of many battles, looking at the fiery, eager faces of the young soldiers, Tuan didn't feel at ease, but a deep anxiety arose in the bottom of his heart. He wondered what would those immature-faced young soldiers be like facing the fierceness, monstrosity, barbarism of war? As a bunch of young sheep, would they still keep their bravery and ideals to endure death, hardship, disease, and countless challenges and obstacles in the deep jungles? Having to overcome the challenges under bomb raids and fighting himself, Tuan always trusted his soldiers, since most of them, the young Vietnamese soldiers, were brave, willing to sacrifice and suffering hardships.

But to get that spirit, they had to be trained, to endure the challenges under bombing raids, the challenges between life and death without having any fantasy. However, at the moment, he let the aura of Pham Tien Duat's poem: *"How beautiful of the road to the battlefield's in this seas*on" sparkled on the young sweaty faces.

Tuan coldly looked at Hao: "As liaison agent of Truong Son trail, overcoming so many challenges, why are you scared that much?"

Hao calmed down: "I am still immature...how can't I be scared, Commander?"

Tuan did not answer. He stared blankly at the scene.

Several thousand meters had been completely destroyed by the B52s. A thick pall of smoke still hung over the burning tree trunks, darkening a corner of the sky. The soil was filled with three-rows of horizontal and deep streaks, one was about 20 to 25 meters apart, stank with a suffocating odor left by the explosions and the corpses of soldiers that littered on the ground, their blood and bones mixed into the soil.

The late teenage soldiers who'd marched so enthusiastically to the battlefield but who had never seen the result of bombs exploding, now seeing with the gruesome images arms, legs, and smashed and Many of them at the sight. , and fear.

The moving through that dreadful, bomb torn tried to cover their mouths with their hands but the sound of their agonized sobbing burst out loudly. They presaged for the first time that random death might seize them, and they moved now as if staggering between life and death, suddenly sensing their own fragile mortality.

Looking at a disheveled, brainless, dissolved, tattered troops marching like lifeless ghosts, Tuan couldn't hold an ungovernable rage. He turned to his troops, pulled his K59 pistol out of its holster and fired three rounds into the air. "I'll shoot the next bastard I see crying," he yelled, pointing his gun at the air and fired: "Bang, bang, bang", terrified the young guys.

All the moans and cries were silent. The young soldiers stopped weeping, they shrunk into different groups, leaning against each other to warm themselves. Angrily, Tuan jumped on a high stone, glancing painfully at the weary, fearful faces of his soldiers, he heavily yelled: "Comrades, as revolutionary soldiers, we have determined to go to the battlefield to fight against the enemy and no one wants to choose to die but all of us must understand that having been in the war, one might sacrifice himself. Look at our comrades lying dead in pain in these B52 bomb sites by the Americans, you know, death spared no one. Who are commanders, who are soldiers…Who still has his whole corpse, who was torn apart?

"Death comes fairly, regardless of age or position, look, in this carpet bombing, how many of our comrades were sacrificed? We don't know, but we must know how to keep our hate towards the American enemy, and we must not be afraid of them, not be afraid of scarifying. The enemy must pay the debt of blood so that we can exist, and to exist in the battlefield, we must know how to love each other, without loving each other, without protecting each other, we can't survive.

"Our comrades' blood and bones are still lying there, we should gather even a handful of flesh, a piece of bones for a proper burial, and then light-up the incense-sticks on the makeshift memorial in the Truong Son's trail-side, praying so that our martyrs would be less cold and lonely!"

And right then, Commander Tuan and Political Commissar Mao rolled-up their pants and rushed to the bomb craters, followed by the soldiers. Together they gathered all the pieces of the remains of corpses, placed them on the stretchers, and carried to a newly dug large grave for a mass burial of unknown soldiers.

Huu passed Commander Tuan a handful of burned

incense-sticks, a thick smoke covering their faces. Trembling and staggering, it took time for Tuan to put the incense-sticks on the mass burial. Kneeling down in the front of the mass grave, he bowed three times, his face twisted painfully, wet with tears, and emotionally choking, "Here we are, the cadres and soldiers of the 26th Police Reconnaissance Company, we respectfully would like to burn incense to pay tribute to the heroes and martyrs who have sacrificed for our Fatherland. You are killed by American bombing raids; we have gathered your remains to be buried alongside with your comrades in this mass burial. As the sacred souls you are, please bless us to spare the barbarous bomb raids from the enemy. Bless us to be strong enough to kill as many Americans as possible to avenge you. Bless us to win over the enemy and be home safely..."

Suddenly, in the hazy vastness of evaporating bombs smoke covering the gloomy and dreary forest, a horrible chirping cry calling out to the horde. Vultures and crows were attracting from the smell of human corpses and blood. The vultures and crows in Truong Son jungle weren't afraid of living people, they even snuggled into the groups of soldiers covering under raincoats, stretching their rotten beaks, sensing, and pecking where the wounds and bleeding parts of their bodies were. The young soldiers cried out loud in pain and exasperation, trying to catch them, and smashed them on the ground. Strangely enough, the crows and vultures living here were also used to the bombs and death like the soldiers, they prey on the dead ones and are still struggling, competing with others for food, even though they might be killed by predators.

Looking at the bunch of crows and vultures jubilantly fighting and tearing the remains of the dead corpse's soldiers laid on the ground, painfully, Tuan couldn't hold his tears. But he immediately wiped them away, ordered the company to march forward, staying away from the bloody hungry birds. It seemed as though even Tuan himself could no longer tolerate the barbarian and the brutality of war anymore...but he had to move-on. Tuan and the soldiers of his Company bid farewell to a friendly army medical unit. Then, hand-in-hands, they silently matched forward, no one saying a word.

2

That night, the Truong Son's sky poured down heavy rain, and the rains saturated its ground. In the soldier's bunkers, although the wall was enforced with tree trunks and the roof supported by trusses and poles, the rains and the floods swept away everything standing in its way. A mixture of soils and mud turned the bunkers into a field of thick dark brown water.

Even in the large size bunker which was dug into the mountainside, made for the Company's cooking kitchen, was flooded by the rainfalls from the top of the mountain that filled up to one's chest. However, during this critical times, the military cooking staffs turned-out to be a savior. They had used tree branches , and cooked several big pots of rice for each platoon. They portioned the half-raw and half-done cooked rice into small aluminum containers for distribution.

Not to get entangled in soaking wet army clothes, the soldiers stripped naked like a chrysalis, one lined-up behind the other, pushing on the guy's back and butt, holding the rice's pot on a slippery slope. They still fell-down on top of each other and spilled the rice on the ground. The brothers, being hungry and cold, told each other to scoop-up the fallen rice, and tried to swallow it instead of starving,

That evening, Hao, the liaison comrade for Truong Son theatre, and Huu went down to the kitchen to get rice and water for the Company Commanders, Hao walked in the front, telling Huu to look at the phosphorus light on the top of his hat to follow. But it was showering, the roads were steep with slippery rocks. Hao stumbled and fell, and the military mess kit flew away. Only Hao's ration and two tin water bottles remained. So, then the ration has to be divided for four people: Commander Tuan, Political Commissar Mao, Hao, and Huu.

Each of them got a small handful of squeezed rice. The hunger Huu and Hao's eyes see dizzying stars, exploding fireflies, and they were exhausted. Tuan, the Company Commander, told Huu to get some raw rice in the reserved sack stored in his backpack and gave each person a fistful. He instructed them by chewing a small pinch of rice slowly with a few grains of salt.

Although in life Hao, Huu, and even Political Commissar Mao from time to time had a stomach full or half-full with rice meals now and then, they had never ever smelled the great aroma of rice like that night. Having consumed that handful of rice, they were awakened, sweating from the warm air, their bodies less shaky when walking, and their lips stopped tickling. Solving the hunger problem by eating raw rice was passed on from the company commander to all the platoons, thus, all were settled.

When it stopped raining and the wind calmed down,

Huu Uoc

the soaking wet clothes on their bodies began to dry out. The young soldiers, many of whom had been suffering from ringworm in the past, now encountered the same conditions, once again catching the symptoms. Ironically, ringworm pimples all "grow" in the intimate area of the groin and the penis. The patient felt itchy, scratched the pimples with his hand, and the rash continued to spread gradually into larger and larger rings with raised, bumpy, and scaly borders.

With Huu, the ringworm grew a rash in bunches covering the penis, making his penis swollen, red, and itch crazily. He couldn't wear pants, stood naked, and kept holding the penis with his two hands, closing his eyes, groaning, jumping up and down until he was so exhausted that he lay down, rolling on the ground. Then comrade Hao had to take the small bottle of iodine tincture to pour onto Huu's penis and groin. Huu screamed out: "Oh no...my penis is burning, Hao! You burn it. Oh dear, I am so painful. I am dead! Hao!"

Comrade Hao laughed and said, "Endure a little pain with iodine when applied, but it will relieve the itch right now! Don't worry, your bird's not burning, and it's not dead. Tomorrow when you see a young girl, the bird will be alive again, immediately..."

Having been treated with a smear of iodine tincture for a while, Huu experienced that the itching was gone. He had t exhausted, his limbs trembling. The Company Commander Tuan gave him a cup of milk to drink, and he really felt like a dead man being resurrected. Huu kept wondering and couldn't sleep, his hands were under the back of his head. He closed his eyes and pensively, perhaps for the first time in his life, Huu was thinking seriously as a mature adult, far from the outcry of his young days before enlisting.

***

Huu's father was a District Chairman. All three of his brothers were students in different universities, so, even though he was the youngest, his father insisted that he enlist in the army. When his mother found out, her heart wrenched with worry. She could hardly sleep at night and lost her appetite. Every night she would cry silently for hours. When her husband came home from the office, she clasped her hands and bowed to him: "Our youngest is small and fragile; how could you make him join the army. He'll be killed on the battlefield."

"You understand nothing about war, woman. Don't question my decision."

"You remember how it was under the French occupation, when this whole place was part of the battlefield. I had to dodge bullets and live underground for months. Don't you remember how many times I was nearly killed? What don't I understand? I know what war means: it means death. It means bombs and bullets. This whole family has fought in the revolution. As your wife, I understand what happens on a battlefield quite well! Even during the land reform, I hid a pot of gold for the revolution and never took a single coin for my children, even when they were suffering from hunger and hardship…. Do you think that means I don't understand sacrifice and what it is to be a revolutionary? Let me ask you another question: what do I get for being a revolutionary?"

All at once, she could no longer control her anger, and began screaming and stomping her feet, "I have been stupid all my life, and now I'm going to stop being stupid, do you hear me? I don't want any child of mine to be killed, that's all. As for you, you'll do whatever you want. The revolution is yours, you men, but what do my children and me get from it? You men get the glory, the power, the right to speak, to right to enjoy eating, to right to father people on earth. Revolution and life…nothing is equal to one's life. I absolutely refuse to let my son to go to the battlefield, and that's the end of it!"

"Do you want to destroy me," the District Chairman roared. "Three of your four sons are in universities. As a District Chairman, if I don't let any one of my four sons serve in the army, how can I be a leader? If I send everyone else's children to the battlefield while all my sons go to universities, how can I even talk to people? Who will respect me, who can I lead, tell me?"

He staggered inside, took a pistol out of his briefcase, and pointed it at his temple as tears ran down his cheeks. "If you don't let your son join the army," he screamed, "I will blow my brains out. Do you want me and your three other sons to continue to live, but to live in humiliation?"

Witnessing his parents' fierce quarrel, Huu rushed out and removed the pistol from his father's hand.

"Look," his father continued, "our three elder sons are naive and gentle, so I got them into universities. As for

Huu, don't worry, he is cunning, nimble and clever, and sure to survive."

Huu calmed his mother down: "Mom, all the families in this village have sons in the army, and not all who go to the battlefield will die. Listen to father. Let me go, I am cunning and clever enough to avoid death. If I don't enlist, it will humiliate the whole clan, and I am sure father would lose his District Chairman position. Even if I didn't enlist, I'd still have to leave this village out of shame, Mom!"

Huu, as a District Chairman's son, understood clearly how shirking his duty would bring shame and ignominy to the family. Perhaps the valiant blood of his ancestors still sizzled in his veins. Maybe he'd inherited something in his DNA that drove him to go to the battlefield, to perform glorious feats of arms. He was eager to follow in the footsteps of the heroes, the warriors whose daring lives and glorious deaths had been taught to him at school every day, and who he saw idolized by society.

The image of Pavel Korchagin in *How the Steel Was Tempered* by Nikolai Aleksyevich Ostrovsky stood in his mind as the shining example of a worthy life. Huu dreamed of living such a life as his hero Pavel, a stormy life that would challenge, temper, and mature him, even though he had no idea of what being in war would really be like. In that way, he knew he was like many young people, filled with frivolous notions and dreams. But he also knew that a young man who wiggled out of his military service or deserted would be shunned and disgraced, and he knew that such turpitude would extend to the whole clan and family.

In his own village, he saw how at 7 am every day,

Huu Uoc

those who were too afraid of dying to join the army or who'd deserted had to form lines and run around the village, led by the Communal Police Chief, and shouting: "One… Two… One… Two… Three. If everyone was like me, we'd lose the country! One… Two… One… Two… Three. If everyone was like me, we'd lose the country!"

Perhaps, for the peasants in Huu's village, their understanding of what it meant to be proud of the fatherland was abstract, something they didn't think about or imagine day-to-day. But the shame of a family having a son too cowardly to join the army or who'd deserted from the battlefield, meant that their family members would not dare to look up to greet anyone when they stepped outside their houses. That humiliation would follow them everywhere, haunting them, clinging to them whenever they sat down to have a meal or lay down to sleep, every day, every night, year after year, without end.

The very afternoon Huu received his enlistment papers at his school was the same moment when everybody got the sad news that President Ho Chi Minh had died. The farewell party Huu's 10D grade classmates planned for him, with one friend contributing a grapefruit, others bringing boiled peanuts, ears of corn, and a few apples, was immediately cancelled. President Ho's passing shocked and deeply pained the whole nation. Everywhere people wept uncontrollably. Huu shared the same feeling of shock, grief, and pain, but he also felt that the occasion of Uncle Ho' death marked the most auspicious moment for him to join the army. He hurriedly rode his bicycle home.

His father had been chopping vegetables to feed the

pigs, standing over a chopping board, bare-chested and in his shorts, looking like an ordinary peasant. It was a breezeless day and his father's back had been greasy with sweat. Huu quickly leaned his bicycle against the wall, and rushed to him, his eyes filled with tears. "Dad, Uncle Ho is dead!"

His father stopped chopping and looked up, his eyes blazing. "Liar," he roared. "Who told you that?" Huu paled, frightened. His father raised the knife and brought it down savagely on the board. A piece of the ironwood flew off into a bush.

"Tell me who told you that Uncle Ho is dead? There is No Way that Uncle Ho may have died! I've just heard an announcement by the Party Central Committee saying only that Uncle Ho was rather ill. I was on duty in the District and have just got home..."

Cowed, Huu didn't dare to come closer to him. His father kept screaming: "Come, tell me. When did Uncle Ho die? Tell me. Where did you hear that? Have you been listening to the enemy's radio broadcasts?" As if those words made him suddenly remember, he muttered: "Oh dear, I forget to turn the radio on. Turn it on right away!"

It seemed to Huu that his father was in shock, unable to accept the truth burning inside him like a giant furnace. Huu burst into tears. "It's true, dad," he stammered. "Uncle Ho has passed away. It was announced in my school, and everybody is setting up a mourning altar for Uncle Ho...."

His father stood silently for a while, then covered his face with both hands and wept, his tanned brown shoulders shaking. Uncle Ho's death was an unbearable shock. For people such as him, life-long followers of the Party and

Uncle Ho, their leader's death was unthinkable, something nobody dared to imagine. Shaking with grief, he wiped away tears with his muddy hands, and glowered at the frightened son in front of him. Without warning, he seized the heavy ironwood board and threw it at Huu's face. Huu had time to dodge and jump into the spinach-clogged water.

Hearing her husband yelling and the loud splash of something falling into the pond, Huu's mother panicked. She grabed a hot brand from the kitchen and rushed out, screamed at her husband. "What have you done? If he dies, who will you live with? What kind of husband...."

The sad news about Uncle Ho's death was real. It was announced by the Central Committee of the Workers' Party of Vietnam, broadcast on the Voice of Vietnam. As he listened to his Chinese Xiangmao Transistor, Huu's father continued to weep, whether he was sitting or lying down. That evening, nobody ate dinner. It was not only Huu's family. Every other family in the village wept in mourning at the enormity of the loss of Uncle Ho, the father of the nation.

That night, Huu's father even forgot the fact that his youngest son was about to go to the war. He cleaned the family altar and wiped off the frame containing Uncle Ho's photo, fastening a dignified border of black cloth around it. He spent the whole night creating a beautiful, richly decorated altar for Uncle Ho, and then burned incense-sticks and worshipped the late President.

As Huu and his mother looked at him, they couldn't stop weeping as well. Huu understood that besides mourning Uncle Ho, her tears sprung from her awareness that he, her youngest son, was to depart to the war, and she did not know when oo if he would return. She quietly took the chicken she had steamed the day before and wrapped it into a banana leaf that she warmed over the charcoal fire. "I have nothing to give you before you leave but this bit of chicken," she told her son.

Huu packed the chicken into his knapsack and then forgot all about it. But later, whenever he missed his home, he remembered the day of his enlistment, and his father, who like the Vietnamese people themselves had lived his life like Uncle Ho, on his own terms, accepting the challenge to survive and prevail, in spite of continual, epic strife, loss, and tragedy.

That was the Huu's situation on the day he joined the army.

As with numerous other young soldiers who had gone into the army as a matter of course, Huu hadn't examined his own life, the way he wanted to live it, the way he should live it, his future if he should survive the war. Like most of his comrades, he hadn't considered deeply what was gained in this risking his life in the fight against the Americans. Like everyone else, he had grown up with the sound of the slogans made by his elders and by propagandists ringing in his ears. The way young solders thought about the war was simple and direct. They must fight the American invaders to save the Fatherland.

The blood in their veins boiled with anger against the invaders that made them willing to leave their bamboo fenced villages, leave the plow and the water buffalo, the fish, and the shrimp in the muddy and marshy pond, to go to the battlefield. That was it. They were enflamed by the Party's idealism, eager and excited to take up the gun and fight against the Americans, filled with an undying pride and a desire to live and die for the Fatherland.

In reality, before they enlisted, few of the young men like himself could have imagined what war and combat was like, what the Americans and the Saigonese soldiers were like, how fierce the fighting would be, what sacrificing one's life for the country truly meant. But a flood of patriotism cascaded through every small alley, down every street, in every village and young men from everywhere volunteered in droves to go to the front, to become part of the eternal history of their nation and its fight for salvation.

***

On the day of his enlistment, Huu had travelled to Hanoi from his village in Hung Yen province. He had been to the capitol a few times since American aircraft started raiding North Vietnam. When there was no bombing, Hanoi seemed as calm and peaceful as a village. A capital populated by people from everywhere, but everybody seemed relaxed and serene with the rustic charm, kindness and familiarity of country people. The streets were lined with trees, and on the corners people sat in the sidewalk teashops, drinking tea, smoking pipes, chatting and laughing without worry. Even when the war intruded in the form of American bombs, they sang to drown out the explosions. "Do everything to defeat the American invaders" was the slogan heard in all the streets and alleys, ringing in millions and millions of minds and hearts, the people's anger welding them into one.

Huu had witnessed the stone and iron will of the Hanoians; he knew that no power, no bombs, could defeat them. That spirit was indescribable. At first, Huu had thought it would only be found on the battlefield, among the young fiery revolutionaries like himself. In Hanoi, he heard heroic revolutionary songs encouraging the people's spirit to fight against the Americans echoing from all the public loudspeakers and was astonished to observe that spirit when the air raid sirens wailed. He watched the way Hanoians remained calm and kept order, with no sign of fear on their faces, not even on the faces of the kids. People walking along the street would quickly jump into the individual bomb shelters, while militiamen and militiawomen put their helmets on, buckled their belts, grabed their guns, and rushed up to the top of the buildings, ready to fire at the American airplanes. Then, when the all-clear siren echoed, the Hanoians went back to their normal cheerfulness, as if the war and the bomb raids had never happened.

Huu went to the war as an open-hearted teenager. His idea of what Americans were remained something vague and strange in his mind. The weapons he trained with and carried did not equip him to imagine the enemy. What did an American look like? Sure they had the faces of devils, hiding from the sunlight. Surely, they were cruel, ruthless killers. That very morning, he and all the other young soldiers had witnessed the horrific deaths caused by American bombs. Huu was more than ready to stick a bayonet right into the enemy's heart.

Still trying to forget the horror of the B52 bombing that morning, Huu went over to Platoon leader The Cuong's tent. The Cuong was a Hanoian who enlisted when he was a second year student of Literature in the General University. He was a very good writer who diligently kept a diary about their time on the battlefield, and Huu figured he might still be awake, writing in his notebook. When he entered, The Cuong was sitting on a bed he'd fashioned from bamboo trunks and was using his rucksack to brace his notebook; he wrote while holding a kerosene lamp in his left hand. Huu stood beside him and tried to read what The Cuong was writing.

30 February 1971,

Oh my Motherland, how much blood of our beloved compatriots has been shed? How many heroic children were killed in the fierce fighting with the enemy to safeguard our nation, and liberate our country. Today, along the majestic Trường Son mountain range, several of your children were killed through the cruelty of the Americans and their allies, their blood staining red this part of our land. I feel pain, sorrow, and hatred boiling in my heart. The Americans and their puppets will never get to rejoice in the tears we shed. Our tears will bring them horror and terror. They will pay for their sins.

Oh my Motherland, don't blame us for our feeble

tears. We have felt so much bitterness and heart-ache for our great loss. Our dear comrades whose names we hadn't even gotten to know now rest forever in this far place. What are we, the living, called upon to do? Dear comrades, rest in peace here. We'll dry our tears and search for revenge for your deaths. Our blood will continue to be shed, and many of us will inevitably be killed in combat. Because of our hatred of the American and their allies, because of our promises to you and to our Motherland, because of our love of our country, we are ready to sacrifice and without the slightest hesitation will move forwards to eliminate the enemy. They must pay their blood debt. They are cruel, but we will be victorious over them. I promise to you, dear Motherland, "Though I may fall, I will fall facing to the South;" that is the oath I swear as one of Uncle Ho's soldiers in this fierce battlefield. Beloved Motherland, we soldiers will never again be weakened and frightened as we were this morning under the enemy's bombs!"

Reading over The Cuong's shoulder, Huu was very touched. "Cuong, you have expressed exactly what all of us are feeling. Thank you for it."

As The Cuong closed the covers of the diary, a dried flower fell out. He hurriedly picked it up.

"This is the jasmine my girl pressed and put in this notebook for me. She's from Hanoi also; before she left to go as a Youth Volunteer to the Truong Son Trails, she wrote to me that she would stay as faithful, serene, and fragrant as this jasmine flower. She knew I'd have to go South through Truong Son, and said she would be there to welcome me on the crests of the Truong Son range. Poetic, right?" He pressed the notebook to his face and sighed, "I miss her so much. I wonder where she could be now, somewhere in these immense mountains."

3

Continuing their trek from the headwaters of Tiger Spring to the cave along the spring where the medical station was located, the 26th Reconnaissance Company had to pass what the liaison soldier guiding them called the "Cowboy" ridgeline. The weather was fickle. One minute the sun would shine, the next rain would pour down. Under the hot sun, even the rocks seemed to sweat with moisture, and when it rained, soil and sand became a stinking morass. They were in the dry season, with the sun shining overhead, when suddenly a storm hit, torrents of rain soaking them and huge gusts of wind shaking the trees and tattering the leaves. The stone-cluttered trail quickly flooded and they were moving in a knee-deep mush even though they were high up on the flank of the mountain.

It was the first time the young soldiers had been in such a situation. As soon as the storm seemed over, the exhausted soldiers spread their ponchos on the mud, removed their rucksacks and weapons and lay down to rest. Along with the water and mud that had flowed down came thousands and thousands of bloodsucking leeches, their proboscis thrust up, flinging themselves onto the men from the rotting leaves from both sides of the trail, clinging between the toes of those who wore rubber sandals, wiggling on to the bodies of the soldiers lying on the ponchos.

Frightened soldiers with no experience of these small bloodsuckers, screamed, "leech...leech!" frantically twisting their bodies around to scratch wherever they felt itching, pulling out leeches swollen with blood. One soldier tore off his shirt and was horrified to see numerous bloodsuckers clinging onto his belly. Crying loudly, men tried to pull each leech out with their hands. But as soon as they saw Commander Tuan trudging uphill to join, they stopped crying immediately.

Huu accompanied Commander Tuan along the line of troops. "Stand up! Let's go," Tuan yelled at each cluster of prone soldiers. "We're in range of the enemy's bombs here. Stand up! We can all be killed!"

"I can't take this anymore," one soldier groaned.

Tuan rolled his eyes. "Take it or not, live or die! Stand up, move out!"

That evening, after crossing Cowboy Ridge, everybody was ordered to fall in. Political Commissar Mao had gathered the Party Commitee to conduct political activities while waiting for the cooks to prepare dinner.

The men lined up in formation. Political Commissar Mao and Commander Tuan faced their soldiers. "At ease! Sit down," Mao called. He regarded the exhausted soldiers, his face stiffened.

"There are over one hundred men in this Company, all of whom are party members and youth group members.

Before joining the armed forces, you'd written applications that stated you will be ready to sacrifice your lives and suffer all hardships in order to defeat the American invaders, liberate the South, and reunify our country. For more than one month as we marched to the battlefield, I have been happy to see how you have remained cheerful, and demonstrated your keen determination to fight.

"However, after only one day and one night facing challenges, hardships, bloodshed, and sacrifice, many comrades among us seem frightened and bewildered. I heard one soldier say how scared he was of the bomb; afraid he would be torn to pieces. And you all have seen how some of our comrades have burst into tears. So let me ask you, comrades, are we a revolutionary army, the army of the Party, or aren't we?"

He stopped, glancing around at the soldiers' faces. Some turned their face, not daring to meet his eyes.

Mao swallowed as if he was trying to swallow his sadness, and not choke on his disappointment.

"Everybody stand up," Commander Tuan shouted, startling them.

The soldiers stood.

"Comrades, I want anyone who is afraid of death and of hardship to have the balls to stand to the side of the line. I repeat, comrades, anyone who is afraid of death and hardship stand aside...quickly! I don't want to say it again!"

All six rows of men remained silent.

"Raise your heads," Tuan roared. "Raise your heads and look straight at me and listen clearly. Our Fatherland, our Party, and our People do not want to hear the sound of

Uncle Ho's soldiers on their way to the battlefield crying, whining about being frightened of the enemy, about hardships and difficulties. In combat, you need to think this way in order to survive. One might not be hit by bullets. If one is hit, he might not die. If he dies, he might not have anyone to bury him. You must think of death as nothing. Our Fatherland or death. The only way for us to survive is to accept the sacrifices, accept the hardships. We might die in the next few moments, but now we sing and we laugh. That is what it means to be the soldiers of Uncle Ho and of the Party. That is victory; so understand, comrades?"

All the soldiers shouted in unison, "Understood!"

Their resounding shouts seemed to calm down the commander. He went on,

"Dear comrades, we have just witnessed the enemy's crimes. How they killed our comrades-in-arm mercilessly and broke our hearts. Do you hate the American enemy and their agents?"

"We do!"

"Dear comrades, do you want revenge for our comrades-in-arms?"

"We do!"

"Is anyone afraid of death and hardships?"

"We aren't!"

"Then, comrades, stand up!"

Tuan abruptly stopped speaking. For a long moment no one knew what he was thinking. Then he suddenly roared, "From now on, I forbid you to look back. Your only duty is to go forward, to fighting against the enemy whenever we find them. Whether you live or die, you must fight.

Whether you win or lose, you must fight. Do you understand?"

"His speech fires me up," The Cuong, Huu's close friend said. "Everybody thinks he's hot-headed and grumpy, but he's actually as eloquent as Karl Marx." He chuckled, "But he's really tough. Mock him and you're liable to be punched!"

"He's a fighter," Huu said. "He doesn't care if he lives or dies. If he wasn't so brave, so determined, how could he lead us? Whenever there is a difficult task for the D12 Reconnaissance Battalion, it is assigned to 26th Company, under his command, right?"

"So why is he still only a Company Commander?"

Huu lowered his voice, "Just between us, it's because he is stubborn, always argues with headquarters, and is really a womanizer. He is married, but it seems not out of love, just to have a wife to take care of his parents at home in his village."

The two young soldiers burst into laughter.

That evening, after checking the soldiers' overnight positions, Commander Tuan came to Huu. "Take the shovel and the flashlight and follow me."

Tuân guided him to a muddy puddle, surrounded by thick bushes. He took his entrenching shovel, its blade the size of an outstretched hand, and dug a 40-cm deep hole with a 20-cm perimeter. Then he covered the hole with leaves and set the lit flashlight down in it.

"We must cover it properly to prevent the light from coming out, to be spotted by enemy reconnaissance aircraft. Meanwhile, the light in the hole will attract insects.

By tomorrow morning the hole will be full, and we will collect them and fry or cook them with salt to preserve them. Remember, before we fry or cook insects, they need to be boiled with sour, acrid leaves. Eating them will increase our immune systems, even against malignant malaria."

This surprised Huu. "Why do we boil them like that, commander?"

"You need to know to never eat the bitter and pungent leaves; they're poisonous. The sour and acrid leaves are safe and non toxic."

"How did you learn all that?"

Tuan laughed, "'From life. Life on the battlefield."

"What about eating insects, worms, mosquitoes, and cockroaches?"

"Eating such insects is like getting vaccinated against rabies. You have to learn such things if you want to survive combat."

Huu listened to him in silence.

"The Americans are losing," Tuan chuckled, "because we Vietnamese people keep up such primitive ways, such as eat salted insects and worms in order to live, to survive. As for them, they stupidly stick to eating and drinking on a mealtime schedule. Even if they are fighting, when it's meal time, they have to stop and eat first. Each has his own ration, so even when an officer has more than he can eat, he throws away the rest. His soldiers are not allowed to have his leftovers. It's a piggish way of thinking! They are machine-like, dogmatic, perceiving the world through cold reason whereas we perceive it through emotion. We know, for example, that to survive in the fierceness of the battlefield like this, we must always sing revolutionary songs.

"They encourage us to love our country, set a fire in our hearts to live and to fight. Another important thing is how we can always find something to eat. The third most important thing is that we always must create and find something joyful. To do that, you have to nourish your spirit. Whenever you have the opportunity, seek out and flirt with the young liason girls, the youth volunteers, the frontline militiawomen, and the female drivers on the Truong Son trails. Remember, try to seduce them whenever you meet them, and if it is possible to make love with a girl, go ahead, don't lose the opportunity.

"In the battlefield, having an opportunity to make love is very rare, man! Making love comes naturally to men and women, especially on the battlefield, where no one knows if they will live or die. We are all human beings!" Tuan smacked his lips, "We all want to be in love and we all have sexual desires. We can survive without women, but it is boring…we are human beings, right?"

He looked at Huu. "Tell me truthfully, if you'd die without knowing anything about girls, wouldn't you regret your life?" He chuckled. "When I was single and in combat for the first time. I didn't know anything about women. Then I saw some of the Youth Volunteer girls wearing their thin cotton trousers and wading across a stream. They had those trousers rolled up nearly to their crotches, baring their pale legs and thighs. All of us laughed and told each other that now that we'd seen those beautiful girls, we could die without regret."

4

After two days of marching through the forest to cross the mountains, the 26th Reconnaissance Company had arrived at their destination in a forested area that flowed around rocky karsts honey-combed with caves. A spring flowed under the immense greenness of the leaf canopies, swirling around ancient stones, and winding by huge senile trees so big that two people could wrap their arms around the moss-covered trunks without their fingertips touching.

But the sheltering natural beauty of the landscape was the backdrop for a vicious struggle to defend this key territory. It was not far from the junction of the legendary Truong Son Trail, one branch of which entered the South from Quang Binh and snaked to Khe Sanh and Quang Tri, another to the Central Highlands and another straight to southern Laos. Close to the forest where the 26th Reconnaissance Company was stationed was the transit route for soldiers moving to and from the three Indochinese countries. On another mountain, more than a kilometer away, sat the Medical Station of Tiger Spring. The company's mission, besides protecting this key intersection of the Truong Son Trail, which was often raided by American and Saigonese forces or Lao bandits, was to protect the perimeter of the Medical Station.

Tiger Spring had been named by the Station personnel after a tragedy occurred. Led by Mr. Ho Pung and his 17 year old daughter Ho Buon to a large cave next to a long stream, the soldiers found it a convenient place from which to begin building a road which led to the Triangle Border.

The next day, while everyone was admiring the white stalactites hanging down from the ceiling of the cave, Ho Buon went out and took a walk along the stream. Suddenly a gray tiger appeared from nowhere, jumped to her side of the stream, seized the young girl in its jaws, and jumped back to the other bank. The soldiers fired a cascade of bullets near the beast, hoping to frighten it enough to let Ho Buon go, but the tiger held the girl in his front paws, raising her like a shield towards the gunners.

"Shoot the tiger, oh soldiers! My daughter is dead," Old Ho Phung screamed. "Shoot…shoot…go ahead, shoot. Kill it, soldiers!"

A B40 rocket hit the rock close to the right side of the tiger, shattering it. Taking advantage of the smoke, the tiger released Ho Buon and ran away to the forest.

Guns in their arms, everybody quickly waded across the spring. Old Ho Pung cried painfully, hugging his daughter's tattered, bloody corpse. Two guardians moved Ho Buon on a stretcher.

"No," Ho Pung cried out, wiping away his tears. "My daughter is dead, but we have to kill this gray tiger; if not it will stalk and kill our soldiers!"

He covered his daughter's face with his old fatigue shirt.

"Plant five or six grenades near my daughter's body. Tigers never let their prey go. It will come back. The grenades will avenge her."

All day, the soldiers waited. Finally, at dusk, the gray tiger soundlessly crept up close to Ho Buon's corpse. The noise of the grenades exploding startled the soldiers, who fired their weapons towards the noise. As soon as the echoes of the explosion had faded away, old Ho Pung and the soldiers rushed over with their flashlights, crying. The grenades had smashed in the chest of the gray tiger just as the beast had reached the young girl's corpse. Old Ho Phung embraced his daughter's torn and tattered body, crying piteously.

The young girl's body was put into a coffin made of the wooden boards of ammunition boxes, and a memorial ceremony was held by the soldiers. Ho Buon was buried right at the very place where she was mauled by the gray tiger.

The story of Ho Buon's death next to Tiger Spring was a dark, heavy cloud that continued to haunt anyone who passed through these mountains; above all, the young girls of the Medical Station and the young soldiers of the 26th Reconnaissance Company.

The climate around Tiger Spring was very strange. There were no clearly distinguished four seasons of spring, summer, autumn, and winter. The weather was only rainy or sunny, windy or stormy, bright or gloomy. During the day, sometimes the sun would shine gloriously in an immense blue sky, spreading golden beams over the canopies of the forest, the leaves fluttering and sparkling in the wind. Then, suddenly, it would be as if the sun shrank as it was enveloped by a dense black cloud. Thick banks of dark clouds would fill the sky, tumbling down from all sides like ghostly evil images as thunder roared and lightning flashed, and the clouds rolled twisting in the sky and then bursting into showers. Afterwards it would rain night after night, day after day, bringing floods that loosened soil and rocks, sending them sliding down the slopes as the air rumbled like an earthquake. Huge trees were uprooted and as they fell, knocked down other trees, big and small, exactly as if they were hit by a B52 bombing raid.

Whatever storms, cyclones, floods or any other of the outrages of heaven occurred, those based in the area knew how to deal with them, to be cautious, to rely on each other, to survive or to die together. No one lost their will or despaired. They considered the vicissitudes of nature as challenges, as ways to train themselves to be steely and determined and they proudly accepted all the dangers of war.

But for the young soldiers, including Huu, and for the eighteen or twenty-year old girls, the worst to deal with was not thunderstorms, tornadoes, landslides, or floods, but the long silences of the night.

Nights were so long, so leaden. It would grow dark about five in the evening. Slowly the darkness would thicken until a suffocating pitch black blanket redolent with the cold, damp, fishy smell of the rotting leaves mixed in the soil would cover everything. Trees, plants, and the whole forest, including the people in it, would fall silent, haunted by a vague, undefined fear. Those ones who got used to the atmosphere could sleep, but for anybody else, the nights were frightening, their silences broken by a strange howl from a wild animal or the caws from a murder of crows, their bellies full of the flesh they fed on from the corpses of soldiers.

The worst sound was the sudden "chick chick" of passing owls, which in the lore of country people foreshadowed death. In the countryside, that sound was not fearful but only evoked the souls of old people who died naturally going to join their ancestors. Birth, aging, sickness, and death were always a natural part of existence. But in a place where bombs fell and bullets flew and anyone could be killed anytime and anywhere, to young people like Huu and his comrades-in-arms, the sound of owls horrified them and racked their nerves with a mixture of vague regret and fear.

When night came, the darkness was weighted with sadness, with complex emotions that could neither be shared nor hidden.

But when dawn broke, even in the fragile light of the first rays of sunlight, everybody shook off the long, fearful silences and doubts of the night. Human beings here were like tiny ants crawling in a wilderness ringed with fire, wondering how they could continue to exist. Yet human beings are also endowed with a mysterious and incredible strength and will to survive, to prevail, even in the face of all the fury of nature. Even more mysteriously, they were able to face the possibility of unnatural death from bombs and bullets. Yet they were still fearful of facing their own loneliness in the silence of the black night, the silence that evoked confusion and terror. It was those silent, endless nights that wore down even the spirits of the young, including Huu.

At night, tormented by the sounds of nature, the resentful buzzing of the cicadas, people would hear the sound of the virgin girl's soul, wandering aimlessly, floating into the minds of those listening to the nocturnal reverberations of the forest.

All those who were based in the Tiger Spring cave had witnessed the specters of dead souls. In their dreams, the young girls at the Medical Station had seen Ho Buon in her black skirt, red blouse, and thick, waist-length hair, drifting nebulously, as if she were floating on the surface of Tiger Spring and then disappearing into the jungle. Now and then, they would awaken screaming and hugging each other, the agonized roar of the tiger echoing in their ears.

On one such occasion, the station's security guards and three platoons of the Reconnaissance Company, fully equipped, searched the jungle, but found not a trace of any tiger. Everyone accepted that the appearance of these souls, human and tiger, in their dreams foretold something that would happen. Each time someone at the Medical Station or in the Reconnaissance Company dreamed of the virgin girl Ho Buon's soul hovering in the air and picking flowers and catching butterflies, the next day would be peaceful.

But if anyone dreamed of Ho Buon suffering and sobbing, someone at the Station would die. And surely dreaming of the roaring tiger meant that the Station would be raided by enemy aircraft. Aware that Ho Buon's soul was as sacred as the soul of the gray tiger—the Lord of the Jungle—was terrible, everybody often placed wild flowers, and burned incense sticks at Ho Buon's grave next to Tiger Spring. Near her grave, soldiers and volunteer girls had also erected a symbolic grave mound for the gray tiger, where bones and canned food were offered. Whoever passed by would pray to Ho Buon and the Lord of the Jungle to bless them, to protect them, to tell them any impending omens of which they could be fore-warned and avoid.

Once The Cuong had a strange dream. In it, Ho Buon dragged him to a devastated hill on which lay the burned, entangled corpses of American and North Vietnamese soldiers. As he ran up the hill, he fell into a deep bomb crater and dropped his AK-47. As he bent to pick it up, he saw the black muzzle of an M-16 held by an American trooper pointing at him. He glanced around for Ho Buon, but she had disappeared. In front of him he saw a tall American woman with pale skin and blond, ruffled hair. She stood between him and the American, stretching out her arms as if to protect him.

The Cuong stared at the American, whose own eyes had opened wide and whose mouth gaped open in surprise at seeing the American woman. As The Cuong raised his AK and trained it on the American soldier, the American woman disappeared. In her place was The Cuong's mother, facing him, her eyes flashing with phosphorescent light, her thin arms stretched out as if to prevent The Cuong from shooting the American.

The Cuong felt a gush of blood covering his body and awoke, his heart fluttering. He sat up, terrified, checking himself, convinced that the sweat soaking his skin was blood. He touched his skin and then brought his fingers to his nose, smelling, to his relief, not the fishy smell of blood but the salty smell of sweat. From a corner of the room a lonely gecko cried repeatedly: "Gecko.... gecko...gecko."

That dream shook him. But he didn't dare tell it to anyone.

Two nights later, the deep silence was broken as usual by Ho Buon's sobbing, occasionally interspersed with the tiger's roar. But the roar that night was quite different. It repeated three times, " hummm...hummm...hummm," like someone beating a battle drum. Then near dawn the sound of bombs and rifle fire thundered from the triangle border, awakening the soldiers.

"Is everybody up," Company Commander Tuan asked. "Let's prepare the food. You need to stuff yourselves in order to get ready to fight. This kind of heavy air raid means that the Americans and the Saigonese soldiers are going to be attacking, trying to destroy the road and our supply depots. They might attack the Medical Station as well. Get ready for heavy action."

Checking that his pistol was in his holster, Tuan told Huu to follow him to the Tiger Spring Medical Station. They rushed into the cave to find dozens of soldiers, their faces and uniforms soaked with blood, carrying in the wounded and dead on their shoulders or with just their hands. Tuan stopped two soldiers carrying between them a wounded soldier who was screaming in pain.

"Where are your stretchers?"

The two soldiers laid the man down. "Damn my Company Commander," he bellowed, with a Nghe An accent.

"He's a bastard. If I get back to my unit, I'll kill the motherfucker!"

Taking in the pistol on Tuan's waist, one the other soldiers recognized he was an officer. "Look, captain, our C.O., made us load up with as many weapons as possible, but he wouldn't allow us to carry our hammocks or take stretchers. That is why we have nothing to carry the wounded with!"

"What an asshole," Tuan roared. "What kind of leader would do that?" He helped carry the wounded soldier into the cave. "Damn him, if I meet that scumbag I'll punch him in the face."

The 26th Reconnaissance Company moved quickly into the maelstrom of bombs and bullets where American Air Cavalry soldiers and the 759th Infantry Company defending the Truong Son Road were locked in fierce, often hand-to-hand combat. They fought for control of a large hill, stripped bare of trees by the bombs and napalm dropped by the Americans. AC130s, F4Hs, and F105 bombers climbed nearly vertically into the sky after they dropped their loads, trying to avoid the anti-aircraft fire from the surrounding hills. Since the 759th Infantry Company used the tactic of "holding onto the enemy's belt," most of the American bomb runs were useless.

Panicking from the volume of anti-aircraft fire, they dropped their bombs and fired their rockets randomly on both American and Vietnamese troops. As the American soldiers began to withdraw, carrying their wounded, they roundly cursed their own air support.

The Company Commander of 759th Infantry Company of Trường Son Corps was about 40 years old, medium height, with a tough, broad face. He fought bare-headed, and was covered head to toe with blood, firing his automatic rifle and jumping from one bomb crater to another, shooting at the fleeing Americans, the other soldiers following him, bayonets fastened onto their AK's. "Kill them, kill them," they screamed, shooting at the soldiers running away and stabbing those within reach, some of them screaming in fright in the bomb craters...

The 26th Reconnaissance Company joined in just as the battle was ending. The gunfire had stopped. They moved onto the hill, evacuating wounded soldiers, identifying the dead, gathering up weapons, and checking each American corpse to see if any were alive and wounded or pretending to be dead. Entering the shattered American Field Command Bunker at the top of a hill, Platoon Leader The Cuong saw several corpses, including one tall American who was lying on the sandbags. When he touched the body, he felt the man's skin was warm. He raised his AK and fired into the roof of the bunker. The American jumped up, swinging a shotgun around on The Cuong. The Cuong immediately pointed the barrel of his AK at the American. Then he remembered his English.

"Don't shoot," he shouted.

"You too," the American replied.

There was an eerie silence. The American field bunker was empty, but the air was thick with the odor of cordite from all the firing, making it hard to breath. The Cuong was sweating heavily, the smell of his sweat mixing with the gunpowder smell. He didn't dare take his finger off the trigger to raise his hand and wipe off the sweat.

"We are both soldiers," the American muttered wearily. "Dying here means nothing. No one will care and no one will remember you and me. But my mother and your mother will suffer for the rest of their lives…"

The Cuong nodded. Both lowered their weapons. Two other soldiers rushed in. The American handed his shotgun to one of them, at the same time staring at The Cuong. The Cuong patted his shoulder. "Don't worry, we won't kill you. You're being taken as a prisoner of war. We will treat you properly, and later we will hand you over to your government so that you can go back to your mother. Alright, what's your name?"

"My name is Thomas Kowalczyk, but just call me Tom. The Saigonese Officers called me Tom, and you should do the same, okay, Mr. VC's…!"

The Cuong turned toward his two comrades: "This American is alright, guys. He is not as cruel as the others. He didn't shoot me, and I don't want to shoot him. He said how our mothers would feel if we kill each other, so we stopped and both our mothers didn't lose their sons." He laughed. He felt good for not killing the American, for not having more blood on his hands.

As his unit regrouped to return to Tiger Spring, Tuan walked with the Commanding Officer of 759th Infantry Company. Tuan respected the other man deeply. "It was amazing to watch you, the way you ignored the bombs, the bullets, the big aggressive Americans. I admire you! You're a role model for me. Like General Zhao Yun, alone on his horse and his lance, saving A Dao."

The Infantry commander laughed. "We officers have to

act like that. Our soldiers take their cues from us; they will be brave or be cowardly, all depending on how their officer acts."

"Then tell me the truth; why are you so cruel to your soldiers?" Tuân asked.

"What do you mean cruel? The Infantry officer, shocked, stared at Tuan. "Why would you say that?

"You didn't allow your soldiers to bring stretchers and hammocks. I saw your wounded soldiers being carried on their comrades' shoulders or between them all the way to the Medical Station."

"You know, when you go into combat, either you will live or die," the infantry commander answered thoughtfully. "Whoever is killed is dead. Whoever is wounded is wounded. By bringing along stretchers and hammocks, you create a mental fear. Everybody who goes to war is conscious of death. Bringing stretchers along just hurts their morale. So, instead of carrying those things, I encourage them to carry more weapons. In my own experience of combat, the worst thing that has happened to me was not having enough weapons, and especially not having enough ammo. It was frustrating because I had to conserve my firing. If you have an extra magazine, you can eliminate a few more enemies. Even if you miss, you can keep their heads down by showering them with bullets."

"He laughed, "As Vietnamese daring to fight against the Americans, if we die, we have to die bravely. To be honest, I was born a peasant, but since joining the revolution, I have been determined to live properly and to die properly. I am not a hypocrite. I always tell the truth to my soldiers.

They are all teenagers going into combat, and I wouldn't lie to the poor bastards!"

Tuan laughed. "To tell you the truth, this morning when I saw so many dead and wounded being carried without stretchers, I was enraged at you and intended to "give you a lesson. But now I understand; especially after witnessing your bravery during the fighting…"

"On the battlefield, who can keep their humanity? We have to face and kill the enemy. Even when I saw one try to surrender, I shot him to save time so I could kill more of them. I wouldn't give them the chance to counter-attack and kill my soldiers. But once they're defeated, I don't kill prisoners. To tell you the truth, I'm enraged at the cruelty of the Americans and the Saigonese. I want to kill all of them, the invaders and their Saigonese henchmen!"

"And to do that you'd sacrifice many of your own soldiers as well?"

The other silently squatted and then sat on a mound of earth. He pulled out his canteen and gulped down some water.

After a while, he spoke. "Whether I 'sacrificed' a lot of my soldiers or not, as a revolutionary soldier, one's goal had to be to win on the battlefield. To have the will to defeat the enemy, you must be ready to sacrifice yourself in order to kill them. I don't care if I lose three or four soldiers for every American we kill. I hate the invaders!"

He continued talking passionately about fighting the Americans until it was time to go.

"Sorry," Tuan said. "We were so busy talking that I didn't even get to know your name."

"My name is Quyet. You can ask anyone who has been marching through the Truong Son about "Crazy" Quyet." He shook Tuan's hand and smiled, "Each time I fight the Americans, I feel so excited it is as if my blood is boiling. I keep applying to the Corps to re-assign me to a mainline unit in Quang Tri, where there's the heaviest combat against the Americans. I'd be happy if even I had to die. But my superiors always refuse to transfer me. I'm really frustrated."

When he got back to the company, Tuan ordered The Cuong and Huu to escort the American prisoner to the Security Team at the Tiger Spring Medical Station, and took a rest for himself, lying on the slope and looking down at the stream section where some of the young girls from the station were enjoying a bath. He pointed to them. "There's a tonic for your eyes," he called out to the soldiers near him.

They cheered and applauded. "One two…one…two…three, hooray for the commander…one…two…three, hooray for the Commander!"

For a soldier on the battlefield, life came in discordant beats. Fierce and intensive under the bombs when the line between living or dying was so fragile that one's existence could end in an instant, or as a lingering suffering in the harsh and unhealthy conditions of the poisonous jungle…it was why the soldiers loved these rare moments of peace, when there were no storms or typhoons, no bombs falling of their heads, the peaceful silence after a deadly battle. This was one of those wonderful moments, lasting only as the tired sun shrunk to nothing more than a small plate perched on the top of the trees, its fragile light glimmering on Tiger Spring where it wound along the edge of the jungle. A gentle breeze ruffled the leaf canopies, sprinkling the tiny, colorful petals of jungle flowers over the deep, clear, transparent water. It was in that section of the spring, different groups of soldiers poured down to bathe.

What made it even better was that down in that same spring, they could hear the pure, cheerful laughter, and could see the white bodies of the eighteen or twenty-year old girls sporting like young mermaids in the middle of the stream. Tuan's heart lightened as he watched his men staring: he saw the bathing girls like a gift given by Heaven to the soldiers of 26th Reconnaissance Company—creation balancing itself like a sudden gush of cool water flowing through the hot, fierce life of the battlefield.

When the soldiers got closer, the young girls screamed and rushed hastily to the bank, giggling. The young men stood in bewildered, regretful silence. To Tuan, they looked like cars racing at full speed that suddenly ran out of fuel. His heart filled with pity for them. He felt his eyes filling, blurring behind a thin haze, and suddenly he burst into tears like a child who had stepped on a sharp thorn.

Tears filled his eyes and spilled down over his high, skinny cheekbones, through his beard and into his mouth, tasting salty, warm as his own breath, then falling nonstop. Tuan cried in silence, trying not to sob.

This was the second time he cried on the battlefield.

The first time he cried had been in a very different situation. They were spending a night inside the cave when the young soldiers were awakened by Dr. Lien. "Hey, wake up," she whispered. "Follow me and I'll let you see "something".

Tiger Spring

The "Something" turned out to be the naked body of an anesthetized girl lying on a table in a corner of the cave, waiting for an appendectomy.

Dr. Lien covered her mouth with one hand and made a sign for the soldiers to do the same. They walked silently, one after another, around naked girl lying motionless in front of them. Each soldier felt a different emotion. Some tightened their jaws and opened their eyes wide as they looked at the girl's body, one even covered his face with both hands, looking between his fingers at her, trembling. There was complete silence except for the sound of ragged breathing. Hiding himself in a corner of the cave, Tuan stared at the serious, tensed faces of his soldiers, and felt choked by a sudden bitter sadness. His shoulders trembled, and he tightened his lips to keep from sobbing.

He cried for these young, baby-faced soldiers of his. He wondered if any of them had ever known the smell of a young girl's sweat or the taste of her tears, or the press of her sweet kiss. He knew that most would have never had the chance to love like that, and by tomorrow, or the day after tomorrow, or the next, some of these innocent young boys would be killed. No one knew how long the war would last. This thought seized him. Tuan felt more bitterness, more sorrow, and his tears kept falling. He staggered back to his hammock. That night he couldn't sleep; he tossed and turned all night long, trying to rid himself of the feeling of sadness. Soldiers had to accept being sacrificed. They all knew it.

Like the need of consuming food to survive, sexual desire was something natural for men after puberty, as his own experience told him. Every time he went to bed with his wife, Tuan would always seek something different, try to discover something new. He was an eager and fervent lover, hugging his wife's warm body in his arms, caressing her smooth, tight breasts as her breath trembled nervously, shyly. As his hand slid down to her swollen, warm wetness, she would slowly spread her legs, expectant, ready. He would enter her and be with her for a very long time, both of them longing for each other, moving together towards the culmination of orgasm, her fingers caressing and clutching his back.

The way she would let out a sharp groan had become a sweet, euphoric memory that came to him whenever his mind wandered to the image of the naked body of the young girl. Now the memory of his wife and the memory of the pale naked body of the girl lying on the stretcher in the corner of the cave intertwined, flared up inside him into painful desire. He let out a sigh.

His mind drifted from his thoughts of the young soldiers and their wasted puberty. He was hard with lust. His hand grasped his erection, caressed, and stroked to relieve his discomfort, his burning desire. As he came, he closed his eyes and uttered a sorrowful moan. As satiated as a hungry child after being fed, he pulled the thin blanket up over him and fell asleep. Sleep arrived suddenly, quickly, gently.

Outside, the leaves were rustling as the wind blew stronger and stronger. A few raindrops fell, the beginning of the change of seasons. The hot, steamy air that had accumulated since yesterday afternoon transformed into a thick fog that covered the whole area. The fog, the breeze, the rain, the flowers blended into a fragrance that permeated and rose from the jungle canopy. Not until now did the jungle start to move and awaken. The insects rustled pleasantly and birds, hidden somewhere until now, burst into the air, singing, cheering up the atmosphere.

The stifling sadness they had all felt was gone. Sleep came easily, lulling the young soldiers like a gentle mother. Then came dawn. At 6 a.m., the sentry on duty blew the alarm whistle, again and again. The 26th Reconnaissance Company poured out of the big cave and got in formation to do their morning exercises, refreshed from a full night's sleep and the chance they'd had to look at naked young girls. All wore green T-shirts and shorts. Seeing the dark stains on their shorts, Tuan knew that these young guys had done the same as he had and masturbated during the night. He chuckled.

Suddenly the sound of the American warplanes broke the silence and a series of ear-splitting explosions turned heaven and earth upside down.

"Bomb raid! Get down," Tuan screamed. He jumped on Political Commissar Mao, pushed him down and lay on top of him, face down on the ground.

The roar of the aircraft and the explosions from the bombs tore the air. Tiger Spring Medical Station was engulfed in fire and smoke. Shrapnel from smashed trees and splintered rocks flew in all directions.

As soon as the raid ended, Tuan, Political Commissar Mao, and all the soldiers stood up and straightened their clothes. His face stern, Tuan turned to Mao, "They may follow the bombing with a raid. You will command Platoon One and Platoon Two on the outer perimeter; I'll take Platoon Three to defend the station and take care of any wounded soldiers…You need to stop the enemy at any cost."

He turned to his men. "Get back to the cave and get your weapons!"

They scrambled inside as fast as squirrels. An early morning mist concealed them from the fighter planes swarming above.

The golden rays of sunlight began to tear apart the mist, but it was thickened by the smoke billowing up in all directions from the exploding bombs. The explosions, the red flashes, and the black smoke mixed into each other like a graveyard full of demons and ghosts with thousands of long arms clawing apart the green, calm forest where life overflowed with joy of the nature, reaching for the young soldiers who had left their families to fight for the salvation of the nation.

A/F 105 Thunderchiefs and F4 Phantoms swarmed above, dropping their bombs, and then swerving away. Silence descended on the immense jungle. There remained only the black billows of smoke, the stink of gunpowder and the wandering mists…

Suddenly the silence was broken by the drumming noise of helicopters flying in from the direction of Quang Tri. They flew in an A-shaped formation; as they landed, they disgorged enemy troops all around the entrance to the Tiger Spring Medical Station.

In his ambush position, Political Commissar Mao and

two elite platoons with more than fifty experienced soldiers were ready to brave death, the determination to fight for victory welling up in everyone's heart and mind. They didn't mind lying prone on the wet, sticky ground, rifle barrels forward, hearts racing, waiting for the orders to attack. Unfortunately, the wily Air Cavalry soldiers had not landed in the ambush zone set up by the 26th Reconnaissance Company. Political Commissar Mao immediately gave the order to split into two directions and pursue the enemy.

Blocking the entrance of the cave, Company Commander Tuan had only one squad of ten riflemen, including Hoan and Huu. The officers and soldiers from two other squads were ordered to go back into the cave and transport the wounded to the rear, away from the fighting. As an experienced veteran, Tuan knew that the enemy's final goal would be to obliterate the Tiger Spring Medical Station, and to accomplish that they would send in reinforcements and call up more aircraft to bombard this area day and night.

More than a dozen helicopters circled overhead like a swarm of bees, their rotors roaring like hurricanes, crushing down the treetops. Tuan wondered why he was not hearing firing from the two platoons at the ambush site, led by Political Commissar Mao. He asked Huu to lean against the slope outside the cave entrance and used him as a ladder to climb up the cliff in front of the cave so he could observe what was happening. He immediately saw the helmets of the enemy soldiers who were moving through the jungle on the right and the left of the hills leading to the entrance

Huu Uoc

of the cave. Tuan quickly turned to Huu, "Run quickly to the rear of the enemy troop on the right and shoot up in the air to alert the enemy's movement to Platoon One."

5

Inside the cave, some of the Platoon 3 soldiers, along with Doctor Lien and several other nurses, hurriedly carried the wounded out. The weapons, first aid kits, IV bags, and hammocks strapped around their waists made the task awkward and difficult. Company Commander Tuan, a pistol in his belt, an AK in his hands, encouraged the injured soldiers. He was sweating but maintained an appearance of courage and calm.

On Doctor Lien's back, a heavy soldier was moaning painfully. She sweated heavily, her legs wobbly under his weight. Tuan bent down and shifted the wounded soldier to his own back. Doctor Lien reached to take his AK, but he held it back. "Let it be. Go ahead and urge them to hurry up; the enemy is right behind us…"

Suddenly, a volley of AK fire exploded on the right side of the mountain, then another on the left. Tuan knew that Hoan and Huu had approached in two directions, surrounding, and pursuing the enemy. The fighting between the combatants of 26th Reconnaissance Company and the American-Saigonese was about to happen.

Exactly as it had been planned by Company Commander Tuan, as soon as Political Commissar Mao heard the warning shots from Hoan and Huu, he had sent Platoon One and Two to pursue the enemy from both sides of the mountain. Tuan's ears were assailed by the sound of B40s and B41s and machine guns, and then volleys of AK bullets...discharged one after another, again and again. His brave soldiers were in active pursuit. Two or three minutes later he heard the enemy's mortars and M16's firing as they started their counter-attack.

Explosions erupted all over the area. Dozens of helicopters darted to and fro, just above the treetops, zig-zagging between the ridges to avoid the fire from anti-aircraft guns. The enemy showered bullets down from the helicopters. A group of three helicopters, loaded with the helmeted, well-equipped troopers, hovered along the mountainside near the entrance of the cave, pouring bullets down. From halfway up the mountain, there was a sharp explosion and a bright flash and a B41 rocket tore through the air like a comet and plowed straight into the first helicopter. It exploded and crashed into the cliff, scattering thousands of pieces of debris together with the charred bodies of a dozen American and Saigonese scouts and commandos. A HU1E hovered and fired two rockets into the area where the flash of fire from the B41 had been seen. They tore into and shattered the undulating ridge line of the mountain, with rocks and soil flying everywhere.

Carrying the wounded soldiers to the rear, Tuan and his comrades-in-arm had witnessed everything, from the

B41 rockets destroying the enemy helicopter to the counter-attack of two helicopter-borne rockets that had killed his brave soldiers. He knew the destructive power of the two rockets and pictured his brave young men whose bodies had been melted into the soil, or flew up with the wind. Tuan took off the Pathet Lao hat, placed it across his chest, bowed down to say farewell to those war-martyrs. Then he turned back and helped wounded soldiers. As the last man in line, now and then he turned around and watched the enemy moving closer at their rear.

Suddenly, as if he'd dropped from the sky, a South Vietnamese commando fell upon him. Both men rolled down on the ground, struggling. Tuan's AK and the commando's M16 flew away from them. The fight between Tuan and the commando, who was the same size as him, was fierce. They entwined, kicking, and punching at each other. All the martial arts training from the Reconnaissance Special Forces used by Tuan was ineffective, both because the commando was too strong and because he was also well trained. He smashed his elbow repeatedly into Tuan's face, flipped him and got his huge body on top of Tuan, pressing his forearm onto Tuan's neck. He was trying to pull a duckbilled grenade from his belt to hit Tuan in the head, when Doctor Lien jumped in. She kicked the commando's face hard, so he rolled off, giving Tuan enough time to pull out his pistol and pulled the trigger. The commando screamed loudly, convulsing as he died.

Lien rushed over to Tuan and lay down next to him, embracing him. "Are you alright, Tuan?"

Tuan closed his eyes and grasped at Lien. "I'm alright,

Lien. You've saved my life. How did you know to return and save me?"

Feeling Tuan's rough hands clutching at her, Doctor Lien was surprised and confused. She moved out of his embrace. Exhausted, she rolled next to him, looking up to the sky.

"We'd been moving away, and I could no longer hear you from behind us. I got worried about you and came back."

Lien gathered her smooth black hair, long as a python, and placed it between them. Tuan reached over and pulled a handful of strands to his face, breathing its scent in deeply, his eyes closing. The light fragrance emanating from Lien's hair enchanted him.

"What kind of leaves did you use," he asked her. "This is so nice!"

Lien gently pulled her hair back. "Wild grapefruit leaves," she whispered.

Tuan half-closed his eyes. It felt as if his soul was wandering somewhere, not quite close, and not quite far away.

"Grapefruit leaves are nice," he said dreamily. "This scent made me miss my mother; she used to wash her hair with grapefruit leaves. Hey," Tuan stretched his hand towards Lien. She pushed it away. Tuan murmured, "Lien, you remind me so much of my mother." He laughed. "My mother doesn't know anything about the Party, the country, the war...but when every family in the whole village, the whole commune sent their children to join the army to fight against the invaders, then she let me go. My mother doesn't know how we fight against the Americans and the

Saigonese... In reality, at the beginning, she hesitated to let me go; she was so afraid that I might die."

"Our mothers are so sweet, aren't they," Lien asked innocently.

Tuan rolled over and put his arms around her. She struggled, trying to push him away. "Let me go! Get your hands off me!"

Tuan didn't release her. "Didn't you just hug me?"

"I was happy that you were still alive."

"Doesn't that mean you like me?"

"Yes," Lien answered, her face cold.

Tuan released her. She sat up, gathered her long hair, and twisted it like a black rope around her neck. Something wet and cold was sticking on her chest. Looking down, she saw a saffron-colored liquid; when she reached down and wiped it away, it felt greasy.

"Did you have an egg in your pocket?"

"Oh, right. Last night Hoan gave me one, but I didn't have time to eat it..." Tuan pulled out the crushed eggshells, sticky with yolk, and threw them away. He stood up, tidied his clothes, and picked up his AK. Just then, they heard the sound of a hovering helicopter over their heads. Tuan and Lien ducked under the rim of a cliff under the canopy, aiming their rifles upwards. Lien clicked off her safety, getting ready to shoot. Tuan pushed her hand down.

"Don't. You'll reveal which way our wounded are moving... this one is looking for the missing commando."

There was a rustling noise of footsteps nearby, coming closer and closer. Tuan patted Lien's shoulder, signaling her to be quiet, and pointed his rifle towards the sound. Two people emerged: a soldier from his company and Ms. Lan, using the muzzles of their AKs to part the bushes. When they saw Tuan and Lien huddling by the cliff, they looked happy.

"One, two, three, kiss...one, two, three, kiss..." Lan teased.

Lien lowered her rifle, rushed to Lan, and hugged her. "Oh dear, Lan! Stop joking!"

The young soldier saluted and then embraced his Commander.

"Everybody was worried that the commandos had captured you and Doctor Lien..."

"How could they! They'd have to kill me before I let them capture me. Are you underestimating your Commander?"

"I beg your pardon, Commander," the young soldier apologized frantically, "We were worried."

A helicopter suddenly hovered above them, its rotors clattering and fanning down all the treetops, searching for the missing commando. Tuan, Lien, and Lan crawled towards the commando's corpse. Tuan took off the man's cartridge belt and passed the magazines, grenades, canteen, and dagger to Lien and Lan. He flipped the corpse over and searched the man's back pocket, pulling out a brown alligator leather wallet filled with Saigonese government bills, a military ID card, and a small photo of a very young girl whose face bore a pure innocent beauty. On the back of the photo was a hand-written note written in a childish hand: "*Wishing my elder brother to come home soon to Mom and me*", and a signature "*Youngest sister Hanh*".

Tiger Spring

Holding the photo, Company Commander Tuan felt a vague sadness. He passed it to Doctor Lien and Lan. As they read the note, both of them became contemplative and quiet.

The sound of the helicopter was growing louder and louder. It soon was hovering overhead.

Tuan stood still, sunk into thought. The photo of the innocent young girl with her note *"Wishing my elder brother to come home soon to Mom and me"*, clung in his mind, haunting him. He looked at the commando's corpse, feeling pity and sorrow. He had been the enemy, but he was a human being. If he and his Lien hadn't killed him, he would surely have killed them. In war, there had to be winners and losers; there had to be justice and injustice. To go to war would always be painful, even if necessary, even if it was a just war, with Tuan and his comrades-in-arm bearing the weight of an historic mission on their shoulders.

Tuan looked at the commando's corpse again, now become the corpse of a man like himself. He wouldn't mind giving the soldier a proper burial, just as he would one of his own comrades-in-arms. But it would be a lost, lonely grave lost in the immense jungles of Laos. After the war, who would know, who would come to gather his remains and bring them back to his mother and his younger sister who had been longing for him? The thought haunted him. "We should return this commando to his mother and sister, even if only his remains," he said to Lien, Lan, and the soldier.

"How could we, Commander," asked the soldier.

"You three hurry on back to the wounded. I'll deal with this."

The three hesitated, reluctant to leave. How could Tuan bring this corpse back to the other side? Tuan saw their concern, "I'm giving you an order. You need to obey it!"

Doctor Lien, Lan, and the soldier picked their weapons up, reluctantly said goodbye to their commander, and moved out to the temporary treatment area.

The helicopter was still hovering overhead. The gunners on each side shot down, riddling the earth and the trees with machine gun bullets. The helicopter stayed right above the treetops, its rotors whirling, creating a horrible, howling roar.

As it drew closer, Tuan dragged the commando's corpse to a small clearing, half carrying it on his shoulders, half dragging it. The helicopter was right overhead, Tuan raised his AK and fired into the sky and then ran as fast as possible into the jungle. Bullets from the helicopter poured down ahead and behind him as he ran. Then he hid under a tree and aimed his AK at the empty field where the torn corpse was lying.

The helicopter circled around the clearing before landing. Six commandos in camouflage uniforms, equipment strapped to their waists and chests, jumped out, and quickly formed an A formation: one in the front, two on the sides, and three in a horizontal line at the end. They were frightened, hesitating. The three in the back pointed their guns in three directions, their fingers on the triggers, their hands shaking. The first one reached the corpse but didn't touch it.

"Take care, the VC may have bobby-trapped it," he said, with a Southern accent.

One of the others ran back to the helicopter where the rotor blades were still slowly spinning. The crewman handed him a rope with a hook on its end. The commando came back to the group and threw the hook over the corpse.

"Get down," their leader shouted.

They backed off and lay prone, covering their ears with their hands. The leader pulled the rope, the hook catching into the corpse. He yanked the rope. Dead silence. Hearing no explosion, the commandos approached the corpse.

Close-by, Tuan clicked off the safety on his AK into the firing position and placed the three duck-billed hand grenades he'd taken off the commando's corpse to one side. He took up the slack on the trigger…and then loosened his finger, tightened on it, again and again, sweating profusely. He wiped his face and sighed, the image of the young girl in the photo, her note: "*Wishing my elder brother to come home soon to Mom and me*", signed, "*Youngest sister, Hanh*" appearing in his mind, along with the image of Doctor Lien, Lan, and his soldier standing by the corpse, and the memory of his own words: "*We should return this commando to his mother and sister, even if only his remains.*"

He felt he was walking in his sleep, stuck in place, the images and thoughts running through his mind endlessly. He knew the right moment to shoot was just when the six commandos got the corpse to the helicopter. Its rotors started spinning faster, fanning down air, the engine roaring as the aircraft rose up.

Company Commander Tuan casually slung his weapon, gathered the grenades, and walked back to his unit. He could no longer hear gunfire. Was he wrong to make sure the commando's corpse would get back to his mother and his sister, did he regret doing it? No, on the contrary, he felt no regret, only relief. He had done something that one human being should do for another human in the true sense of the word human, though the commando was his enemy and the enemy of the country. Of course, one had to kill the enemy, but he was not cruel or callous to them, especially when they had lost. But still, he had had the enemy right in his sights; why hadn't he shot? These were the same evil, bloodthirsty commandos who had committed so many crimes against his comrades-in-arm and even to himself. Only just recently he had escaped death from them. Why didn't he shoot them? Why didn't he kill his enemy, the enemy of the revolution?

As he calmed down and thought about it, he kept wondering why, in that fragile moment, when his finger was hooked on the trigger, he didn't have the courage to squeeze it. Was it that he just didn't want to kill, or that he wanted to be certain the man's remains got back to his mother and his innocent younger sister? The commando's poor mother and his poor youngest sister were innocent. The war had caused the suffering of so many Vietnamese mothers and children. Mothers lost their children, wives lost their husbands, younger brothers and sisters lost their siblings.

And as for Tuan, he had hesitated, had not squeezed the trigger because he thought of those mothers, wives, brothers, and sisters. He let the commandos go without regret. But deep in his heart, he wished that the fact he'd let the body be retrieved, spared the men who had come for it, that somehow those commandos would know, and the glimmer of their humanity would be awakened, and make them aware of the painful consequences of killing each other...

He'd wished that those commandos would stop being bloodthirsty, stop being crazy, stop being happy to massacre fragile young girls like Doctor Lien, Lan, and these baby-faced young soldiers of his.

6

The Tiger Spring Medical Station in "Gecko" cave looked disordered and chaotic due to the swiftness with which the wounded had had to be evacuated. Medical equipment and personal belongings were scattered everywhere, stuck in every nook and cranny of the cave.

Using only the dim sunlight coming through the cave entrance, Huu, Hoan, and a young private named Toan, searched through the cave, painstakingly recovering both the personal items and everything they could take to a new location.

Toan came across a pair of panties and a faded green bra in a cranny, where Doctor Lien and Lan had slept. He stood motionless and embarrassed, his face red. For some reason, he stuffed the bra into his pocket, but still clutched the panties. He closed his eyes and pressed the fabric to his face, inhaling its smell deeply. A strange feeling surged through him, making his heart beat faster, erratically. He felt excited, overwhelmed with a desire to taste the strange, poetic fragrance of a young girl, which was now dissolving on his face.

Daydreaming, Toan stood still for a long while, his shoulders trembling. Then the young soldier shivered and removed the panties from his face. In a sudden panic, he looked down his crotch and saw an opaque liquid blotch had soaked out through the fabric of his trousers.

At that very moment, Hoan called out: "Toan, where are you?"

"Yes, here I am. Inside."

Hoan came over to the cranny. He saw Toan hastily stuff the panties into his pocket.

"What are you doing here? Searching for gold?

"I just wanted to see how the doctors and nurses live."

"There's nothing to see. On the battlefield, the lives of male and female soldiers are equally tough. Get out of here now."

As Toan moved out, Hoan saw the dark wet patch at his crotch.

"Did you just come?"

Toan blushed, lied. "It was that awful bomb raid...it scared me so much I wet my pants".

They slung their weapons and walked out of the cave.

Meanwhile, Tuan searched the cave methodically, gathering anything usable and putting it into his rucksack. He shone his flashlight into dark recesses, looking carefully, all the while calling, "Cluck...cluck...cluck". His mood was strange, frantic. After a time, he stopped taking care and just began running here and there, kicking at whatever he saw. He looked like an insane Don Quixote fighting with the windmill.

Just when his boredom and frustration were at a height,

he saw the plum-flowered hen slowly emerge from some dark nook. He lunged happily at the hen, and then hugged her tightly in his arm like she was a precious treasure. He caressed her feathers and cuddled her, holding onto her as if he was afraid that if he loosened his arms, the hen would run away again.

The hen was also beyond fear. It lay on Tuan's chest, enjoying the warmth, raising its head as if it was about to ask something. Hearing the sound of footsteps, Tuan hung onto the hen with his left hand, while raising the AK with the other; he got behind a rock, aiming at the sound. The dim light in the cave was just bright enough for him to recognize his three soldiers. He stepped out, startling Hoan, Huu, and Toan who spun around and pointed their rifles at him.

"Hey, it's me, Tuan!"

"Commander!"

The men hugged each other happily.

"Commander, where are Doctor Lien and Lan, and the wounded," Huu asked.

"This station has been exposed. I've moved them to the new location, at Orang Outang."

"Are they all OK, commander," Hoan asked.

"They're all fine." He laughed. "If Doctor Lien hadn't come back to look for me, I would have been "swallowed" by a commando. I'm big, strong, and good at martial arts, but I was losing to him, to my shame! Ha...I have to say that their scouts and commandos are well trained by the Americans and the Saigonese, especially in hand-to-hand combat."

He passed the hen to Hoan. "Take this to your unit, and when we move the medical station, ask Lan to raise it. Take good care of it, yes? I wonder if it will still lay eggs, after that horrible bombing."

Hoan took the hen from Tuan. He took a rice ball out of his rucksack, chewed a few grains, and then fed the hen by pushing them into its beak.

On the way back to their garrison, Tuan told them how he had returned the commando's corpse and spared those on the rescue helicopter. The three men were horrified. Huu, who was always outspoken, said what was on his mind.

"What a golden opportunity! If I was there, I would have "swallowed" them right away! I'd shoot all those dogs."

"Me too," Huu said. "That was a once-in-a-lifetime opportunity! I would have shot all of them! The American soldiers and the Saigonese commandos are thirsty for Communist blood. They're crueler than beasts! I've heard they drink Communist soldiers' blood and eat their livers like they are drinking water and devouring the flesh of wild animals." Huu's face turned burgundy red with anger.

"Seeing them like that, I'd have to do the same, commander! Even if they'd been surrounded and helpless, I'd shoot them. You know how I hate those bastards. They are not only evil but really brutal. Once I went into a Laotian ethnic village after they had been there. They had killed everyone, the elderly, women, and children..."

Company Commander Tuan let them speak their minds.

"I also hate the commandos to the marrow of my

bones," he said thoughtfully. "You're still new, and don't know everything about them. But we veterans have been fighting with those commandos and the Lao bandits for a long time. They're cunning, evil, bloodthirsty, and brutal, as if they were trained only to kill..."

"Then why did you spare their lives," Hoan asked.

"Yes, even now when I think about it, I don't understand myself. I only had a split-second to decide whether to shoot or not. My conscience was telling me to return that commando's corpse back to his mother and his youngest sister. Why do people keep spilling blood for blood, doing evil to avenge evil? To be honest, at that time I didn't want to kill anyone, even though they were my enemy. It was that simple. Who knows, the fact that I let them recover the corpse and didn't shoot them, might make them understand a little about the humanity of our Communist fighters. I believe that no matter how evil they are, somewhat they still have a bit of humanity in them. I always hope so.

"Hey there," Tuan stopped walking, making the others to stop as well. "I order the three of you not to talk about this to anyone in the unit," he said. "Especially Political Commissar Mao. If he knows what I did, he will report me, and I will be punished right away. He is very "bonsevich" orthodox, and principled, you know. The punishment for sparing the enemy is expulsion from the Party, discharge from the military, and a court martial. What I told you is not for joking, babbling, or gossiping about, got it, you three?"

The three young soldiers stamped their feet and saluted, "Yes, Commander!"

Tiger Spring

Touched, the Company Commander stretched his long arms out and embraced his three soldiers. There was no more gunfire to be heard. The jungle was calm again. A soft wind rustled the branches. But still the immense greenness of the jungle now scripted with the images of war. Everywhere was devastation from the bombing, burned patches, ancient trees felled, and others stripped bare of bark, with gray or blackened branches, standing like lonely, The desolation outside of "Gecko" cave tore the heart. Rocks. Hills, trees, and vegetation had all been torn, melted, mixed, and piled as if by a giant into scattered heaps around the entrance. Dark pools of coagulating blood permeated the area with the fishy, pungent smell of human flesh. Company Commander Tuan felt his heart bleeding with the immense sorrow as he looked at the mournful scenery. How horrible the war was; it didn't only kill numerous people, it also murdered nature, all the inanimate species that had brought beauty, greenery, and happiness to human beings.

Why did the enemy come from far away to rain death on this lush green forest, filled with life? And why did people who had the same yellow-skins, who spoke the same language and who shared the same blood, have to divide, and slaughter each other?

The human blood mixed now into the debris piled around the cave entrance: which of it had been shed for the just cause, which from the other side and the invaders? As he mourned the devastation around him, the thought flared in Tuan's mind that he hated war. Human beings had begun the war, but why? Why didn't they come together to speak with a common voice of kindness, of love, of compassion, of human happiness...

The rain started beating down on the ruined scenery. Rain and fog dampened the jungle and dispersed the black noxious smoke left from the battle, floating melancholy in the air, loaded with sadness.

Company Commander Tuan and the three young soldiers arrived at the base by early afternoon. Political Commissar Mao was calling the rolls of Platoon One and Platoon Two after their fierce fighting with the nearly one hundred paratroopers and commandos of the American and Saigonese armed forces.

Lined up In front of the six rows of troops were the bodies of six war martyrs. They had been covered by a hammock.

Company Commander Tuan flipped the hammock up. He recognized five of the dead: these brave soldiers of his, baby-faced, eyes closed as if they were dreaming. The sixth, whose name he hadn't known, was the one who'd lugged the B41 gun up the mountain and shot down a helicopter carrying nineteen enemy soldiers. He had been hit by two rockets from another helicopter. All that remained of him was a piece of uniform, a clump of hair, and a fragment of rock stained with dark red blood. Tuan, overcome with emotion, covered his face, and burst into tears.

Political Commissar Mao, his face blackened with cordite, his right arm bandaged from shoulder to elbow, allowed Tuan to mourn the dead war martyrs for a while, then he moved forward and put a hand on Tuan's shoulder. "All fighting creates loss and sacrifice, Comrade Company Commander. Be brave in front of your officers and soldiers. Our duty ahead is still very tough. Your weeping will weaken the fighting spirit of the whole Company. Get back to your position!"

Tuan quickly wiped his tears away and marched to the front of the company. He made his right hand into a fist and raised it up. "Stay determined to defeat the American invaders and the traitors," he shouted.

"Determined! Determined! Determined!" All the soldiers in the formation raised and shook their fists in the oath of determination. It echoed resoundingly against the immense jungle around them, generating an excitement and an unshakable iron will in the soldiers' souls. Then the men lined up, their weapons slung on their shoulders, and, along with Company Commander Tuan and Political Commissar Mao, walked steadily by their six comrades-in-arms, taking off their hats, and saying farewell to these soldiers who had heroically sacrificed their lives for the Motherland.

Suddenly both Tuan and Mao realized they had forgotten the tradition of offering each dead person a bowl of rice with a boiled egg on top, together with burning incense-sticks. Tuan turned around and asked, Each squad was always issued two bundles of incense-sticks to light whenever someone passed away or was killed and buried on the battlefield. The soldiers assigned to keep the incense-sticks took them out of their rucksacks and gave them to Tuan. Tuan extracted 18 sticks, and trembling slightly, lit them and then passed them to Mao. Political Commissar Mao put three sticks on top of each war martyr's remains. He bowed down three times, and then all the other soldiers did the same, wishing their comrades-in-arms to rest in peace.

Faint trails of smoke rose from the burning incense-sticks and undulated in the breeze, deepening the silence and grief of the moment.

"Huu, cook some rice and put it into six bowls," Company Commander Tuan ordered. "I don't want our brave war martyrs to leave us without offering them a bowl of rice." He waved Hoan closer, grabbed the hen, and without saying a word, broke its neck and handed the chicken back to Hoan. "Boil this quickly so I can offer to our war martyrs."

The six war martyrs of the 26th Reconnaissance Company were buried on a gently sloping hill next to the Tiger Spring. A shrine was erected from rocks covered by leaves, and the boiled hen put into it as an offering. It would stay there until it decayed and began to stink, at which point Tuan would throw it into the Spring for the fish.

As night fell, a heavy silence descended on the area. It had been a tough day and a hard battle with the enemy. Everybody in the 26th Reconnaissance Company, together with the wounded soldiers and the medics and the American prisoner, stayed that night in "Gecko" cave.

No one knew who had named the cave, but everybody heard the geckos croaking nonstop all night, like pupils slowly counting one-two, over and over again, the lizards undisturbed by the explosions of falling bombs. Their combined croaking created a chorus of high and low-pitched notes that came in regular intervals of fifteen minutes, four times an hour. Their noise was maddening to the American POW, who was suffering from malignant malaria. Whenever he started to fall asleep the geckos taking their turns to croak woke him up and frightened him so that he screamed. The malaria was torturing him. He was emaciated and shook with fever. Lan injected him in the buttocks with a gram of Quinine and three shots of Nivaquine each time. He yelled out in pain, tears falling from his eyes, his nose running, his entire body soaked with sweat. The medication and his sweat made his thick, heavy American uniform stink like the rotting corpse of a dead mouse.

Doctor Lien worried that this American POW would soon die. He was unable to eat anything, not even a spoonful of porridge cooked with bits of canned meat. Each time he tried to swallow he would vomit. He would yell English words that no one understood. The croaking of the geckos made him delirious, and he would panic, covering his ears with his hands, his long bony legs kicking wildly. Doctor Lien asked Company Commander Tuan and The Cuong, the temporary interpreter to come to him.

As they approached, the American was still panicking, delirious, yelling out something.

"What is he screaming about," Tuan asked.

"He is calling his mother." Tuan asked Lan to pass him a hot towel. He wiped the American's face and used his hard-pincer-like hands to press acupressure points on the nape of his neck. The American stiffened, then grew quiet and slowly opened his eyes and looked around.

The Cuong tried to remember his English. Apparently

the POW recognized him as the one who had taken him prisoner.

"You, good VC, right, good VC, right?" He burst into tears.

The Cuong lifted the American's shoulders and pulled him onto his lap, trying to comfort him. The American looked up and grabbed The Cuong's arm, "I am afraid of that animal sound. It keeps crowing that ghostly sound. I can't sleep! I am going to die, oh my God, I'm going to die!" He crossed himself.

"He is terrified of the sound the geckos make," Lien said.

Tuan turned to The Cuong and Doctor Lien. "Take him out of the cave, erect a tent for him over an A shaped foxhole, assign someone to guard him, and let one nurse take charge of giving him the proper medicine. If he survives and recovers, we will send him up the Trail to Hanoi."

Tuan took the bowl of porridge from Lan and gave it to The Cuong, "Feed him. If you spoon feed him, he will eat."

The American remained silent. His head still resting on The Cuong's lap, he closed his eyes. But when The Cuong put the spoon into his mouth, his eyes opened wide and he spat the porridge out all over The Cuong's face and chest, saying something at length in English. The Cuong drew back his hand to slap him, but Doctor Lien stopped him, "Don't hit him. He has malignant malaria, so everything tastes bitter to him, and he can't eat it; that's why he's angry. Poor guy. For two days now, he hasn't been able to eat, and is so terrified by the gecko's noise that he can't sleep."

On the third day, the American POW—Tom, was se-

Tiger Spring

verely ill. He didn't only refuse to eat, drink, but also refused to lie still in bed. He kept wandering around the cave, going from this nook to another cranny, and choking while walking at the same time. When being too tired, he then bent down, raised his hands pretending to be holding a gun and shouted boom...boom...boom...as he was shooting in desperation, then suddenly rushed into a nook, bowed, raised his head up and roared like a cow.

Comrade Nurse Lan put down the medicine injection box and thermostat on the ground, she came closer to the POW and helped him to stand up. Tom was ecstatic, dumbfounded, dull, and naïve as he stared at Lan like a pious lamb. Lan quietly smiled in return and gently patted Tom's shoulder:

Nurse Lan continued to examine his health and wellness, only to discover that Tom's condition had deteriorated...She said, "Tom, you have an injection or you might die. Behave, please!" Then she made a sign for The Cuong to be her interpreter.

With her gentle voice, she patted on Tom's head to bend down, pulled his pants down revealing his thin skin to the bony butt. Lan slightly rubbed alcohol on one side of his butt and quickly gave a dosage of medicine. Tom jumped up, screaming! Suddenly, the American POW saw an AK-47 gun that Comrade Cuong was leaning against the cave wall, he quickly jumped-over and grabbed it, aiming at Cuong and Lan and shouting loudly, "Boom...boom...boom, boom...VC...VC...boom...b oom..." Lan calmly and bravely stood in front of the gunpoint to shield The Cuong, she then slowly walked closer to Tom, looked at his eyes while she raised-up both skinny pale hands towards him, and making a peaceful gesture to Tom, "Come on, Tom! Please listen to me…I beg you to give me the gun! Stop making fun! Are you going to kill me too?"

Standing behind Lan, The Cuong wasshaking and with his trembling voice, trying to translate for Tom. Tom just looked up bewilderedly, while holding the gun, he walked backwards to the end of the cave. Just then, the whole cave suddenly rumbled with the sound of footsteps rushing in, the sounds of guns loaded and locked by the soldiers surrendering the cave…pointing all the barrels aimed at Tom.

Panicking and nervous, Lan turned right, turned left, turned back, swerving forward, stretching her arms…, she screamed out loud with her tongue twist shouting, "Hey guys…Don't shoot! Please, don't shoot him…I beg of you!" As she burst out into tears for being anxious and fearful, she shouted, "He has malignant malaria and high fever that turned him into a psychotic, but he is not a bad guy, and he doesn't cause harm to us. He used to be nice and appreciate us. He is an intellectual and affections, for sure he doesn't want to kill anyone, especially me."

Then she turned to a grumpy woman and ordered, "Get back to your duty everyone! Let The Cuong and I deal with him. I will bear all the responsibility for Tom." She then waved to Tom, "Tom, come over here!"

Now that Cuong comes along with Lan slowly walking towards Tom, and says calmly, "Hey there, listen to Lan, Tom!"

Lan calmly came closer, she then reached out and

grabbed the gun in one hand and hugged Tom with the other, almost pressing his head to her chest. The POW let go of the gun. Lan took it and placed the AK 47 on the ground, with her hands she frantically caressed Tom's head. A mixture of strong foul and stinky smells from his head and his clothes horrified her that caused her to regurgitate and just about to throw up.

She had to raise her head, take in a full lung of fresh air, hold her breath, and release him. Then Lan directed The Cuong, "Please do give the POW a bath with boiled lemongrass leaves for his treatment since he has severe malaria! If we don't try to rescue him and if he dies…, so you may have wasted your chance not to shoot him then?"

The Cuong pushed Tom to the cave bathroom, then smiled and said, "Let's try to save this priceless American in exchange for gold and dollars from the US government. I'm told that the US side must pay as much gold that is equal to his weight to our government…if he is safe and alive! Is it not by coincidence that our superiors ordered us not to let him be hungry, cold and die. Everybody's caution and plans to escort him safely to Hanoi to return to the US government in exchange for gold and dollars. We are poor, we really need gold and dollars to buy weapons to fight against the American and the Saigonese troops."

Doctor Lien and Tuan nested in a nook of the cave. That night it grew colder and colder. When it was almost dawn, Lien awoke, shivering, and tried to dispel her sleepiness by boiling a pot of leaves and inhaling the steam. She moved close to the fire, putting more and more wood onto it, but still her body kept trembling and sweat drenched her clothes. The heat of the fire was not enough to warm her. Tuan knew that she had suffered from flu and then a painful bout of malaria. He covered her with a thin blanket and hugged her tightly, so that she would sweat more. The warmth from his strong body eased her pain and stopped her trembling. She tried to go to sleep in his arms.

Feeling her thin, fragile body in his arms, Tuan felt deeply sorry for Lien. He lightly caressed her, all over her body, warming her. Lien opened her eyes. "My breasts and buttocks are flabby, aren't they," she asked softly.

Company Commander Tuan's face twitched, and he swallowed heavily, as if trying to clear a lump that was painfully swelling in his throat.

"It's because you don't have your man with you. When you are with a man your body will be fresh again. Don't worry, let me massage you." Tuan kneaded her breasts, feeling her skin growing warmer under his hand. Lien closed her eyes, breathing faster. She put her arms around Tuan. "I'm feeling uncomfortable…Don't…don't, let me go, please!"

At that moment, Lan, Hoan, and Huu entered. Tuan said, "Doctor Lien caught the flu, and then developed malaria," Tuan said. "I had to hug her to warm her up. She's doing better now. Lan, please take my place and hold her in your arms, let her sleep a little more. When she wakes up, give her some milk. Thank you. I'm going to get some sleep. I'm very tired."

Close to Doctor Lien's nook, there's also the one for Tom and The Cuong. That afternoon, The Cuong and the nurses gave Tom a bath in hot water with boiled lemon leaves, then gave him some milk, some porridge to eat, and followed by a dose of antimalarial. The fever stopped and Tom could sleep for about three or four hours at times during the day. At night, he woke up, feeling quite well. While next door, under the light of the kerosene lamp, The Cuong was in his deep sleep snoring loudly.

A natural human sexual phenomenon...and it happens. Flashing back on what happened in the morning, when the soldiers' barrels pointed at Tom and Lan, the slender young and pale lady, her voice choked from begging the soldiers not to shoot. And the feeling of being hugged in her maiden arms, with the smell of grapefruit leaves on Lan's hair pressed on his face. A feeling...likely ecstatic, stiffened him. The male instinct hormones arose, Lan's image kept flickering in his mind, making him stir inside the thin blanket.

Then he held his hairy hands and shook his limp penis in the crotch. He was in imaginative and excited, feeling ecstatic, overwhelming of joy. tingle hot flashes all over the body. Tom suddenly let out a groan that awoke The Cuong.

Thinking that Tom had malaria again, The Cuong hurriedly turned on the flashlight and went to Tom's bed. He reached out and grabbed the corner of the thin blanket covering Tom's body and pulled it up. Under the light of the flashlight, The Cuong clearly saw Tom's loose shorts in withered grass color was pulled down to his knees, his two hairy hands were holding his penis, shaking it in moaning. From the corners of Tom's hands, a little bit of white liquid flowed out and landed on the thin blanket. The Cuong released Tom's blanket and shook his head, said pitifully:

"You have such severe malaria, how could it be erected that you do it yourself, Tom? Don't you know anything about malaria? Malaria parasite eliminates the sperm, and it's hard to ejaculate."

Listening to what The Cuong said, Tom paled, trembling. In a sudden, he burst into tears, holding tightly on The Cuong's arm, bewildered, "It mean that I can't make love with woman anymore…yes?"

The Cuong patted on Tom's shoulders, "Don't worry, now you are in severe malaria that weakens you. Back home in the United States, having good food and being cured, you will be normal again."

Then Tom smiled, shaking his head, "Oh dear, malaria in Vietnam is so terrible. It can kill your penis. Oh my God!"

7

Their victory in the battle with the Americans and Saigonese force meant that the 26th Reconnaissance Company had succeeded in their mission of protecting the safety of the strategic route that passed through three fronts: the Central Highlands, the Southeast region, and southern Laos. The hundreds of wounded and sick soldiers at the Tiger Spring Medical Station had been evacuated to safety and had now been brought back to the cave. The number of the enemy's casualties couldn't be accurately counted but could not be less than forty or fifty killed in action, including the helicopter that had been shot down while carrying nearly twenty men, and the three helicopters full of dead and wounded that had been seen flying in the direction of Quang Tri.

But the losses sustained by the 26th Reconnaissance Company were substantial. Beside the six war martyrs, there were twenty wounded, and all the unit's tents, food, and military equipment had been destroyed by the enemy. Before their withdrawal, they had insidiously planted leaf mines, which would kill or maim any soldiers who didn't remain vigilant. All the soldiers' lives felt completely disrupted.

The company CP had been shifted to a new location, and each squad and platoon no longer camped at the edge of the jungle or cliffs, but instead dug small foxholes along the mountainside. Each foxhole housed three people and were dug 10 to 15 meters apart to be a more difficult target for enemy bombs or rockets.

It was the rainy season in southern Laos. The incessant rain caused floods and avalanches which nearly paralyzed efforts to bring food, supplies, and reinforcements from Vietnam. The whole company depended on grated tubers, wild vegetables, and fish from Tiger Spring for sustenance.

Now, Huu had his chance to show off the talent for catching crabs and fish he had honed during his school days in the salt marshes of his home province. In the early morning, along with a spear head fashioned from a steel gun barrel and inserted into the end of a bamboo stick, Huu asked Captain Tuan for permission to take Hoan with him. Huu was very familiar with the habits of the local fish — at night they entered the underwater cave and at first light they would swim out with the current to search for food.

When it wasn't raining or flooding, Huu found Tiger Spring to be lovely in the morning. The fresh, cool air was permeated with the fragrance of young leaves that had just budded, their scent a part of the essence of "mother forest" and its innumerable blossoms of all colors that bloomed overnight. Flowers and young leaves, incubated in the nighttime dew, were lifted and scattered everywhere by boisterous or gentle breezes fanning through the ravines, gently plucking petals and sprinkling them over the crystal clear stream. Tiny flower petals fluttered on the water as if they were dancing, their motion enticing the fish to swim out and chase those gifts the forest had blown to them. All Huu had to do was choose the biggest fish and thrust his fishing spear into it, The fish would wiggle helplessly again the barbs on the spear and Huu would lift it up so that Hoan could slide it off and place it into their rucksack.

The fish that dwelt in the caves and streams of Lower Laos were a cross between grass carp and mud carp, with a long body, a white head, and shiny white scales. The biggest fish were just over a kilogram. Every morning, Huu and Hoan struggled with the fish for more than an hour before filling the rucksack with enough fish to feed the company for a whole day.

But while this source of fish was abundant for ten days, it gradually ran out. In addition, Political Commissar Mao ordered Huu not to catch female fish so that they could lay eggs to reproduce and thrive. Huu had to use his initiative to collect ingredients for nutritional dishes which could be provided for the soldiers of the 26th Company.

The affection, trust, and expectations of his comrades-in-arms imposed a heavy burden of responsibility on Huu. He spent more than a few sleepless nights, tossing and turning, searching his childhood memories for ways of finding food in the poor countryside. He knew that where there was water and soil, there would be plants, flowers, life. He knew if human beings would love nature, they would survive. With that knowledge always in his consciousness, he would wait for the sun to rise and the forest to wake, for the birds to sing and the flowers bloom in fragrance. He and Hoan, rifles and rucksacks slung over their shoulders, would go foraging for food. Nature was always a generous mother for her children. One could learn to read her secrets, hidden deep underground, or under the trees in the rotting leaves, or on the tree tops in the buds of young leaves, or in old leaves or new petals, or the withered flowers of the mountain. If one never went into the forest—he never thought of it as "jungle".

If one didn't love the forest passionately, he would never discover the sacred and miraculous that existed in their surroundings. Every time Huu entered a forest, he felt an urgency and eagerness in his heart, a strange, willed excitement at integrating his life, his breath, with the rhythm of the forest, discovering anew its magnificence and mystery. With just a short hoe and a dagger in his hand, as he searched and dug, Huu was gaining a great understanding of what nature meant for human beings.

After many days spent discovering the generosity of "mother forest," Huu was proud to teach what he had learned about surviving to his comrades-in-arms.

His first lectures centered on the underground life of the forest. The forest floor, which seemed silent and inanimate actually teemed with life: the birth and death cycle of countless species of insects that constantly renewed the earth. The fertile land was filled with life, its lush trees constantly budding, blooming, and bearing fruit that sustained many different creatures. Under the trees, under the mounds of silent termites, were colonies of earth bees, thousands upon thousands of them, each the size of a little finger, shiny and round, with waxy abdomens filled with fragrant honey. There were rats, pythons, snakes, turtles, toads, and frogs.

Huu taught which of the flowers, fruits, and leaves could be sweet and nourishing and which were poisonous. Only someone who understood the forest knew that the leaves that seem to be very bitter, very sour, would contain no toxins and that could cure many of the diseases of soldiers on the battlefield.

The growing knowledge and appreciation for the forest they absorbed from Huu lessened the other young soldiers' apprehensions about surviving in this wild mountainous place. Huu's enthusiasm for the nature all around them was catching; they were seduced by it, eager to connect to the forest and discover its immortal magic. The more they learned, the more they felt a strength, courage, and pride in their own abilities.

To obtain honey from a beehive, to hunt a python, a rat, or a wild animal, to be able to find and gather ten kilograms of yam or a rucksack filled with edible vegetables and leaves, was not only arduous, but also required perseverance, courage, and ingenuity. They knew if they committed one small mistake, they might have to pay for it in blood, or even their lives.

What they learned of the generosity, greatness and vitality of the forest assured the soldiers of the 26th Company that they did not have to starve to death in this unwholesome environment. Even on the days when they couldn't find other food, their "saviors" were worms, insects, and larvae that became "trapped" at night in the water holes they'd dug. Such insects and bugs were boiled thoroughly with bitter and sour leaves to detoxify them. Hungry as they were, the young soldiers gulped them all down.

While foraging helped resolve the food issue for the company, information was received about dire circumstances in Bong Va village, home for people from the Van Kieu ethnic group in western Quang Tri. Village land straddled the Laotian border, an area that was continually carpet-bombed by B52's and sprayed with toxic chemicals. The villagers had stopped farming the poisoned soil and had sheltered into caves. Many Van Kieu had died of hunger and malaria; the company received orders instructing them to find ways of helping the villagers.

Company Commanding Officer Tuan and Political Commissar Mao drew up a plan. It would take five days for someone familiar with the trails through the forest to get to Bong Va; the question was how much food could the company contribute, including the rations to be eaten by the rescue party along the way. After careful calculations, Tuan and Mao decided that the company could spare ten kilograms of rice, three kilograms of salt, and seven hundred grams of monosodium glutamate as emergency relief for people in the two hamlets.

Instead of the usual team of three, a two-person team would go, saving the rations that would have gone to feed an extra mouth. There was no question that the best men for the mission were Hoan and Huu, especially with Huu's knowledge of how to forage in the forest.

Tiger Spring

Tuan went with Huu and Hoan as far as the river bordering Vietnam and Laos. It was flood season, and the water flowed rapidly and rough, spilling over the banks and sweeping along clusters of dead tree trunks, branches, and leaves in its current. Huu and Hoan took off their clothes and placed them, along with their rucksacks and hammocks, into big plastic bags.

"You two do your best," Tuan said compassionately. "I know it will be an arduous and difficult journey, but I hope that you will get most of this meager amount of rice and salt to the children, to the elderly, and to the ill from these two hamlets. For them, a kernel of rice or a grain of salt is more precious than gold…"

Unembarrassed, even though he was naked as a savage, Huu hugged Tuan's muscular shoulders.

"Don't worry, boss. The two of us won't eat more than one bowl of rice: five bowls in five days should be less than two kilograms." Huu laughed. "That will leave 15 kilograms for many of the starving."

Huu and Hoan shook hands with Tuan, slung their AKs on their backs, held onto the big plastic bag containing the rest of their things that each carried, and jumped into the flood. The river here was not too wide, and Huu was a good swimmer, so he had no difficulty carrying a bag and his weapon. But Hoan, a young Hanoian, was familiar with music, but had no experience diving into a muddy, torrent. Taking Hoan's plastic bag and kicking, Huu pushed Hoan inch by inch though the current. Finally, with Huu's help, Hoan was able to reach the other bank. As soon he got back on the ground, still pale with fear, Hoan screamed joyfully and waved both arms at Tuan, who stood watching from the other bank.

As soon as he put the bag down and slid off his rifle, Huu dove back into the river. When he came up, he was holding a large carp in his hands. "Great, you're great, Huu," Hoan shouted out happily, looking at Huu with an admiration Huu pretended not to notice. Using his dagger, he slit open the fish, threw its intestines into the water, and marinated it with some salt and then packed it into his rucksack. "It's enough for a nice meal for one day," he said calmly. "Come on, let's go!"

After passing the river, they entered the forest. As a result of the carpet bombing in this area, it appeared shriveled and tattered, with fallen trees, blackened from catching fire, scattered everywhere. From here and there, they could hear the sound of geckos clicking their tongues, a painfully sad sound that was interspersed with the mournful laments of birds calling each other. The birds all seemed timid and fearful as they searched for places to roost, starting nervously whenever they heard a noise from afar. The rain of American bombs had stripped away the natural and ancient instincts of the animals and the birds. They no longer sang, twittered, danced, or flew innocently and wildly in their flocks as they always had.

Occasionally the two men heard the sound of flapping wings, or the footfalls of some animals, very light and hesitant, like ghosts walking in the dark. The atmosphere became more and more gloomy, permeated with a sense of tragedy. A constant drizzle kept the soil wet, and there were snails and leeches everywhere. Huu told Hoan to take his sandals off and stow them in his back pack; they only wore anti-leech wrappings tied tightly up to their knees.

Instead of walking, they trotted slowly, not giving the leeches enough time to fasten on them. It was the right move, but whenever they had to pass through areas where the trees were dense and climb up steep slopes, both men would still find leeches fastened in between their fingers. They were impossible to pull off and had to be pried out at knife point, the leeches falling to the ground swollen with blood. They were fortunate that Political Commissar Mao had given them a vial of ointment to stop bleeding.

As if struggling with leeches wasn't tough enough for them, they were attacked several times by some of the thousands and thousands of cluster flies and gadflies feeding on the rotting corpses of people and animals. On hearing the two men approaching, the flies would rise and swarm them, violently buzzing like bees whose hive had smashed, emitting a horrible stench that made Huu and Hoan want to vomit.

Whenever they saw a corpse, both men would just dare to glance at it and then would run past, their heads down. Having not yet fought in many battles, they were unused to such tragic and horrific sights. Huu couldn't help staring obsessively at the sight of a dead Van Kieu mother and her two children. The mother looked emaciated, with sores all over her face and her eyes still open. She was hugging a less than one year old baby, his legs hanging loose, his tiny hands clutching his mother's skinny, monkey-like body, his mouth still tightly latched onto her shriveled nipple, and another dead child, a little older, curled up at her feet.

Huu Uoc

As they ran past those hideous corpses, Huu felt dizzy, and staggered, the burnt tree trunks and the sky turning upside down, spinning and dancing around him. As a human being, he felt ashamed and powerless in the face of the untimely death of these unfortunate and innocent people. Unable to control himself, he started weeping, even as he continued to run. Hoan, who was a few steps ahead, turned back to him. "Are you afraid of death? It's war. Death is normal, so stop being so emotional..."

He grabbed Huu's hand, yanking him into a faster run through that tragic mournful forest.

That night, they found an ideal location to have a rest after the shock of seeing such scenes. It was a clean, deep cave, filled with a natural fragrance and hung with beautiful stalactites. The small entrance may have concentrated and funneled the scent of flowers and leaves, of heaven and earth from time immemorial that permeated every corner of the cave. Huu and Hoan felt immersed in the fresh, wonderful atmosphere of the forest.

They made a fire, and Hoan boiled water in the mess kit, poured it into two canteens and left some inside, adding two handfuls of rice. When it was done, he scooped the rice into two iron bowls and turned one upside down on top of the other: a traditional way to make an offering bowl of rice. Taking the fish out, he cut it into half, skewed a stick into its belly and grilled it. After a day spent running, without food, they filled their stomachs with water, but the smell of the grilled fish didn't tempt them. They quietly carried the offering bowl filled with rice and half of the grilled fish to the entrance, placed it on a flat rock, and murmured prayers for the dead, for the wandering souls who had now become ghosts in this desolate wasteland, which awaited its liberation.

Outside, the wind howled, its sound mingling with the shrill caws and flapping wings of the crows as they flocked to the corpses. Where did crows that big and that fat, as large as the gourd ducks raised in fish ponds back home, come from? Murder after murder of crows, attracted by the smell of blood, the smell of death, flew in from all directions, excited, frantic, cawing noisily. Swooping down, they pounced on the swollen corpses, pecking, poking, gouging, and tearing off patches of rotting flesh and filling the air with the stench of human blood.

Huu watched the crows hovering and circling above the dead forest, its blackened soil pocked with new bomb craters, like suppurating sores on a human body. He pictured them tearing at the corpses of people who once had been loving couples, old men and women, young mothers and their children, all the poor human souls whose lives had been suddenly severed by bombs like trees suddenly snapped in half by a typhoon.

They were in a good place that night, warmed by the fire and the smell of the grilled fish still in their nostrils, but still neither man could sleep, even though they both knew they needed it in order to make it through the next day, continue to Bong Va where people were waiting and longing for the rice and salt they would bring, waiting to be reassured that they would never be abandoned by the Party and the Revolution. Each man told himself to sleep. But in his hammock, Hoan kept turning and tossing and sighing, and Huu stared at the fire and looked out of the cave entrance, listening to the whispering wind gusting against the cliffs and shaking the leaf canopies in front of the cave as if it was the crying of wandering souls.

Huu remembered when he was a student and would encounter floating lights, looking like jack-o-lanterns, in the village cemetery when he had to lay eel pipes, and fish and shrimp traps near that place. While waiting, he would sometimes fall asleep atop a grassy grave mound. His sleep would be restless, especially during rainy nights when he would see ghosts hovering like human shadows. Sometimes he saw five of seven shadows gathered together, talking, whispering, lamenting, or singing lullabies.

Usually in those moments, Huu would close his eyes, clamp his hand over his eyes and whisper prayers: "I beg you, spirits, don't take me; I am still so young and I will not harm any of your graves…" Still terrified, he would eventually fall asleep, waking when the sunlight shone on his eyes and he would hurry to check the traps and gather the fish or shrimp he had caught. Eventually he became used to seeing the lights and stopped being disturbed by them.

But tonight, along with the cold wind rustling through the cave, he heard long howls, one after another. They did not sound like the noise an animal would make; they sounded clearly human: endless, lamenting, lonely howls. One howl, then two, three, then five, seven, like animals calling each other after being dispersed and now trying to regather. Huu lay motionless, listening. Suddenly the howling stopped, only to be replaced by bursts of laughter as high-pitched as the squealing of pigs being poked with sticks. One peal of laughter, then two, then five, then seven, all of them merging together in the middle of the dark night and pouring into the cave, raising goose bumps on Huu's skin. He shivered in fright, sweating so much it soaked his hammock.

Looking over, he saw that Hoan was still tossing and turning.

"Did you hear the howls and laughter out there, Hoan?"

"I did. Are you scared?"

"Yes, I am. I'm afraid! I've encountered ghosts before, but I've never heard ghosts' laugh like that."

"They aren't ghosts; they're the souls of those who died unjustly, which is what makes their laughter sound so strange and so wild." Huu clicked his tongue. "The war's worst victims are ordinary people. They have been shot and bombed and poisoned, along with all the usual natural calamities they have to face. There used to be more than a thousand people living in Bong Va; now there may be only a dozen or so survivors, living in caves."

"When will this war end, Huu?"

"I ask myself the same question. The war can last five years, ten years, twenty years or longer, but the Vietnamese people are determined not to be afraid. Nothing is more precious than independence and freedom. We'd rather sacrifice everything..."

"Exactly as Uncle Ho said..."

"I remember Uncle Ho's appeal in 1965. Who knows when this war will end? I wonder if you and I can survive until the end of the war?"

"Come on, stop saying inauspicious on life and dead! It

isn't fun. Try to get some sleep; we have three more days to go."

In his half-unconscious, half-dreaming state, Huu left behind all the shadows, all the souls, all the nameless, unidentifiable corpses of people who might have been soldiers or civilians, enemies or friends; left behind the ghostly howls that both terrified him and wounded his heart. He had found that the true tragedy of the war in which he'd found himself came not from the fierce battles between soldiers but in the accusatory silence of the mothers, fathers, wives, lovers, and families longing for the soldiers to come back home. And the greatest pain for the soldiers in the midst of battle lay in their memories and longings for their homes, for their loved ones, for the memories of the past that were slipping away, so far away.

But in his dreams that night, Huu's mind avoided any painful memories; instead, his mind drifted to his teenage years. He dreamed of the road he would take through the immense greenness of the rice fields when they were in full bloom, the bright sunlight shining on the stalks. He dreamed of clumsily holding the hand of a seventeen-year-old girl with two ponytails and big, round eyes, the girl that he'd secretly loved and now deeply missed. He felt her panicked breath, saw the image of her slim back as she walked further and further away from him, shouldering two baskets of paddy, and he frantically ran after her, calling "Ly! Ly! Wait…wait!"

Suddenly Huu awoke, still looking around for the young girl with the two ponytails and the big black eyes.

The cold wind rushing in from the entrance of the cave, the ghosts' mournful howl brought him back to reality.

At dawn, they pulled on their rucksacks, slung their rifles, and continued crossing the dead forest. As the sun rose, the first golden rays of the new day brought some of the vitality of the nature to the forest as it began dispelling the opaque mist which lay on the land like a patchy shirt.

The sun poured its warmth on the ground, chasing away the thick milky mist, revealing the burned soil of the forest. For the two men, it was wonderful to see, amidst this immensity smoldering with death, life sprouting, fresh and tender. Tens of thousands of seedlings of all kinds were germinating and pushing shoots and plants up through the ashes. Their young green leaves, wet with shimmering dew, fluttered in the early wind as if they were welcoming a new day, revealing the tough, immortal vitality of the forest.

From caves and craters and dead tree trunks, numerous species of birds flew out, flapping their wings and singing to greet the new day. Their sound, so warm, so noble and sacred, wove together different melodies, some high-pitched, some low; sometimes soft, almost to whispering, sometimes bright and lively, chasing away the gloomy atmosphere of the ruined forest, the stench of corpses and the wandering souls lurking around, all the noises that had tormented Hoan and Huu all night long.

There in the scorched earth, among the germinating verdant plants, Huu recognized the tips of Okinawan spinach, a life-sustaining vegetable for soldiers. "Okinawan spinach, Okinawan spinach, oh dear!" Huu and Hoan both shouted simultaneously. Without another word, they bent down and picked the leaves. Soon they had two big bunches of vegetables packed into their rucksacks. They moved forward. After that long night filled with so much sadness, and fear, both had the same thought: that in this horrible war, where there was only destruction, starvation, death and wandering souls, would the future be just a continuation of such darkness, each day, each month, each year, year after year? The future seemed like a dark tunnel with no light at the end, no way out.

Soldiers did not ask questions nor expect to receive answers. They only knew to fight and to survive. Their existence endured with their belief that they had chosen the right path. The country was in danger: foreign invaders were destroying their homeland. The desire to fight for national salvation was like a bell, awakening millions and millions of people's hearts; their longing to take their places in the immortal epic overwhelmed any feelings of cowardice or the selfish desire for hedonistic living. It was sacred and magnificent and gave soldiers the strength and determination they needed.

As they encountered the harsh, painful reality of the war, soldiers needed the belief and pride that made them ready to fight and sacrifice for the country. But they also needed to see and feel the vitality of nature in their daily lives. It was for Huu and Hoan at this moment: the sunrise, the fresh and fragrant morning breeze, the birds singing in the forest and the germinating buds of the plants poking up through the ashes that chased away the fear, and despair they kept in the dark, hidden corners of their souls.

For Huu, nature inspired a belief in the future, in the

renewing life all around him that was embracing and protecting him. For a moment, the cold darkness in his soul was gone. But then came back, stronger. He realized suddenly that he had never ever been able to live and to love as fully as he had in these very miserable moments. He vowed he would never subject himself to self-pity and self-doubt again.

A day passed and then two more beautiful days passed, even though his thighs ached, and his face was bruised from tripping and falling on the rocky path to Bong Va.

On the fourth day, they felt buoyed by their quest, like two Don Quixotes fighting a windmill in the middle of mountains and forests where no man had walked. They didn't speak of it, but they had come to feel that they had overcome a cowardly acceptance of and surrender to fate, to become true human beings, true revolutionary soldiers. It was what kept them going from early morning until dark until they stopped to rest next to the musically murmuring water of a shallow spring. There, Huu spent a night without nightmares, without swaggering ghosts, without streams of blood and rotting corpses, and resentful lamenting. In the hammock next to him, Hoan was snoring. After four days struggling with starvation, thirst, with the obsession of death, with the howls and cries of wandering souls, both were exhausted. They slept soundly.

They woke at dawn the next day, knowing they had one more day of walking to Bong Va village. Their breakfast was boiled Okinawan spinach with a pinch of salt and a little glutamate. As it steamed, it emitted a pungent, unpleasant smell, but it was full of vitamins. Huu and Hoan enjoyed feeling the warmth of the vegetable soup entering their intestines. But when their stomachs warmed up, a craving for rice arose, and suddenly they felt nauseous and then very tired, a heavy fatigue seeping into their bodies.

"Let's cook some rice," Huu said. "I'm dying for rice. For the past two days, we've only eaten this Okinawan spinach. My stomach is getting upset."

Thinking about rice made the saliva well up in Huu's mouth. Better to not think about it. But in this situation, they needed to do what was necessary to complete their mission. Without eating rice, no matter how pure spiritually he and Hoan would be, it would be very difficult for them to have the energy for another day's climbing up the mountains and crossing the ridgelines. And who could predict if they would be bombed today.

Huu opened the mess-tin lid, poured in a bowl of water, and then pulled a full sack of rice out of his rucksack. He put three handfuls into the mess-tin. Feeling tense, he bent over and blew on the fire to cook the rice. When it was done, he scooped it into the steel bowls, and handed one to Hoan. Hoan took it hesitatingly, as if reluctant to eat. Huu gave him a few grains of salt.

"Eat up and let's go. People are waiting for us."

Hoan put a few crystals of salt in his mouth, and then picked up the rice. He finished about half a bowl and gave the other half to Huu. Huu also put salt into his mouth before eating the rice. He chewed and swallowed slowly. Perhaps because the rice was too old and no longer had any scent, or perhaps because of having to eat rice this way, he felt his craving for it suddenly disappear, to be replaced by a bitter feeling of self-pity. Tears flowed out of his eyes, slowly drop by drop, rolling into his mouth, and increasing the feeling of bitterness. He tried not to let Hoan see that he was crying. Hoan was dividing the other bowl of rice in half, wrapping each portion into a banana leaf. He put them in a side pocket of his rucksack and told Huu to get going.

The fifth and last day of their journey to the Van Kieu ethnic people in Bong Va hamlet went quite smoothly. The weather was cool, and the fog contained the scent of flowers and grass. The rest of the road went over gentle hills, with no big trees, but only groves of myrtle, filled with purple flowers. After a full night's sleep, and a good meal of spinach and half a bowl of rice, they were eager to come to Bong Va hamlet. They ran rather than walked towards the village.

Late in the morning, the sun shining harshly on an area full of myrtle bushes and corn flowers, they heard the rumbling sound of an approaching aircraft. They ducked under some myrtle bushes and scanned the clear, cloudless sky. Two jets, darting like giant dragonflies, tore through the sky. They didn't strafe or drop bombs, but Hoan and Huu spotted four plumes of white smoke pouring from the wings like meteor trails. Panicked, Huu shouted: "My God! They are spraying toxic chemicals!"

"What can we do now?" Hoan asked.

"Take your towel out, pee on it and cover your face."

"Damn the American sons of bitches!"

They quickly pulled the towels out of their rucksacks, hastily unbuttoned their pants, and strained out a few drops of cloudy yellow urine to wet their green towels.

Huu Uoc

In the sky, the two planes, like two evil monsters, dove towards the hills. The smell of wild flowers that had permeated the whole area was now tainted by the strong, unpleasant smell of pesticides. A few buffalo ran out crazily from the tree line. Two of them, as big as war horses, trampled through the myrtle bush where Huu and Hoan were hiding, defecating as they ran and leaving a trail of steaming shit behind them. Grinning, Huu told Hoan to help him scoop up the hot shit and spread it thickly on one side of their towels. They pressed the towels soaked in urine and buffalo shit over their noses and mouths, and then hurriedly gathered their rucksacks and moved somewhere downwind, trying to avoid the toxic fumes from the dioxin chemical poison the planes were pouring down from the sky.

Suddenly a pair of bulls, as big as buffaloes rushed up behind them, panicked by the roaring of the airplanes. Afraid that the bulls would run them over, Hoan fired off two shots from his AK. The bulls both defecated immediately and then turned around and ran off in the other direction.

Huu and Hoan ran over to the two new piles of excrement, which stank and emitted dark green fumes. The men had been taught by Tuan that the urine and dung from bulls were "magical" drugs—drinking them would make people immune to chemical toxins and resistant to all diseases—but only if one squeezed out the liquid and drank it hot and fresh. Huu and Hoan quickly scooped the bulls' dung up with their towels and squeezed out drops of fecal liquid into their mouths.

Tiger Spring

They kept running downwind. By the time the sound of the planes finally faded away and the bitter smell of poison in the wind subsided, they were exhausted and fell to the ground like two chopped banana trees. They lay face down in the black, stinking towels. The stench, baked by the sun and mixed with their sweat, became unbearable. Both men puked their guts out. They pulled out a water bottle and washed out their mouths and faces. The horror had faded, but the nausea remained. Huu suddenly remembered that he still had wild spinach in his rucksack. He took some out, gave Hoan a handful, and they chewed each leaf slowly, very slowly. The bitter, sour, pungent taste of this kind of vegetable usually made it impossible to be eaten raw. For soldiers and people who lived in the jungle, it was to be boiled or cooked properly. But in this situation, the unpleasant taste was a wonderfully effective antidote against the discomfort and horror welling-up in their throats. It allowed them to relax and lay face up to the sky, breathing in some fresh air.

It was late afternoon, the sky cloudless. Since Huu's first day in the war, he had never been able to look up and enjoy a sky as beautiful and spacious as this. In the west, the sun was now a small golden disc hidden behind the distant mountains, the sunlight, as it weakened, sending shimmering pink rays over the undulating hills, stirring a poetic, yearning echo in his breast. Purple and pink myrtle and melastoma flowers stretched as far as he could see, scattered among the sparkling blades of green grass swaying in the light breeze of the afternoon. From the myrtle and melastoma groves, from the rocks, and mounds of

Huu Uoc

decaying leaves piling high from time immemorial, small warblers flew out, chirping, hopping, running, and singing, filling the whole space with their cheerful sound.

Suddenly Huu and Hoan heard a rumbling noise, very close to the stream at the foot of the hill. They hurriedly gathered their belongings and quietly approached the stream. The rumbling grew clearer, interspersed with the sound of heavy panting and bellows from an animal. Hiding themselves behind myrtle bushes on the crest of a hill, they saw a pair of elephants passionately making love on the gentle slope beside the stream at the foot of the hill. The young female elephant was comparatively small, her clay-colored tusks just sprouted like two lotus buds. Her male partner was twice her size, with a shiny black back and fierce bloodshot eyes, glowing with eagerness. It was in a frenzy, using a trunk as big as a banana tree to push the female elephant onto the slope, happily trumpeting at the sky.

It started to drizzle, a spring drizzle so light it wouldn't wet even butterfly wings, and the shallow stream was gurgling lazily. Droplets of water on the leaves started to bead and trail gently into the clear water, not even dappling the surface. The breeze rustled the myrtle petals, and sprinkled tiny purple dots on the flowing stream, attracting all kinds of fish to leap and play with them. Butterflies of all colors contributed to the beautiful sunset by darting back and forth to show off their brilliant wings. They swooped down and tried to cling to the male elephant, who was madly in love, intoxicated with passion; he swept the butterflies off with his tail. It rained a little heavier, and the male elephant seemed to gain more strength, rising and crushing the poor little female elephant under his forelegs. Silent, eyes closed, she accepted the violent thrusts of her partner.

Huu and Hoan remained motionless, their hearts pounding as they lay on the ground, nervously watching the elephants. They understood that the male elephant was in the throes of passion and would crush the life out of anything that dared to disturb his carnal pleasure.

But their fascination with the love life of these elephants was suddenly interrupted when a pack of gray wolves rushed out of the dense jungle just past the ravine, splitting into two groups as they came. One group of five was led by the largest male wolf, its head big as a lion's, its bared fangs flashing like sword blades as it howled.... Another four came from the other side, led by the second largest wolf. They rushed in ferociously, also baring their sharp teeth, howling....oooo oooo....The sound was chilling, so wild that it made Hoan and Huu shiver with fear, hug each other tightly and close their eyes, not daring to watch the wolves attack the two elephants.

Hearing their howl and the sound of the branches breaking under their footpads as they came, the male elephant let go of his partner. The two elephants shifted around until they stood back-to-back, shaking their heads, and swinging their trunks from right to left. The male elephant trampled and smashed the rocks under his feet, trumpeting, each cry like pounding surf shaking the forest. As if in response, the whole pack of wolves howled "....oooo oooo," the sound like cold steel striking stones as they attacked the elephants from four sides, biting and slashing at their backs and buttocks in a frenzy.

The male elephant roared painfully, its two fan-shaped ears swollen and bleeding as it kicked out with deadly accuracy, as if its feet could see: forward, behind, left, right, each kick hitting a wolf. It wrapped its trunk, which was as long as a banana tree, around the gray wolves that were jumping on the back of the female elephant and tossed them off. The wolves, their eyes sparkling and green, plunged their fangs into the neck or back or bottom of the female elephant. The male elephant got its trunk around one wolf after another, piercing them with its sharp tusks, and then tossing their bodies down into the ravine and the creek. The female elephant didn't have the same power, but she had the instinct to keep swinging her trunk defensively, wildly spraying water on the hideous wolves, trampling and kicking out in all directions. The battle between elephants and wolves became more and more fierce, the corner of the forest in which they fought becoming as damaged as if it had been hit by a cyclone.

In the midst of all the tumult, suddenly Huu clearly heard the ringing of the small copper bells that the ethnic minority people often wore around the neck of the domesticated animals. "Come on! These elephants are domesticated," Huu told Hoan, "They must have run away from home because they're in heat. We have to save them. Remember, domesticated elephants are very smart, they will help us."

Before Hoan had time to respond, Huu had jumped out from behind the rocks and fired a burst of AK rounds, three shots at a time. Hoan followed him from behind the rock, and, knowing that wolves were very cunning and sensitive, pulled the pin of an American grenade and threw it at the wolves. The explosion, together with the burst from the AK, scared the wolves and they ran off into the forest.

The male elephant, his muscular body like a huge gray rock, his hide covered with thick black hair as hard as a bull's hoof, was stained with dark red blood from the wolves' attack. The female was even more pathetic; her thinner hide had been mauled and slashed all over by the wolves' fangs, exposing patches of red flesh. Fresh blood flowed from wounds on her back, belly, and legs.

As Hoan and Huu approached them, both elephants trumpeted:"ah ah ah uom…" a sad, depressed sound. Hoan and Huu understood that they were in pain and needed help. Huu, remembering how when he had once gone to see a circus in Hanoi, a young actress had distracted an elephant just by gently patting his ears in a clapping motion while looking at him with a friendly, sincere face, and it had obeyed her. Huu came up close to the male elephant and looked at him lovingly while gently patting its ears. The elephant rubbed his head on Huu, and gently raised his trunk to touch Huu's hand.

Hoan imitated Huu, reaching out to stroke and pat the female elephant's ear. She mewled "rrrrr…rrrr", in pain and sadness, and wearily sprayed water with her trunk onto the bleeding wounds on her back and abdomen. Hoan and Huu understood that she was begging for help, and that they had to act immediately to treat her wounds. They took bottles of penicillin and their medical kits from their rucksacks. As the male elephant looked at his partner, tears streamed from his eyes, and he stretched out his long trunk and rubbed his burgundy nostrils over and over her wounds. A white liquid like saliva flowed from his trunk nostrils onto her bleeding wounds, as Hoan and Huu sprinkled them with penicillin as well.

To further help the elephants, Hoan and Huu gave them spring water mixed with a handful of salt. Then both men jumped on the male elephant's back, and followed by the female elephant, rode to Bong Va hamlet.

8

All Hoan could dream about during the rest of the journey to Bong Va hamlet was having a guitar. He felt his surroundings were so beautiful, so evocative of Spring that they could only be captured by the sound of a guitar. Even though he and Huu were in the midst of a ruined forest, travelling through the dead fields of a no man's land, he could feel the inherent natural vitality of the land around them as it struggled against the effects of bullets, bombs, and poison to survive and thrive. The beauty of nature, the promise of rejuvenating life had eased the two men's pain, weariness, boredom, and even fear, and had rekindled in Huu and Hoan to a belief that life would endure, that happiness was possible, and that the future would come as long as they could continue to believe in the love of life.

Buoyed by that good mood, feeling Spring all around them, they rode the two elephants into Bong Va village, arriving just when it was getting dark. The village was deserted and silent. They called out but the only response was the mocking echo of their voices from the forest and the mountains, a wild, ghostly cry of "hooo, hooo: carried on the night wind.

After a while they heard an answering cry and saw a flame flicker and flash in the distance. It looked bright and lovely against the dark dead forest and the human cry dissipated the dark gloom, sowing a seed of hope that human existence continued in this unwholesome environment, ravaged by chemical poisons and bombs. Huu and Hoan's hearts raced, dispelling the long suffocating moment they had waited in anticipation of seeing their fellow human beings, longing for a sign that there were people living there.

Hearing that weak cry and seeing the sudden flash of fire made the moment seem magical and both of them ran frantically towards the sound. Under the dim light of the bamboo torch that a small Van Kieu ethnic man was holding, they saw tears flowing from the man's deep black eyes.

"I thought that the revolution had abandoned us," he said in a distorted voice.

Hugging the man tightly, Huu felt like he was embracing a living skeleton. A vague pain, regret, and pity welled up in him.

"The revolution is sorry...sorry for our villagers," Huu said. "I...I apologize on behalf of the revolution."

The Van Kieu man kept crying, sobbing convulsively. "Most of the villagers are dead, oh you soldiers of the revolution...Huh huh." He pointed at the two elephants: "They belonged to old Ho Pung, soldier! They ran off when they were in heat, and old Ho Pung cried day and night."

Huu and Hoan were thrilled to hear about old Ho Pung. Scenes from their memories about this old man appeared in their minds like slow-motion movies. "Where is old Ho Pung?" They asked.

"He stays in the cave with the villagers, I will bring you over." He sobbed. "Most of the villagers are dead…Oh Heaven, oh Heaven!"

Hoan took the torch from his hand and helped him to sit down. Trying to help calm him down, Huu passed him some water, and Hoan gave him a rice ball the size of three fingers and a few grains of salt. He put the grains of salt into his mouth and held the rice, but only licked around it instead of eating.

"Please eat," Huu said. "Aren't you hungry?"

"I'm very hungry. But I can't eat. Not while my father is starving to death in that cave. I will bring the rice back for my father…"

"Eat please. We have rice, salt, and medicine for the villagers. Eat and let's go…

"No, I won't eat. Let's hurry so that I can feed my father, or he might starve to death…hurry up, please."

The air was light, fresh, and cool in the dark night. The Van Kieu man seemed reenergized, running ahead as if he'd forgotten his hunger and pain. Huu and Hoan exhausted themselves trying to keep up to him. It wasn't until midnight that the three of them came to the cave where the Bong Va villagers were sheltering. Before, the population of the village was over two hundred; now there were forty-four left, all of them puffy-faced and pale, their skin barely covering their bones, their breathing shallow and labored.

The cave was large but stank of human feces and urine.

The dead had been placed in a cranny in the rear of the cave. Fortunately, since the corpses were nothing more than dry skin and bones, they had not decomposed further and did not smell.

The first thing Huu did was to cook a big pot of porridge. He threw in a handful of salt and some glutamate. Then he and Hoan scooped up the porridge and divided it into small bowls. A dozen kids huddled together around the pot, and Hoan had to move them back, to make sure the porridge was cool enough. The Van Kieu who accompanied Huu and Hoan to the cave hurriedly carried a bowl of porridge to the side of his father who was breathing heavily. Just as he reached him, the old man's eyes closed, and his legs stretched straight out. His son put a wooden spoon of porridge into his mouth. He could still swallow. But suddenly he rolled his eyes, and with his remaining crooked, rough teeth, he bit down on the spoon and froze in that posture. He was dead. His son burst into tears.

"Oh Heaven, Heaven! My father is gone…huh huh! Why did the revolution come so late, oh Heaven!"

Huu and Hoan stood dumbfounded, the angry lamenting cries of the Van Kieu like sledge hammers hitting their hearts. They turned away and tried to hide their tears of regret. Huu felt himself to be a traitor, a thief caught red-handed who didn't dare to confess his own sins. He knew it was the war that caused such evils, struck tragic, horrible blows on innocent people, but was frustrated that he, a revolutionary soldier, couldn't do anything for the people. Sadness and pain swirled through him; he felt choked up and hurting to witness other people's suffering.

Tiger Spring

The Van Kieu was hugging his dead father, crying silently. He was drained of energy after all the time he had suffered from hunger and cold. He closed his eyes and his weeping gradually died down and then stopped. Looking at him, Huu forced himself to overcome his melancholia, his regrets and illusory pain, and face the reality in front of him, the death and life of the villagers.

With Hoan's help, Huu spooned some spoonful's of porridge into the mouth of the Van Kieu. They quietly removed the dead old man from his arms and placed the corpse in a corner of the cave. The villagers—from the elderly to the children—were eagerly gathering around the pot of evaporating porridge. Hoan and Huu gave each one bowl for the moment.

Meeting the two revolutionary cadres, the villagers instantly forgot the tragedy and death they had endured for so long. They'd thought that they would have no future, no hope, and would one by one die of hunger and disease. Huu and Hoan's arrival hadn't only brought them food and medicine, but also, and most important, had rekindled the flame of belief that the revolution hadn't abandoned them.

When the villagers had finished their porridge, Hoan and Huu gave each one with malarial symptoms a dose of Quinine. The next day, together with some healthy villagers, the two men helped carry the corpses out of the cave and dug a deep trench to be used as a mass grave. Afterwards, everyone returned to the old village.

When they returned to Bong Va, the sun was shining above the distant cliffs. Old Ho Pung, always the happiest person, kept laughing, his mouth hanging open, revealing the few front teeth he had left. He bounced up and down as if dancing on the back of the male elephant. The atmosphere was no longer gloomy and tinged with death and sadness, though survival would still be a challenge for the villagers. Everyone returned to the bombed and napalm blasted ruins of their former homes, trying to salvage whatever they could from the broken pieces of pots, pans, dishes...

People called out sporadically the names of chickens, dogs, and clacked together two bamboo sticks, making a sound used to urge buffalos to hurry home to their masters. Those calls to the lost, dispersing in the breeze, was at the same time sad and yet tinged with a fragile hope. Miraculously, a few dogs, cats, and chickens that had survived the bombs and napalm emerged shakily from their hiding places after hearing those calls. The dogs and cats were ecstatic to see their humans. They shook their bodies and wagged their tails and ran up to wrap themselves around their owners' legs for protection and pets.

A few chickens ran around also, staring blankly at their surroundings. From where they had remained hidden in a canyon, three buffaloes galloped towards the familiar sound of the clacking bamboo: one female and two males. They stopped in front of the person holding the bamboo slats, thrusting their three torn, singed heads at him. Villagers tenderly patted all over the bodies of the three buffaloes, soothing their scorched fur, speaking to the buffaloes and to each other in a dialect which Hoan and Huu didn't know. It was apparent to them how happy the villagers were to have the buffaloes back.

Tiger Spring

The extremely difficult situation now for Huu and Hoan was how to feed the Bong Va villagers. They divided the rice, salt, and glutamate, and saw that there were a sufficient number of chickens, dogs, and cats left to be bred. Their biggest asset were the three buffaloes. Huu and Hoan suggested that the villagers sacrifice one male buffalo to solve the immediate problem of hunger, especially for the sick, wounded, elderly, and children.

But the villagers refused. "It is not permitted to kill a buffalo," Old Ho Pung sobbed. "We can stand the hunger. We'll go to the forest and dig up tubers, banana tree bulbs, and earthworms, and catch snakes while we wait for help from the revolutionary cadres. The villagers and I know that the revolution won't forget us, cadres! I won't let you kill our buffalo!"

But his insistence only lasted another two days. When the tubers and banana tree stalks they gathered were mixed with the thin porridge, the mixture caused their stomachs to growl loudly and their intestines to hurt. For a whole night sitting by the fire in the makeshift shack they'd constructed for the oldest and most ill villagers, Huu and Hoan, and the Van Kieu whose father had died of hunger begged old Ho Pung to sacrifice the buffalo and save the villagers. But he kept shaking his head.

By the end of the next day, Huu had found a solution: he wrote a bill of sale for the buffalo; it promised when the revolution was successful, the villagers would receive a quintal of salt, five hundred kilograms of rice, and ten kilograms of glutamate. At those terms, the village elder agreed and the male buffalo was slaughtered.

Huu Uoc

At dawn the next morning, when the sun had not yet risen, all the villagers woke up. The damp cold of the morning dew and the breeze silently moving through the trees made the napalm-seared forest feel illusory and weary. But when the fire was lit, it dissipated the glittering mist covering the poor little village. Everybody, the sick, the old and the young, especially the nearly naked children ran around the fire, their eyes shining as they looked at the cast-iron pot simmering with cleaned buffalo intestines that had been dropped in along with the last kilogram of rice and a handful of salt and some glutamate. The aroma of the fresh meat was enticing, so inviting that even the dogs and the chickens ran around the fire, the chickens comically pecking the ground with their beaks and the sound the dogs made, no longer a panicked mournful wail, but a chorus of cheerful barking. The cheering children, and the jubilant adults and animals made the occasion into a festival.

Only old Ho Pung was not joyful. As he huddled in a dark corner, about ten feet away from the fire and the porridge pan, looking at the children and his co-villagers slurping hot porridge and laughing, his heart felt numb. He was a human being, and his people were human beings. Why had life been so cruel to them? Was it their fate? Was it the fate of human beings to be exiled, to suffer, to die, if not from the vicissitudes of nature then from the wickedness of other human beings?

He understood that he himself and his co-villagers were not the only ones who had to suffer natural disasters or being killed by wild beasts or from bullets and bombs. He thought of his own beautiful daughter, mauled by the gray tiger, and even though he had avenged her by killing the tiger, still he had to bear the pain of her loss for the rest of his life. That a wild animal killed was its nature, but what about the evil done by human beings? He could not understand why human beings—why another nation—would want to usurp the ancestral land of a people who had lived on it for many generations. Why did the green-eyed Americans kept bringing bombs and bullets here to kill his fellow villagers? Why are they so much crueler than wild animals? "Oh Heaven! Oh Heaven!" he cried out.

The old man watched the miserable remnant of Bong Va village celebrating joyously at receiving a meal that would be sufficient only for this day. But tomorrow, and the day after tomorrow, what would they live on when their great, benevolent, generous, and tolerant mother for many generations, the old forest that had nurtured and protected his people through the centuries, was now ravaged and destroyed from one end to the other?

His people had first fled here, from the centers of humanity to the remotest mountains and forests, yet even here the Americans had found them, hunted, and harried them. His people had supported the revolution because of the simple and innocent reason that the revolutionary people they saw owned the same muddy hands and feet as their own, and had shared their suffering, their cries from the pain of loss, and even their joy. In the most difficult and desperate situation, Ho Bung and his villagers' last hope, last belief was that the revolution would never abandon them.

And in reality, it had been two revolutionary soldiers

who had come to rescue them. But slaughtering the buffalo and taking payment for its meat in order for the villagers to survive was painful. There was no precedent for eating buffalo meat, whether it was on New Year Day or the day of worshiping Heaven. For the Van Kieu, the buffalo was their closest and dearest friend. It not only plowed fields and transported all their burdens, carried children and adults to bathe in the stream, and frolicked with the children in the afternoon sun; it also embodied the power of nature, of the mountains, of the forest. The buffalo created a harmony with the natural scenery of the majestic Truong Son Mountains.

After the recent napalm attacks, most of the herd of nearly seventy buffaloes had been burned alive, with only three survivors. What sadness could be greater than that? Seeing the joy of his fellow villagers as he looked at the pile of red buffalo meat, divided into many parts on those ragged banana leaves, then at the pan of porridge, steaming with the smell of buffalo intestines, he felt heartbroken.

When Huu offered him a bowl of porridge, old Ho Pung received it indifferently, and then suddenly he began crying, silently, tears slowly flowing from his deep red eyes, rolling over his dry, thin cheeks, and falling lightly onto the bowl of porridge as it cooled.

Then before anyone knew what he was thinking, old Ho Pung put his bowl aside, stood up and walked towards the pile of meat. He picked up the biggest, most delicious-looking chunks and put them aside.

"This meat is for the army," he told everyone. "The soldiers are also very hungry. They share rice, salt, and glutamate with us, even when they don't have anything to eat. You two, dry this out and bring it back to the soldiers in your unit, on behalf of our villagers."

Huu and Hoan were astounded; they stared at old Ho Pung, unsure how to react. If they took it, they would be depriving the people of the meat. If not, the old man would be very angry. At that very moment, there was a howl from the bottom of the hill, followed by two and then three more. The howls resonated. They seemed to conjure the mystery of the mountains and forests. Not only the villagers were cheered up, but even the dogs and chickens, their bright eyes bewildered, turned in the direction of the howling. The dogs' nostrils flared.

Suddenly one dog, baying with joy, bounded down the slope. The other dogs, wobbly as drunkards, ran after it. The villages could see five men, led by Political Commissar Mao, all waving staffs and herding five buffaloes, each of which was carrying heavy goods on its back.

"The revolution has arrived, oh Heaven! We are saved, oh Heaven!" Someone in the back shouted out. Everyone, from the elderly to the women and children, cheered and it seemed as if the dogs and chickens were also dancing for joy with them.

The cadres of Huong Hoa district, representing the People's Committee, Police, Military Office, and Health Department had brought food, blankets, clothes, and medicine to Bong Va village. Upon learning they were to be given five more buffalo, two males and three females, Old Ho Pung was the happiest villager. The first thing he did was to appoint a family to take care of the buffaloes, and then to distribute the food, clothing, and medicines.

The representatives from Huong Hoa District stayed on to stabilize life for Bong Va villagers. Huu and Hoan handed over their duties to them and said goodbye to old Ho Pung and Bong Va villagers and went back to their unit.

Throughout their time in the war, Huu and Hoan would encounter many nostalgic and tearful farewells. But their farewell from the upstanding and kind hearted Bong Va villagers, especially Old Ho Pung, who had suffered from the starvation and destruction of the catastrophic war, stunned them. Old Ho Pung had become cheerful again. Though he would not eat himself, he packed dried buffalo meat tightly into Huu and Hoan's rucksacks and hoisted them onto their shoulders. Only then did he smile, a distorted but happily satisfied smile. He patted Huu's shoulders, and touched his skinny calf. "I'm worried about your feet—how can you have enough strength to cross these mountains again? Another five tough days…"

He made a sign, and the two elephants walked up from nowhere. Old Ho Pung patted the male elephant that put his trunk tightly around the old man, gently lifted him into the air, shook him a few times, and then put him down. The female elephant kept rubbing her head against the old man, emitting a soft cry, and then gently spraying old Ho Pung with her trunk. In his life there had been two most precious things he'd loved: his daughter Ho Buon, who had donated her body to the revolution to eliminate the evil tiger. And the elephant couple he had been raising for more than ten years, but who he now offered to the revolution since they would help the revolution to do a lot of work, and also to thank the two revolutionary cadres who had saved them from the gray wolves.

Huu hugged the old man in his skinny arms with reverential love. The warmth of giving, sharing, trusting, and loving each other, had chased away fear and weakness. The old man seemed to transmit warmth and strength to Huu, making him feel both happy and healthy. The power of kindness and love seemed to be fueling and inspiring him to continue on the difficult and arduous journeys ahead.

Later, when writing down what he'd experienced during the war years in Truong Son, he remembered, as if it were happening at that very moment, the feel of that flat, skinny chest and warm breath which embodied for him the overflowing love he had felt from the Old Ho Pung of Bong Va village, on the morning of their parting from the villagers. Yet underneath that overwhelming reminiscence of human love, he felt as well a bitter regret, a painful torment scratching at his mind. He was holding the paper on which he had written his promise to the Bong Va villagers to pay five hundred kilograms of rice, one hundred kilograms of salt, and ten kilograms of glutamate, for the buffalo they killed for meat. He'd forgotten. He forgot that promise, as he had forgotten many of the journeys and footprints of life that he had gone through.

He knew that such an oblivion of memories was common in a person who'd suffered so many traumas in the war, in life. And forgetting the details of something that had happened in one sudden moment during the war, in the distant past, could be forgiven. There were so many instances of life and death, bitterness, glory, heroism, and humiliation during the war. The fact that Huu still owed a debt to the Bong Va villagers was like a dream from childhood that easily faded with time, even though it was a sin. A common sin of those who had become successful like himself, who became focused on the scramble for fame and wealth and the busy details of ordinary life.

Huu felt a deeply regret as he thought about the life he was living today. To whom else did he still owe a debt? Could he say that his life was so filled with pain, unhappiness, sadness, and regret that he could forgive himself? Huu closed his eyes, sighed, and dared not think of anything else.

9

Riding back to Tiger Spring from Bong Va village on the elephants, Huu and Hoan followed directions from the village elder, and so avoided the dead forest, which had made their hair stand up and given them goosebumps. They were able to follow the bare trace of a trail through a part of the forest that had not been sprayed with toxic chemicals or destroyed with napalm by American aircraft.

The forest was eerily quiet, and a cold wind blew through it, but it was covered with endless flowers blooming in an immense greenness. The two men could travel leisurely, rest whenever they wanted, enjoy their meals, and then sleep peacefully at night among the fragrant flowers and grass. Occasionally, they encountered wild deer running like the wind in the woods. Once Hoan had been ready to take a shot, but Huu stopped him, afraid that the gunfire would alert any enemy soldiers who might have set up ambushes somewhere in the forest.

It took only four days for Huu and Hoan to return to the garrison of the 26th Reconnaissance Company. They had run out of things to tell each other about themselves and missed the company of their other comrades-in-arms.

Each night, when they lay on their two hammocks, they kept reminding each other about things that had happened with Company Commander Tuan, Political Commissar Mao, about Ms. Lan, and Dr. Lien—stories with no beginning and no end. What they remembered the most was the love affair between Tuan and Dr. Lien in the banana grove one night—thinking of it, they couldn't help but to burst out in laughter.

That night, they had been accompanying Dr. Lien on an emergency rescue mission for Political Commissar Mao, who had come down with severe malaria. On their way back to Tiger Spring Medical Station, they passed through a clearing crowded with many banana plants, not far from their campsite. Suddenly Tuan shouted: "Tiger! Tiger!" His shout startled Huu and Dr. Lien, who screamed and tripped over a banana plant, Huu started to alert his comrades-in-arms when Tuan's steely hand squeezed his arm and pulled him back. "There's no tiger," he whispered. "Go back to base and let me be with Lien."

Huu understood immediately and returned to the camp. When he got there, he called Hoan: "Come with me, and I'll show you something nice. But we have to love with absolute secrecy…" The two moved like cats stalking mice; as reconnaissance soldiers, they had been trained to walk without making a sound. There was a breeze, but they sweltered in the heat coming from Laos, feeling suffocated and sweaty. When they pushed through mimosa bushes, thorns raked their faces and skins and made them itch like crazy. They clenched their teeth and endured the suffering as they approached the plant where Dr. Lien had tripped. They smiled, their hearts pounding as they saw Tuan and Lien entwined like two pythons. Both were frantically panting and clutching at each other. Tuan released her from the embrace of his long, ape-like arms, and clumsily, frantically, began undressing her. "Slow down," Lien whispered, giggling. "You're tearing my clothes; my friends will laugh at me if they know."

Tuan had ripped his own clothes off and discarded them like a bunch of rags near his pistol, engrossed in making love in silence. His lips were tightly sealed to Lien's sensual, lush lips as he moved her body from the banana plant to the grass.

A huge moon appeared in the sky. It seemed quite close, shining just above the couple. The clear, blue light danced silver glitters down their naked bodies, twined together, writhing in love next to the banana plant. The magical light of the moon was so clear that Hoan and Huu could see Tuan's bare back covered with small, round, glittering drops of sweat.

Lying on top of Lien, Tuan searched her body, brushed his hands over her sensual areas. Lien writhed, struggled, and groaned loudly or sweetly, her slender hands clutching and scratching Tuan's muscular back as Tuan vigorously pumped against her.

It was the first time in their lives that Huu and Hoan had seen what making love looked like. Their natural male instincts were aroused; they burned with desire. Huu felt a pain in his lower abdomen, and his whole body stiffened unbearably. In front of him was a man and a woman madly making love with each other, giving, and receiving, happily satisfying their youthful desire.

As for him, he was satisfying his curiosity about what no one taught anyone, and everyone wanted to know. Witnessing that couple achieving that human right to satisfy themselves, how could he not be ecstatic, how could he not fall into the illusory state of being human? Hoan shared that mood as well, as both came to understand what it was to make love.

As they looked at Hoan's sweaty face, his eyes slowly opening, and stared foolishly at Tuan and Lien's intercourse, both Huu and Hoan tensed. They pressed their faces down into the soft grass wet with the dew that softened the blades and molded the scent of heaven and earth, pure, cold, and clear against their faces.

Now Tuan and Lien were lying on the soft grass, looking up to the sky. The moon played for that couple, its light dimmed and then shining bright, revealed by scudding clouds that embraced and then released the orb and let its light flow over the mountains and the forest, making them look dreamy and magical.

Lien's voice sounded as if it were falling into the void, as she sighed and then whispered sadly: "Am I too bad?" She turned over and lay face down in the soft grass, crying. Her painful sobbing astonished and frightened Tuan. They had never spoken to each other about love, but surely Lien knew how much he liked and loved her, and he was sure she felt close to him and somewhat liked him. Why was she crying? Why was she upset? He hugged her, trying to comfort her. But her crying panicked him. He held her tightly. "Lien, I am sorry...I am sorry, please don't cry, I can't take it."

Lien tried to hold back her tears, but as Tuan wrapped his arms around her, she couldn't stop sobbing. Now Tuan understood that what he was hearing was the sad, regretful cry of a young girl who had lost her virginity. And both were aware that after enjoying that short natural happiness, they would separate from each other. Tuan and Lien were on the same side in the war, but not in their hearts, in their feelings for each other. Although Tuan wanted to hold onto their relationship, he knew that Lien's heart never belonged to him, even though he had taken her body. He held her a little longer, wanting to comfort her as she continued to tremble, her face glistening with sweat and tears under the moonlight. Tuan could sense something falling inside her. Her eyes were dulled, staring at nothing. She looked like a sleep walker, as if she were soothing her heart by pretending that what she had just experienced was a painful dream.

A woman's status in war was very fragile, as fragile as a leaf imbued with the fragrance of flowers, of nature, but that still was just a lonely leaf floating along the fatal stream of life. Lien felt cold, even in the warm and strong arms of Tuan. She loosened her arms from his body, her eyes still glued to his as she waited for him to say some sweet words to her, to soothe the bleeding wound inside her. But this man who always seemed to be so quick and smart, now looked quite stupid. He couldn't seem to find anything to say to her. Something again collapsed inside herself. She slipped out of his tight embrace, sat down on the grass, and wept bitterly. In her pain, she came to realize how much she hated war. War was always a painful wound that never healed. What happened to her here was because of war. What was lost was lost and could never be regained. Without the war, she would never have been in this forest.

Tuan didn't know what to say. His face was a blank screen on which mixed emotions of happiness and pity played. Satisfaction but also shame, confusion, and disappointment. He helped Lien get dressed, got his own clothes on, and lifted Lien on his back to carry her home. The road from the banana grove to Tiger Spring cave was not far and he was not too tired to carry Lien. But her sobbing, and her tears soaking on his back made him feel too heavy-footed. He was carrying the weight of regret and guilt on his back. He vaguely understood that now Lien would always stay away from him, but also would walk through his life forever.

Reaching the entrance of the cave, he put Lien down, hugged her, and whispered: "Kiss me, kiss me to say goodbye. I promise not to hurt you again, though my promise is too late now."

Tuan held Lien tightly and sealed his lips to Lien's tear-salted lips. She felt suffocated, but before pushing Tuan away, Lien lightly kissed his thick, smelly beard and looked directly into his depressed face, filled with disappointment and pain, and then walked into the cave.

Having witnessed the two of them madly making love, and then now hugging each other in pain and sorrow as Tuan sat helpless as a wooden statue, Huu and Hoan burst into laughter, and then realized they had revealed themselves. Huu made a sign to Hoan: "Let's run!"

As they ran from their hiding places, they heard Tuan shout fiercely. "Huu, Hoan, is it?"

Back at the camp, Huu was so scared that he crawled under his mosquito net with all his clothes on. Soon Tuan walked in, he turned the kerosene lamp on, took his pistol and dagger off and threw them on the bamboo cot. Then he shone the flashlight on Huu's mosquito net.

"Wake up," he shouted.

Huu, trembling, got out from under the mosquito net. Before he even had time to put on his sandals, Tuan had grabbed him by the shoulder and dragged him out of the camp. He felt like a pincer was grasping his shoulder. The pain made his eyes fill with tears.

It was past midnight, but it was still quite hot. The hot wind blowing from Laos was discomforting and suffocating; it made people feel like they were breathing fire. The eternally bright green of the trees was replaced by a dry yellowish color that made them look burned out and tired. The pain he felt in his shoulder from Tuan's grip seemed to him an extension of the heat. After dragging Huu out, Tuan ordered him to go to Platoon 1's camp and bring back his accomplice, Hoan. Then Tuan made the two of them stand with their backs against two trees.

"Both of you are reconnaissance soldiers in the Special Forces. Now you will practice some qigong."

The two were terrified. Huu stammered out a few words, in vain.

"Grind your teeth," Tuan shouted. "Horse stand now."

Legs outstretched, hands clenched. Take a breath and stretch your belly out fully. Ready?"

Huu and Hoan nervously assumed the position.

"One, Two, Three," Tuan shouted, and drove his right hand like a sledgehammer into Huu's stomach, as he hooked his left into Hoan's belly. Both men saw stars and fell to the ground, their heads knocking against the tree trunks, which, fortunately for them, had been softened by the heavy rain. They felt dizzy, the back of their necks numb, and their ears humming like they had a flock of cicadas singing inside their heads. Tuan grabbed both of them by the necks, lifted them off the ground, and then released them, and let them fall to the tree stump.

"You two know what you did, right?"

"Yes, I do," Huu stuttered. "I am so sorry." Tuan yanked Hoan up.

"And you?"

"Yes…yes…I do…I apologize to you, boss." Hoan sounded like he was going to cry.

Tuan pointed at both their faces. "Just remember to keep your mouth shut about tonight." Then he turned to Huu, his voice was less severe: "Go to the camp and get me something to eat. I'm starving."

Huu had idolized his commander so much that whenever Tuan slept in his hammock, in his shorts and T-shirt, Huu would stare at him and sigh, comparing Tuan's long, firm, hairy legs with his skinny ones. His most lasting image of Tuan was of the commander standing proudly in front of the company formation, his waist encircled by a cartridge belt weighed on one side by his holster and pistol

Tiger Spring

and his lieutenant's insignia pinned on a blouse the color of mountains and forests, barking out orders, as dominant and majestic as a general. As a lowly Private, he could only dream of one day being as commanding and formidable an officer as Tuan-the-Beard, on the battlefield, or on the training base. How proud he would be!

10

After the night they had been severely punished by Company Commander Tuan for spying on his love-making, Huu and Hoan bonded even more closely. But another reason for their growing closeness was their mutual interest in two of the nurses at the Medical Station: Ms. Lan and Ms. Le. Lan had been at the Tiger Spring facility for a while, but Le was new. Hoan and Lan had fallen in love at first sight when he accompanied her singing on his guitar when they performed in a cultural program arranged by the 26th Reconnaissance Company for the doctors, nurses, and medical aides.

Lan was not beautiful. She had an oval-shaped face but was a bit thin and had sharp eyes that made her seem tough and fierce. On the other hand, she had pale skin, and thick, silky long hair that reached past her knees, framing a slim, tall, and attractive body. Hoan said that he loved Lan because of her character: she was honest and strong and, he thought, somewhat different from the girls he had known in Nghe An province.

Lan had volunteered to join the army when she was

seventeen years old. She had been sent to Tiger Spring after a six-month concentrated nursing class. She had never held a gun to shoot at the enemy. For her, the enemy were the ones who launched the war, and for her the war was a horror and abomination, a wild, fanged beast full of venom. The war had devoured countless numbers of her comrades-in-arms. Every day Lan witnessed the painful deaths of wounded young soldiers covered with blood and stinking of rot. The most pitiful for her were the ones who were hit by napalm bombs from the American planes, their faces and limbs blackened, their skin burned like crispy roasted pork.

Some with eye-wounds had sockets filled with blood and pus and maggots; they would grit their teeth and howl with pain when she pulled the maggots out of their eye sockets with forceps. She noticed that often, before dying, the young soldiers didn't speak any final words, but instead screamed for their mothers, their wives, or their girlfriends. Each day was heavy as a month, long as a year. She cursed the enemy every night and shed tears every day. Her maternal instincts as a woman ached to be fulfilled. When the severely wounded soldiers, before dying, called for their mothers, Lan became their mother. If they called for their wives or they called for their girlfriends, Lan became their wife or their girlfriend.

She held their heads in her arms, stroking them and singing lullabies. There were times when the wounded soldiers, in a delirium, cried out for their mother's breasts or to hug and kiss their girlfriends, and she let them do whatever they were dreaming of. As they did, she could see their pain and their last thirst for life subside and they became calm. Once a soldier clutched her young virgin breasts like a drunkard, and then his hands loosened, loosened, and released her...when she looked down at him, he was dead, but the corner of his mouth was upturned in a satisfied smile. She wept, understanding that the soldier had completed his role as a human being...

There was one other act she performed in her duties that none of the other young girls were brave enough to mention. But, seeing Hoan's sincere love for her, she shared the truth with him in a choked painful sob, a confession that came from the bottom of her heart. When the Station had to give emergency treatment to too many wounded soldiers, and there was only a limited stock of anesthetics, Lan used her own body as a magical anesthetic to control the soldiers pain before and during surgery. In some cases, she used her hands to stimulate a soldier's penis, leaving him numb and sedated, in others she pressed her mouth, or even her breast, onto the mouths of the soldiers who were writhing under the surgeon's knife. She did it despite the whispers and objections of some doctors, nurses, and aides, including some male doctors who were very fond of her. She seemed to accept that her life had been permanently attached to these wounded, bloody, and agonizing soldiers.

Until one day, a living memorial ceremony was held for a young soldier who was about to martyr himself in what he knew to be a suicidal mission.

Lan was not allowed to be among those present in that sacred ceremonial event, but she witnessed it all, heard the voice, the firm oath, saw the head held high and proudly, the right hand placed over the heart. Life was a precious, wonderful treasure given by the Creator. But why was this young soldier going so gently, so peacefully, into death? Maybe she was too young to understand it all. But she did understand that the young soldier was entering death for the sake of the survival of the country. The country is the mother. Motherland and mother are the most sacred.

Lan burst into tears. She admired the young soldier, who as about the same age of hers, and who would go into battle and accept his foretold death. Maybe he had been like her, had never kissed a girl, didn't know if it would be sweet or salty. He had never reached his full maturity, even though he contained all the elements of a grown man: beliefs, ideals, ambitions, and dreams. It is said that in the hidden corner of a woman is a silent undercurrent, that a woman's heart was like a sensitive and vulnerable divine eye. Lan's heart felt strangled by a painful knowledge of the soldier's fate. Her heart and her womanhood told her to give herself to him so that he could go to eternity without regrets for not having experienced what it was to be fully human.

She would offer him her virginity, even though she knew that a young girl's virginity was sacred and holy, gifted from her parents' hardships. it was a treasure of creation, of heaven and earth. For the first time, Lan became a woman on a starry night in the middle of Truong Son Trail, amidst the howling and rumbling of American bombs. In each other's arms, the two soldiers remained silent, both in tears, making love clumsily, devoting themselves to each other, rejoicing even amidst their pain and regret. When it was over, the young soldier cried and hugged Lan tightly. Lan never asked for his name or the name of his hometown.

Although she had been at the Tiger Spring facility for less than two years, Lan had met many soldiers; they were young but battle-hardened; they had dealt with hardship and death. The issue of sex was always there, running through conversations and imaginations, and it was not difficult for Lan to understand why Hoan, a Hanoian gifted in singing and playing guitar, had become so infatuated with her. She acknowledged that Hoan loved her to the point of confusion and madness, as if there was nothing more beautiful in life than his love for her.

On every patrol or in hunting for Saigonese commandos, no matter how far from the Tiger Spring station he was, he always searched for her namesake flower, a kind of wild orchid, to bring back for her, placed on the top of his rucksack. His sincere love gave her sleepless nights. In her heart she knew she belonged with him. She thought about him constantly and felt overwhelmed with happiness when she was with him...but she struggled with his desire to go to the very end of love.

She was no longer a virgin, and the loss of her virginity was part of a different story than her relationship with Hoan. She had given herself to that young martyr one time, but that time had awakened her capacity for sexual desire. It had become a need so raging, so pressing that at times she just wanted to plunge into the spring, dive down under the deep water or run wild in the storm to forget the fiery furnace of longing burning in her.

But she kept procrastinating. She didn't have the courage to do what both Hoan and her wanted, lusting after each other like long-starved hawks hunting for prey. She had thought of hiding the fact she had slept with the soldier from Hoan, and instead just enjoy being a normal couple starting to fall in love with each other, intensely and sincerely. Let what was in the past stay in the past. But she spent many restless nights, racked with guilt, even as she tried to suppress the sacred but sad memory of her time with the martyr.

At times, she wished she could escape the love she and Hoan felt for each other. She knew that no matter how great their love was, it was destined to be temporary, the way it was for all soldiers in the war who wouldn't know what tomorrow would be, no matter that they were together today...and so on, and so on. She kept suffering, struggling, procrastinating, tormenting herself, but still she couldn't escape burning in the flame of love, in the sound of his sweet, pure, voice, full of charm, in the magic of his guitar. Finally, on one rainy night, she decided that what she had to do was to just let it go and tell him the whole truth.

That night, a thick blackness covered the forest and Tiger Spring. It was so dark that even though they were walking hand in hand, they couldn't see each other's faces. Hoan shone his flashlight on the ground, giving them enough light to recognize the familiar path to the secret rendezvous.

It was on a gentle hill, the century-old trees there very large, spreading out luxuriant canopies. In the afternoon, at sunset and before dinner, Hoan, Lan, Huu, and Le often would gather there in the afternoon, at sunset and just before dinner. They would lie on hammocks, some of them resting, others singing as Hoan played guitar. It was a beautiful spot, with fresh breezes blowing through it, and many birds sitting in pairs and chirping to each other on the branches in passing branches, each couple leaning their backs against each other, spreading their wings to caress each other. Some seemed were deeply in love, poking their beaks towards each other as if they were kissing, creating a poetic, romantic and fanciful scene.

But this night, Lan and Hoan went to the dark forest without the others. As soon as they had tied up their hammock between the trees, it started raining, something which didn't faze a Truong Son Trail soldier like Hoan. He quickly lay a plastic tarp over the hammock and used parachute rope to fasten its four corners to a pair of stumps. By the time it started raining heavily and the wind started blowing faster, they had finished making their small roof in the middle of the forest.

Hugging each other in silence, Hoan and Lan sat on the hammock, dangling their feet down into the soft grass. Their two hearts were twined together in the midst of these wild, cold mountains, yet they felt lost and lonely. Even though they clung together, their hearts beating fast and their breaths merging...Still, Lan had never felt so sad, felt such a heavy burden on her soul, as she did while being warmed by Hoan's embrace. She felt sorry for Hoan, and for herself. She knew that what she would tell him about that hidden corner of her life would be a sad, bitter truth for him. She wondered if he could stand the fact, she wondered if his tight embrace would slacken... and so on... the worries jumped back and forth in her mind. It was only in the darkness that she would have the courage to look into his eyes to tell a truth which would horrify him.

The cold night raindrops kept falling on the parachute material and flowing down into the soft grass under her feet. She trembled, feeling it chilling her heart. Hoan hugged her more tightly.

"What's the matter? Are you too cold?"

His warm lips traced Lan's trembling lips. It was very dark. Lan raised a hand and put it over his mouth to stop Hoan's passionate kiss.

"Please l I need to tell you something..."

She told him why and how she had lost her virginity. She spoke calmly, clearly, braced for whatever reaction he would have.

He sat stiff and motionless. His embrace didn't loosen, nor did it tighten. He remained silent. It seemed as if the cold raindrops were penetrating every vein and muscle in him. Yet he was aware of her words, her calm voice. He felt cold, a numbing cold spreading into his heart, while at the same time two warm tears flowed from his eyes, rolled down his cheeks, and fell onto her hand, still covering his mouth. Lan shivered.

He slowly removed her hand and bent to her, holding her tighter in his arms. His tear soaked all over Lan's face and fell on her closed eyes. Suddenly, he put his arms around her slim body and turned her so that she was laying on the hammock. He pressed his large body on top of her, burying his face into her breasts.

"Don't say anything more. I understand. I love you very much, and I am sorry…" He didn't know when his tears had dried. All that remained inside him was compassion for her and a storm of love boiling in his heart. He had never felt his passion burn so strongly. He frantically unbuttoned Lan's uniform…but when his rough hand reached to touch between her legs, her sad voice stopped him.

"Don't. Not now…I have just had a nightmare, I am not ready to make love, please understand…Not now."

Hoan felt drunk. He stretched one hand out into the open air and palmed some rain, slapping it onto his face. The sound of that holy rain woke them both up, as if they were regaining consciousness from a coma. For him, he understood what it was for soldiers to fall in love on the battlefield, the romance and magic that came from wondering whether there would be a tomorrow. For the moment, both of them were like the two children playing a hide-and-seek game in a dense forest.

From then on, the wild beast of love kept burning in the heart of the romantic artist Hoan. His love for Lan was as wild and unrelenting as a typhoon. Whenever night fell, or the political activities were over or whenever everybody fell asleep, Hoan would ask Huu to carry his rifle and sneak out with him to his and Lan's trysting place. They would wrap themselves in each other while Huu waited nearby, stuck in a hammock, listening to the wind, and watching the stars. Feeling lonely, he would hum softly, or recite poems.

Tiger Spring

Whenever he accompanied Hoan and Lan to their love-making, he would act as a diligent bodyguard, cradling his loaded AK and on the lookout for a surprise attack by the ARVN commandoes. Hoan and Lan were very grateful to him and tried to hook him up with Le. But his heart stayed closed; he had not felt any attraction when he was next to Le, even though she was also very charming, eye-catching, full of femininity: discreet and delicate. Many times, Lan and Hoan encouraged Le to go out at night with the three of them.

One night Le accepted.

It was quiet and peaceful, the wind so light that one could imagine the sound of dew falling softly on the leaf canopies and hear the clatter of branches, all mixed with the chirping of the birds...the forest in early Spring. Above, the full moon was like a round plate radiating a clear light that splashed down to the treetops swaying in the wind, sparking countless glittering rays, illuminating the two couples entering their familiar sanctuary.

Hoan and Lan walked hand in hand, skipping happily, like starlings. Behind them, Huu and Le walked more slowly, Le still hesitant. Now and then, Hoan made signs to Lan to stop and wait for them to catch up.

Huu, wanting to imitate his friend, innocently held Le's hand, and then tried to put his arm around her shoulder. She pushed him away. "It's not going to happen, OK?" she said softly. Huu felt like a thief caught in the act. He withdrew his hands and shoved them in his pockets, whistling as if nothing had happened.

They reached the rendezvous point. Hoan and Huu unslung their AKs and skillfully stretched out two hammocks between the trees, and then stretched out plastic tarps to form "roofs" over them. Lan cheerfully sat down right on Hoan's hammock, her legs swinging. But Le stood still, her eyes wide and unblinking, staring at the other three. Then she moved backward and turned around to leave. Lan rushed over to her and took her hand.

"Why do you want to leave? Huu is really willing to be with you...please stay!"

Leaving her hot, trembling hand in Lan's hand, Le calmly said: "I just have sympathy for him. I haven't fallen in love with him yet, and he doesn't love me either. Let me go."

Then she turned away. Lan stopped her, almost crying.

"Why are you so serious? He is not a carnivorous, he can't eat you."

"I'm afraid," Le said, trembling. "I never did anything like this before. I feel so frightened, Lan. I'm going back now."

Observing Le's mood, Huu slung his AK again and walked over to the two young girls. "Let Le go back. I'll take her..."

"I can go by myself. I'm not afraid of ghosts. Just lend me your flashlight," Le said calmly. She had stopped trembling.

"What if you bump into a commando?" Huu asked.

"I'll run, what else can I do?"

"Then let's all go back," Lan said. "If Le goes back, it's no fun being here."

Hoan and Huu went over to roll up their hammocks.

But Le just pulled a pistol out of her belt. "I have this. You guys stay and have fun, and don't worry about me…"

Hoan laughed: "If you go out with boys and carry that gun on your waistband, who would dare try to seduce you!"

Huu and Lan laughed as well. Le cheerfully snatched the flashlight from Huu's hand and ran, leaving them behind, still laughing.

"You don't know how to act with girls," Hoan said to Huu. "Men have to be proactive. If you like someone, you have to attack immediately like Commander Tuan and I…"

Lan raised her voice: "Hey…come on, what are you saying, man? Stop your boasting!"

Hoan didn't reply. Instead, he jumped onto the hammock where Lan was sitting. The tarp they had hung above it covered both of them. The hammock swayed from right to left, faster, harder…

In the next hammock, Huu lay motionless, in no mood to sing or to recite poetry. He didn't care about his two friends, madly in love over there. With Le gone, he felt lost and empty. He took a deep breath and let out a long sigh. For the first time in his life, he had felt a passionate love that had welled up inside him from the bottom of his heart. Now he had lost her. In the past, at school, he had liked several young, beautiful, and charming young girls. A few times he'd felt both radiant and dumbstruck, his heart throbbing and his eyes glazing over when a certain young girl gave him a sympathetic look.

But those feelings were just the shadows of passing clouds, the natural feelings of a growing teenager experiencing the emotional enjoyment of being close to a young girl in what was innocent and pure friendship. For young soldiers, comradeship between boys and girls was held up as a great and noble ideal to be lived up to and praised. But he felt both a burning desire and a poetic, and idealistic immortal love for Le, and it had not moved her one bit. She seemed emotionless, totally indifferent to the overflowing emotions that brought tears in his eyes when he read poems about the fate of soldiers, their pain, their lives, their moods, their hearts...poems that evoked the fire and smoke of war, with life and death only a few inches away.

But he loved also when someone would sing a heroic song or recite soaring words describing the greatness of the Fatherland, or about two lovers: poems that made all that sadness and even fear disappear at once. Every time the 26th Reconnaissance Company came to the Tiger Spring Medical Station, whenever he recited poetry, his eyes would always turn to Le, longing for a sympathetic look, or some token of affection from her. But he was always disappointed. It was as though Le had no sense of poetry. She would keep chatting to soldiers next to her as her eyes darted around the room. Now and then she covered her mouth and laughed as he recited poems with such enthusiasm that sometimes he even screamed the words and burst into tears.

When all the other soldiers cheered, or applauded, her reaction left Huu feeling sad and hurt. His self-confidence as a soldier felt threatened. It angered him, but it was also the reason Huu cared for and paid more attention to Le; she remained discreet and delicate in her relationship with all the young soldiers, and that pleased him very much, as did her behavior tonight when she left them after seeing that the relationship of Hoan and Lan had gone too far past the bounds of comradeship while Huu and she had not yet committed to each other. Thinking about it, Huu, from the bottom of his heart, felt bitter, ashamed, and regretful. He, Hoan, and Lan did not understand Le, and their behavior to her had been wrong, really wrong towards her.

It was true that in war, especially on the battlefield, soldiers' lives were always lived in a hurry. Operational alert, slinging on rucksacks and weapons in order to hurry to a battle was normal. Eating, sleeping, brushing teeth, washing one's face, and even going to the toilet was all done quickly. But to learn to understand someone, to sympathize, to share, to fall in love with someone; that was not a process that could be rushed, not like a sudden downpour that ceased within minutes. Thinking this way, Huu began to feel worried whether Le had gotten back safely to the Station.

A sudden loud thunderclap interrupted the flow of thoughts fluttering in Huu's head. He looked up. The bright moon had disappeared. Dark clouds tumbled in the sky, which now and then was torn apart by a cold blue-white light from the flashes of thunder and lightning. It started showering harder, the rain quickly seeped into each tree trunk, and soaked the leaves to their tips. The wet, soft grass trembled under his feet, making him feel cold and numb.

Under the flashes of blue light, the whole forest seemed

to be swaying, creating a feeling of desolateness and coldness.

On the battlefield, life and love were as harsh and unpredictable as the weather, now sunny, now rainy, now hot, now cold. Pity poor Huu, clutching his AK, diligently guarding Hoan and Lan and feeling very lonely as he was presented with that young couple, so fresh and full of energy and vitality, so excited and resilient in their wet hammock. Their passion seemed to rise up like sparkling sunlight, dispelling the darkness and gloom of the forest, burning strongly, despite the storm, rain, wind, and cold. Their hammock shook strongly, inclining to one side then the other by the couple's shifting weight, their heavy breathing was heard under the tarp sheet that was tussled by the wind and struck by the rain.

That tarp was precious to the couple, like a mother stretching out her fragile, body to shield these two small human beings in the middle of a dark forest. The tarp rose and fell with the motion of their bodies under the wind and the rain until it finally went still. It was almost dawn. The three unfastened their hammocks from the trees and rolled them up with their tarps...

While Hoan and Lan were happily falling in love, Commander Tuan was perplexed, still worrying about Doctor Lien's mood after he had carried her on his back to Tiger Spring cave. A few days before, Lan had told Hoan and Huu that Lien refused to eat or drink. After she performed surgery or otherwise cared for wounded soldiers, she would go back to her cave and weep. Lan and Le were bewildered, wondering why Lien tossed and turned and seemed to be suffering so much. Huu and Hoan, though they knew what happened between Tuan and Lien in the wild banana bush, still could not phantom why Lien was so miserable.

Tuan knew what had happened, but he was still shocked, wondering if she were upset because he had taken her virginity. As the saying went: "A young girl's virginity is worth a thousand taels of gold. Unable to figure out what was happening with her, Tuan took the risk of going to the surgical cave and seeking out Dt. Lien's quarters. Both Lan and Le were startled to see Commander Tuan's heavy, bearded face as he strode in, a pistol and grenades dangling from the belt around his waist. They followed him back to the corner of the cave where Lien slept. Tuan pulled aside the plastic curtain. Doctor Lien was sitting on a bamboo mat, her full rucksack on her knees, writing on a sheet of paper placed atop the rucksack. They could see she was crying as she wrote, her tears falling drop by drop of tears on the page. Other pages on which she had already written were lying next to her; they were also stained with tears. Tuan snatched them up and read. A letter to someone.

"*Dear Toan,*

Please be calm when you read what I have to tell you. Afterwards, please think of me as having died, even though your love will be in my heart forever. I know that from now on it will be painful, bitter, and hateful for you to think of our love. I know it is my fault that I will lose you forever.

I don't blame it on the war, but because of the war, we promised to go to the battlefield, to live or to die together until the day the South was liberated, and the country reunified. Day after day, night after night, I hoped to see you on your way to the battlefield, passing through my Medical Station where I am working to help heal our comrades-in-arms. You must understand that if I wasn't in love with you, I would never have come to the battlefield to wait for you, to share bomb-raids, hardships, and risk death with you.

My wish was that we would sacrifice ourselves and dedicate ourselves together. As an educated Hanoi girl, my ideals and dreams were to offer my full love to you. Perhaps because of those mixed emotions of love, idealism, and romance, when I was madly in love with you at university, I tried to preserve myself and not give myself fully to you. I'd wanted to keep my love pure and faithful until the day I wore a wedding dress. Whenever I imagined our wedding, I didn't picture myself wearing a long gown with a veil, nor you in a formal suit, splashed with perfumed scent. Instead, we would wear the green uniforms, soaked with the blood, sweat and tears of two soldiers, smelling of bombs and bullets.

I dreamed of the wedding of two soldiers, and no matter how long it took, I swore to myself that I would keep my chastity and virginity until then. But, oh dear Toan, I couldn't preserve what I was willing to finally offer to you. To tell you the truth, I was not depraved, but that night I met a hero of the battlefield and I fell irresistibly into his arms, even though my heart didn't want to. I lost the most precious possession of a young girl, the love that I wanted to preserve for you. I lost everything, oh Heaven, dear Toan…

Was my mistake due to the war? I don't know. It's so cruel, my dear. I looked forward to the day I met you on the battlefield, but instead, here I will lose you forever. I pray that I will never see you again. But I hope that one day you'll forgive me.

Oh my Toan, my love, when you receive this letter, I will no longer be in Tiger Spring Medical Station, I will go further into the battlefield so that you will never see me. From now on, healing and saving wounded soldiers will be my greatest consolation. Farewell, dear Toan, my love, and the last thing your Lien wishes is that you will be safe, go through this war and back to Hanoi, have a new love, and a happy family…

My dear, what I swore to you has been lost forever…"

Tuan felt Lien's pain; he understood now why Lien was so distraught. She had been willing to preserve her virginity out of love. But it was not to love that she had lost it.

She had stopped crying, and was sitting cross-legged on the bamboo platform, expressionless, looking up at Tuan's drained face.

"Have you read all?"

"Yes," Tuan answered sadly.

"Alright, then go away, and don't come here again. You won't see me anymore."

"Where are you going?"

"You don't have to know!" Lien slammed her hand down on the rucksack in front of her. "Go away!"

Tuan stood motionless, his red-rimmed eyes staring at Lien with exasperation.

"You don't want to go away," Lien screamed. "If you don't, I will shoot myself…" She reached up and grasped the AK on the rack next to her platform. Lan quickly grabbed her hand.

Right then, Huu rushed in.

"Commander, we have to return to the company immediately; we have an urgent operation order!"

When they got back, Tuan saw that Political Commissar Mao had ordered all the company, fully armed, to stand in formation waiting for him. To the right were the two elephants given by old Ho Pung to the unit, flicking their tails, sacks of goods, weapons, hammocks, and food on their backs. Company Commander Tuan tried to ready himself for the fighting to come, but his mind was lingering with Lien's image. He sighed, thinking that it was the sorrow of war, the sorrow of fate.

Mao walked up close to him to exchange tasks. Tuan nodded, listening to the commissar tensely and thoughtfully, and then walked up in the front of the company formation. "Check your rucksacks and your weapons! Be ready!"

As everyone followed his orders. Tuan continued: "Attention! You know that we are going to battle. We are going to provide reinforcements for the 759th Infantry Company of the Truong Son Corps which was besieged by two companies of Saigonese scouts and one company of American

Tiger Spring

Air Cavalry. The American and Saigonese want to wipe out the battle tested 759th, which has been very successful in making the Truong Son painful for them They call it the Steel Company, just like our 26th Reconnaissance Company which was called Blue Tiger Battalion by them." Tuan raised his voice: "All march by twos, from right to left! go!"

11

The battle between the 759th Infantry Company of the Truong Son Corps with three companies of American and Saigonese had entered the third day on an unnamed hill with very few trees, and no sand and soil: only rocky slopes and streams that were bombed and strafed by American airplanes day and night.

The fighting occurred over a large area, with complex terrain, which made it effective to divide the troops into small groups which could either be used to attack, defend, or stay in reserve. Company Commander Quyet was familiar with the area and with fighting the American and Saigonese forces and was aggressive in counter-attacking them daily. The worst part of the fighting was dealing with ground-attack airplanes...F-4As and gunships such as OV-10s and AC-130s. They coordinated their attacks rhythmically like a symphony orchestra synchronizing its brass and woodwinds.

For the past few days, the gunships had been hovering over the unnamed hill, now and then pouring fifty-caliber machine gun fire and 12mm rounds down on the surrounding roads. Quyet telephoned in his report to Corps headquarters and requested permission to allow his unit to dig fortifications and trenches. Initially, he assumed that the enemy would only drop one or two companies tasked to find and destroy the branches of the road from East Truong Son to West Truong Son, which the Americans had not been able to locate by aircraft. If they were surrounded, they would send troops to support or to rescue by helicopter. The American military advisers' tactic was to always send the Saigonese army in first to clear the way for a big battle with the North Vietnamese Army.

But this time, at 9 am, two groups of planes, three F4As and three AC130s, swooped down to drop explosive bombs, penetrating bombs, and napalm and to pound the hill and the high points around it with volleys of 50 caliber and 20mm rounds. Streams of red tracers, each round as big as a hurricane lamp, cascaded down from the American aircraft and were answered by streaks of fire from the anti-aircraft artillery which shells sent forth beams of red light, flashes of lightning soaring through the air, exploding like fireworks, encircled the American airplanes and forced them to soar up. But as soon as the AC130s cleared the way, a flock of about thirty helicopters dropped their troops in a landing zone. Above them, a flock of F4A fighters circled, protecting the helicopters as they landed.

There were three platoons in Infantry Company 759. The first two dealt with the two Saigonese companies of commandos and scouts. The third was personally commanded by Commander Quyet and was tasked to "welcome" the American G.I.'s.

As soon as the F4As flew off and the American helicopters had disembarked two-thirds of their troops onto the landing zones, Commander "Crazy" Quyet yelled to his men to attack, while at the same time firing wildly towards the American commandos. As was his custom in combat, he would cradle a submachine gun secured by two slings around his arms and charge in the frontline, rushing forward and screaming: "Shoot...shoot...kill...kill...shoot.... Kill them all, comrades! Kill...kill...shoot!" His terrifying screams thundered and echoed down the mountain slopes, filled with a cold hatred that drove the enemy crazy and made them panic.

Quyet fired bursts from his submachine gun, and then single shots, sometimes up to seven, sometimes two or three, but always accurate and tightly grouped, his firing focusing all his accumulation of hatred and anger to its climax. Before each battle, he would always say the same things to his soldiers: "Comrades, pour your hatred through your gun barrels."

During the fierce battle, after the thunderous salvos from Quyet's submachine gun, in the midst of the echoing bomb explosions, the North Vietnamese soldiers heard the enemies' terrified screams—the screams of fear from men who knew they were about to suffer a painful and tragic death.

Before the battle, Commander Quyet had radioed clearly how he intended to fight to the Commander of Truong Son Corps: "Company 759 will be resilient in holding the point. We will hold every inch and millimeter of ground to the end, and cling to the enemy's belt to fight. We will maneuver the American company into one area so that the newly reinforced missile detachment and the Reconnaissance company can support us. We will also consolidate the fortification trenches as the battle may be prolonged."

Commander Quyet very well understood the strategic situation, even though the General did not explain or ask how much longer the 759th Infantry Company could resist the American aircraft and the Saigonese commandos. He understood that although the General could mobilize a division, thousands of troops that could "boil" these three enemy companies on this majestic Truong Son Trail, he would fall into the American trap: the American B52 flying fortresses used the 105mm, 150mm and 155mm artilleries and could eliminate the whole division in five or seven minutes. The General would not be willing to sacrifice his soldiers' lives for no gain.

Quyet never forgot the General's image when he visited his Company right at the meal when the soldiers had only had dried cassava cooked with a few grains of rice and a bowl of spring water mixed with salt for soup. The General took a handful of rice to taste, choking with tears: "How can you live and fight against them while eating like this?"

That image had warmed Quyet's heart.

So, in this deathmatch with the enemy, Commander Quyet was outnumbered and against the odds by at least two to ten, with 35 soldiers of his platoon who would have to stand-up and fight against nearly 200 American and Saigonese best armed commandos. He decided that the best chance for his men to fight is applying the guerrilla warfare tactic…, to launch a quick and deadly strike, then withdraw immediately, long enough before they call-in close air or artillery support.

The pre-emptive battle against the American "Gray Wolf" Brigade only lasted for about four or five minutes. Many of the Americans died or were wounded. Then the soldiers spread out and took cover among and behind the natural mounds of rock and earth from which they fired intensively at the North Vietnamese Armed Forces. Commander Quyet ordered the third platoon to withdraw to its fallback position, about a kilometer away from the main battlefield.

Before letting his soldiers take a break, Quyet assessed his troops. No one had died, and he had the two wounded evacuated, but the Platoon Three deputy commander was missing. Quyet transferred the command of Platoon Three back to its Platoon Commander, and he and one soldier went back to look for the Deputy Platoon leader. Meanwhile, the Americans called in F105s and F4s to bomb points along the suspected Vietnamese line of retreat while the American company consolidated its position and formed a line that moved horizontally towards the area cleared by the bombing.

Under the smoke, fire, and exploding bombs, Quyet and the soldier finally found the Deputy Commander of Platoon Three lying unconscious in a bomb crater, covered in blood from shrapnel wounds that had shredded his shoulder and almost detached his arm. The soldier with Quyet applied a tourniquet to his arm and lifted him onto Commander Quyet's back. Quyet staggered under the weight as the soldier kept sweeping the barrel of his AK right, left, front, and back, on the watch for American soldiers.

Suddenly an OV10 hovering overhead dropped a smoke grenade about five or six meters away from the three of them. Immediately afterwards, a barrage from the Americans' M16s and their M79 grenade launchers bracketed their area. "The Americans are here," Quyet said. "If we fall back to our prepared positions. Perhaps we might still escape!"

Carrying a wounded officer on his back, Quyet and one other soldier moved under cover of the smoke lingering from the bomb explosions until they found a small foxhole, about two meters square, dug to about their chest level. Helped by the soldier, Quyet placed the wounded man on a plastic tarp he laid on the wet ground. Awakening, the Deputy Platoon Commander whispered: "Oh Commander, I am thirsty, hungry..."

Quyet helped the wounded man drink from his canteen and asked the other soldier to cut up some dehydrated rations and feed them to him slowly. It was very hot. Slowly, the sounds of firing and explosions faded, as if both sides were exhausted after the two days and nights of fierce fighting. In the cool earth of the foxhole, the Deputy Platoon Commander's shrapnel wound stopped bleeding.

"Dear chief, tell me the truth," the other soldier asked Quyet dreamily. "Before going to the front, did you get a kiss?"

Quyet smiled. "I'm H'mong. Our people love each other but we don't kiss. Only you Kinh people kiss each other."

The soldier asked the wounded man the same question.

The Deputy Platoon Commander had started to show symptoms of malaria: he was trembling, his teeth chattering. He answered sarcastically: "No one in my platoon has a girlfriend that they could kiss or not. More than half of them are dead. I don't know what they'll do after the war, but how many of them can survive this kind of fighting…"

As he looked at the wounded soldier, Quyet felt his eyes well up with tears. Not willing to let the others see, he turned his face to the wall of the foxhole and wiped away the tears. It was getting very dark, and it began to rain heavily. As the rain fell, mosquitoes and the leeches surrounded and attacked them. Quyet helped the wounded Deputy Platoon Commander to sit up and wrapped him tightly from head to foot to keep the mosquitoes away.

"Let's find a way back to our unit," he said.

He lifted the wounded man onto his shoulders. The other soldier pushed on his ass to help him move out of the foxhole.

As Quyet carried the wounded Deputy Platoon Commander, the soldier kept pushing him forward. There was no road, and the burned trees were scattered across the big and small rocks, making Quyet stumble and, fall down and get up time and again. Fortunately, along the way there were many rotten trees that produced many kinds of insects, including fireflies, and Quyet was able to follow the trail thanks to the insect's lucent phosphorescent lights, walking carefully while the other soldier followed behind.

It wasn't until three in the morning that Quyet carried the Deputy Platoon Commander back to the assembly

Tiger Spring

point for the 759th Infantry Company and gave the order to urgently transfer him to the Tiger Spring Medical Station.

12

On the second day of the battle, Tuan's company suffered the loss of twenty soldiers supporting Company 759 as it tried to repel the three American and Saigonese companies that landed on the unnamed hill. Many Americans and ARVN soldiers also died and were wounded, the latter of which could be heard raising a great din of screaming and crying. One group of helicopters or another hovered overhead as if they were dancing: gliding down, landing, and picking up dead and wounded soldiers. Both sides were in intermingled positions, right on top of each other, and had to reinforce trenches and foxholes.

Huu and Platoon Leader The Cuong worked for a day and a night with Commander Tuan digging out a hole they could fortify. They had not yet finished. The ground was very rocky and while two dug, the other person had to keep a lookout for the enemy. All of the company's positions were very close to the enemy, so they couldn't cut down trees or dig rocks easily. Also the rainy season had started in the Truong Son range, and while it didn't rain heavily, it still came down non-stop. They did not make much progress at night, with one man guarding and the other two crammed down in the narrow hole trying to sleep. For two days now, The Cuong hadn't stopped crying. Tuan fully understood The Cuong's pain; on the first day of fighting, the remaining eleven soldiers in his Platoon had been killed. Only The Cuong survived. Tuan had asked The Cuong to stay with him as they dug out the fortification, so they would be close to each other, and he could encourage The Cuong to overcome this loss. Whenever he could stop crying, The Cuong spent his time writing in his diary, trance-like, his eyes shining as his fountain pen kept scribbling on the pages of the small, yellow-covered notebook.

February 10, 1971

During my one year in the battlefield, there have been so many cataclysmic changes. I am 22 years old now, but I already have some gray hair because of the hardship, bitterness, and grief I've experienced. Eleven soldiers from my platoon will stay forever on this land. More broken families, more mourning, pain. So many thoughts and so many issues that I myself do not know for what I am being tormented. So be it! I must move forward with all the strength of my youth, be patient and tough. Perhaps my heart had become hardened enough to endure bitterness, loss, and pain, just as my feet have become calloused enough to step on the enemy's spikes and thorns and obstacles and still keep moving forwards.

I don't clutch at my feet and groan, and I'm not

frozen in terror; I keep walking. I go forward because I believe firmly that victory will come to the revolution and to the just, to people who rise up, and do not cower in shame. I keep going forward because my heart is still pounding in my chest, producing bright red blood that fills my body. I am proud of myself because I am worthy to be a Party member, worthy to be with my comrades, worthy of my father and my brothers, of our homeland and our loved ones. I will continue towards the bright future that calls me, towards the red color of the victory flag beckoning me.

My sacred promise to our beloved Uncle Ho is still burning in my heart, and any hardships and sacrifices cannot extinguish it.

Oh, my homeland, my beloved country, all my sacrifice, loss and pain will only increase my intense hatred of the US imperialists and their henchmen. By acknowledging my intense hatred for our enemy, I affirm that I deeply love our beloved homeland, and our loved ones.

This hatred and this love have given me a profound understanding of myself: they have taught me how we must fight, sacrifice, and to endure everything, how to fully dedicate our beautiful youth. Even if I am the last to fall before the cease-fire, I am ready because I understand better than anyone: there is no victory without loss and sacrifice. Today I have to accept sacrifice, suffer loss and pain so that tomorrow the whole country will regain a peaceful and happy life forever. Those who know how to live in a way worthy of a human being

Tiger Spring

cannot escape the great, heavy, and glorious responsibility" (Original from Nguyen Tien Binh's battlefield diary)

The most terrible thing for Tuan, The Cuong, and Huu was that there was a corpse of an ARVN commando about seven meters below the ledge of their fortification. Beside the corpse there were two mortars, three M16 rifles and a rucksack which held some canned food, dried rice, and some letters written to his girlfriend. In every letter, he wrote about his tragic fate, his fear of death, and his desire to end the war soon to go back and get married. He had prayed for God's help, but God was not there since God wouldn't love those who carry guns to kill innocent people.

That corpse had been lying near Commander Tuan's foxhole for three days but the three of them couldn't find the soil to cover him. In addition, the American trenches and ambushes were very close to those of the 26th Reconnaissance Company. Even supplying meals to their posts was extremely difficult for the cooks. Three bags of rice balls with some salted wild turnip, a box of canned meat, and two cakes of field rations served for one day or two. For water, they gathered rainwater, and food resupply was always done at night. Each cook would be accompanied by two guards, all of them crawling from one post to another. For the last three nights, two cooks and four guards had been shot dead in American ambushes.

Early on the morning of the third day, two cooks crawled over the ARVN corpse to bring food to Tuan's foxhole. The corpse was swollen, its face: ears, nostrils, eyes, and mouth, was covered with white squirming maggots. The smell of the corpse was unbearable, and the two cooks broke their crawl and stood up, just as an OV 10 swooped in, hovering low and dropping bombs. The sky darkened with explosions. Smashed rocks and soil mixed with the fire and smoke and boiled up into a huge column of smoke, its dark gray thick clouds drifting, floating in the air, covering a wide range of mountains and hills of the battlefield. Taking advantage of the large black clouds like a country haystack, the two cooks threw away their sacks of food, and rolled down the rocky slope. On that day, Tuan, The Cuong, and Huu had to survive by eating dried rice and a can of canned meat taken from the dead corpse, with the faint stench of the dead man clinging to everything.

By the fourth day, the corpse was covered by all kinds of flies. It was as if all the flies from all the other corpses on the battlefield flocked over to swarm this one body. Tuan told Huu to cover his nose and mouth and they crawled over to the corpse and with an entrenching tool scraped off some dirt mixed with small stones and shoved it into the bloated belly of the corpse. The bloated stomach burst open and a flood of white maggots, each the size of half a finger spilled out, along with a gush of yellow liquid. Seeing the maggots, Huu vomited his guts out. Tuan put the entrenching shovel back on his belt, pressed Huu's head down, and pulled him back to their hole.

Unable to bear the disgusting smell any longer, Tuan decided to abandon this position and fall back to the rear. At one in the morning, Tuan, The Cuong, and Huu made it back to the second line of resistance. The cook gave them three bowls of rice, and a canteen of cassava leaf soup cooked with some squishy bullfrogs. As soon as he put the rice into his mouth, Tuan vomited right into the bowl. The stench of the corpse and the image of the maggots and flies emerging from it still lingered in his mouth. He stopped eating and asked two guards to accompany him to the nearby shallow stream to bathe.

The stream was very shallow, and the water was usually crowded with soldiers who came to bathe or wash their clothes after fighting, so the water stank from the odor of people and rotting leaves. Still, Tuan stripped off his filthy black uniform, still permeated with the stink of the dead ARVN. He bent over to wash his hair, holding his breath to avoid the stench. Fortunately, the guard who accompanied him had a bar of soap, and Tuan happily scrubbed his whole body, trying to get rid of the lingering stench of the dead.

13

A ground missile detachment joined up with Commander "Crazy" Quyet's 759th Infantry Company and elements of the 26th Reconnaissance Company. At that same time, communication between the Truong Son Corps Command and the troops based on the unnamed hill was restored.

The order from headquarters was: "The 26th Reconnaissance Company will block the two Saigonese commando companies on the right and left flanks. At the center, the ground missile detachment and 759 Infantry Company will focus on eliminating the company from the American "Gray Wolf" Brigade, understanding that the American troops would withdraw by helicopter, and afterward they would use their air support to destroy the entire battlefield and erase the traces of their disgrace. The rear elements must strengthen and consolidate their fortifications. Over."

The plan was clear. Tuan the Beard hugged "Crazy" Quyet and only asked one word: "Win?"

"Win. Sure, we'll win. But as for using the Soviet ground-based missiles attack for the first time during the attack. I don't know what will happen."

Tiger Spring

The leader of the ground missile detachment was lying in a hammock, chewing dry rations, and reading a copy of the Military Arts Magazine. He began belting out a song: "No enemy can stop our forward marching…", but forgot the next verse and switched to another song: "The two of us are hanging our hammocks in the Truong Son forest, we are at the two far ends. The road to the battle is so beautiful in this season, and East Truong Son misses West Truong Son…"

"Who's this guy," Tuan asked Quyet. "Is he in your unit?"

"No. He's the platoon leader of the ground missile detachment that will coordinate with us tomorrow…"

"What's his name?"

"I haven't asked. He just arrived…"

Tuan went over to the hammock. "Get up, comrade."

The soldier sat up and pulled his pants up lazily, looking up at Commander Tuan.

"Are you the leader of the missile detachment? What's your name, and what rank?" Tuan asked.

Seeing the firm face with a tough voice of Commander Tuan, the man hesitated, then stood at attention. "Second Lieutenant Nguyen Dan, in command of the ground missile detachment, reporting."

"I'm Senior Lieutenant Hoang Van Tuan, Company Commander of 26th Reconnaissance Company, and this, comrade," he pointed to Quyet, "is Lieutenant Quyet, Commander of the 759th Infantry Company of the Truong Son Corps. Tell me truthfully, have you ever fought the Americans and the Saigonese? "

"Not yet, commander."

"Have you ever been attacked by American airplanes?"

"Not yet. The Soviets have just equipped us with new weapons: ground missiles and anti-tank missiles that can destroy bunkers and fortifications. Their range is up to 3,000 meters, and with direct line control, every shot is a hit. There are two vehicle-mounted missile arrays with four missiles each in my detachment, and each array consists of six soldiers, for quick and compact maneuvers…Please don't worry, when the ground missile battle starts, the Americans and the Saigonese will be horrified, you'll see, Commander!"

Commander Tuan smacked his lips. "New weapons, modern weapons can be highly effective and can create surprise, but the battlefield is not a training ground; anything can happen. Let me ask, what will you do if your missiles have not been fired but you are being strafed by enemy aircraft, pouring bullets down at you?"

The squad leader's eyes dulled. "To be honest, we haven't figured it out and I'm not sure what we would do about it."

Listening to their conversation, Quyet stifled his laughter, putting a hand over his mouth. He patted the missile squad leader's shoulder. "Fighting the Americans is no fun, man. Their weapons are the best in the world, take care!"

Looking at the squad leader, Commander Tuan became a bit depressed and worried. "You studied at the Artillery Officer College, right?

The squad leader's face cheered up. "Yes, After I graduated from the Artillery Officer College, I was sent to attend a six-months training course in the Soviet Union, and then assigned to test new missiles on the battlefield In this battle, it's the Americans who must take care!"

"Alright. We'll see. Go to sleep; tomorrow we'll have to fight. Try not to die!"

That night, it drizzled. Tuan entered the command bunker. The sleeping space was covered with plastic sheets so that rainwater didn't leak inside. It was cool, and after having a bowl of hot rice with braised stream fish and wild figs, along with a bowl of vegetable soup, Tuan told Huu, "I'm going to bed now, getting ready for tomorrow, since it will be a big fight. Prepare yourself, go to bed early too, OK?"

He lay down in his hammock and soon was snoring.

Huu went outside to pee. Nearby was the Command Post of the 759th Infantry Company—actually just a tent roof covered with green plastic sheets and supported by eight ankle-sized tree poles. Inside he saw Commander "Crazy" Quyet sitting on a plastic sheet spread on the ground; with him was the commander of the missile detachment. They were having tea cooked in a can of meat. A bamboo water pipe lay next to Quyet. Quyet heard his footsteps. "Who goes there?"

"Huu, liaison for Commander Tuan of Reconnaissance. "Great, come in!"

Huu entered and saluted the two leaders. Quyet took out a few dried papaya and cassava leaves from his backpack and gave it to Huu: "Piss on these leaves for me. Do it slowly, in order to let the leaves absorb the urine; this is how you make *Thuoc Lao*, Lao-drug, water pipe tobacco. Just stand there, look carefully at the leaves and pee. There's nothing to be ashamed of... we're all men here, we all have dicks!"

Huu held the dried leaves and slowly urinated on each one. He was glad he hadn't peed outside; then he'd have nothing left to cure Commander Quyet's tobacco and Quyet would be annoyed at him.

He gave the urine-soaked leaves to Quyet.

"Commander, how can dried leaves soaked in urine replace water pipe tobacco?"

Quyet crushed the leaves with both hands. "Urine gives them the pungent smell of *Thuoc Lao*; otherwise they're flat."

"Then why don't you use your own pee instead?"

"You young people know nothing. I'm almost forty years old, I eat whatever filthy food I can find, and I sleep with women, so my urine is dirty and stinky, not pure like yours, understand?" Quyet took out his *Dieu Cay*, long bamboo bong pipe, stuffed some crushed leaves into the bowl, and lit it from the kerosene lamp. He inhaled twice, deeply, and then exhaled with an air of satisfaction.

Putting the pipe down, Commander Quyet reached into his rucksack and pulled out a bottle. He opened the top and sniffed.

"This wine is very fragrant and doesn't have a sour smell yet." He poured wine into an old milk can, and took a big sip, laughing merrily, his eyes bright. "Good wine. Long time no drink. I invented this wine — please have a sip, you guys!" He passed the can to the missile detachment leader, and then to Huu.

Huu drank the wine slowly. There was a strong aroma

of alcohol, but the drink had a sour taste. Huu returned the can to Quyet, who took two more sips.

"I made this wine myself. I make yeast from spoiled rice and cassava brewed for a week and then mixed with sour leaves, rolled into small handfuls, then dried in the sun. Then I find a wild banana tree, make a large hole in it, and insert the ball of yeast into it. Then I drill a small hole in the bottom of the tree to catch the tree's water that soaks through the yeast to become wine. You'll be addicted to it if you drink it for a long time, and you'll get drunk as well. Come on, we three will finish this canteen and then go to bed, ready for tomorrow's fight."

Out of respect for the ethnic-minority Commander, the detachment leader, who was about twenty-four or twenty-five years old, tried to take a few more sips. Huu, who had never drunk before, refused, and asked for permission to go back. It was a moment of rare silence on this active battlefield: there was no sound of bombs exploding, no artillery shells being fired mid-range, only the "chick...queck...chick queck" cry of a wild bird.

It made the missile detachment leader feel strange. "What kind of bird is crying like that, Commander?"

"A pig-bird." answered Quyet, tilting his head back to sip wine.

"In my hometown, each time the pig-bird flies over and cries, we know someone will die."

Quyet smiled. "In war, there is not a day where no one dies; if not our enemy, then us...come on, life and death are just a matter of destiny. For me, I always know that I live today, but I may die tomorrow...Look at this...!"

He unfolded a letter from a notebook in his rucksack. "This is the letter I wrote for my wife, to only be sent if I die. I say farewell to her and tell her that if she gets remarried, she should take care of my elderly parents for me...unfortunately, we don't have children yet..."

He laughed cheerfully and finished the last drop of wine in the canteen.

The missile detachment leader looked pensive. "Last night, I had a dream that I went to see Thao, my girlfriend in the Teachers' University. We met each other in her dorm room. She was sitting on the top bunk bed. Instead of being happy to see me, Thao kept chasing me away, saying, 'Leave me alone; you're a ghost now. Don't come back to ask me to follow you. If you feel sorry for me, please go away, and I will pray for you for the rest of my life.' He smacked his lips. "Maybe just missing her so much and being so obsessed by the idea of death put that kind of strange dream in my head. Couldn't that be right, commander?"

Hearing the sound of the pig-bird, and listening to the two officers' strange conversation, Huu had felt anxious and worried, afraid that something would happen tomorrow or the day after tomorrow...that night, he squirmed in his hammock, unable to sleep.

At four a.m., Tuan-the-Beard came to him, "Relay my orders to the platoons to deploy to their assigned positions."

Huu slung his AK and went off into the dark, trembling, and fearful the whole way. When he finally located the Second Platoon, he asked them to pass the orders to the Third Platoon, for the Third to give them to the First, and finally for that platoon to give them to the Fourth Platoon. He returned safely to the CP bunker but remained feeling nearly paralyzed with fear and still trying to shake off the dread he felt hearing the cold, deathly cry of the pig-bird.

At a quarter to five, the sun rose on the hill with no name; the sky was cloudless. The golden rays of sunlight sprinkled a dazzling light on the burned, splintered tree trunks scattered on the rocky ground that had been plowed by American bombs.

The missile array vehicles, each with four rockets, were placed in an area surrounded by an abatis made of large tree trunks stacked and woven together. Company Commander Quyet told the missile squad leader that it would be difficult for him to determine the target locations since the American and South Vietnamese would keep shifting their positions.

"They will use their helicopters to take the high points and will shift their forces quickly from one point to another in order to avoid close combat with us, since they need to keep a distance so their fighter aircraft can provide support. Remember that surviving American air power is not a piece of cake. After you fire a salvo, move out of your position immediately and maneuver as quickly and as much as possible."

Company Commander Quyet held his submachine gun in one hand. With the other, he firmly shook the missile squad leader's hand. "The order to begin firing is the sound of my weapon! Remember to hit the targets accurately! With these new weapons, when you guys knock out dozens of their bunkers in a few seconds, the Americans and the Saigonese will be so frightened they'll shit themselves. If they run down the hill, we will "welcome" them. We will be victorious...hee hee..."

Quyet slung his submachinegun back over his shoulder and waved his soldiers forward. The entire Area of Operations was spread over a large area of rocky hills and thick forest. The American soldiers and South Vietnamese commandos did not know how to effectively defend and conceal themselves from the North Vietnamese troops, while the North Vietnamese troops could not scout out the enemy's defenses except for the high-priority targets "reserved" for the ground missile detachment to destroy.

When it was exactly 5 AM, according to his Russian Poljot watch, Commander Quyet ordered his Second Platoon, along with five additional soldiers to fire their mortars and throw grenades at the enemy trenches and bunkers. As they did, Quyet sprayed the enemy with his submachine gun bullets. The American and Saigonese commandos immediately returned mortar fire and automatic weapons fire at our soldiers. As soon as they heard the machine gun fire signaling Company Commander Quyet's attack, eight rockets from the missile battery streaked out like bright meteors into the eight American bunkers on one hill. The horrifying explosion destroyed the key enemy positions and the panicked Americans jumped out of the trenches and rushed down the hill. At the same time, American reconnaissance aircrafts, L19, OV-10s roared overhead, swarmed like flying bats on the unnamed hill and poured smoke-rockets down. A group of HU1E helicopters hovered, searching for a landing zone. Waiting for the panicking American soldiers to run down the hill screaming, Commander Quyet grabbed his submachine gun and rushed forward.

The American tactics in both retreating and fighting back was very effective in a counter-attack. They run in a zigzag formation of three to five men, with the first man—while covered by the ones behind spraying automatic fire, and then rolling to the ground behind any cover he could find and loading another magazine and providing covering fire for the soldiers behind him to advance. They in turn would run forward, roll down behind stumps or rocks and shoot at the North Vietnamese troops, allowing the soldiers now in the rear to leapfrog forward.

The frontal attack led by Commander Quyet rushed into the battle like a whirlwind, shooting down many of the enemy, but meeting fierce and methodical resistance from skilled American soldiers, the North Vietnamese soldiers collapsed, one group after another, in the first moments of the battle. Quyet sprayed a volley from his submachine gun at the fleeing enemy, waiting to hear the second batch of ground missiles being fired. But he heard nothing.

He didn't know that after the first salvo, the detachment leader had been so excited that he stayed in place instead of shifting positions immediately, and instead had his men load up a new series of missiles in order to fire a second salvo. Suddenly, two F4s with heat-seeking radar detected the coordinates of the missile squad and dived down, dropping bombs. All twelve soldiers and both rocket launchers were obliterated, the noise of their destruction so loud both sides were momentarily shocked.

The fighting was so fierce: the rifles constantly firing, grenades exploding, mortars, B40 and B41 rockets, heavy machine guns rapidly charging into the targets creating loud explosions like chaotic thunder. There may have been about 200 Americans, and many of whom were now dead and wounded, but there still remained too many surviving ones. They ran towards the makeshift landing zones where a few helicopters were waiting, stopping to take cover behind rocks, panicking, unloading the supplies, and loading the dead and the wounded into helicopters. While above in the sky, the gunships circling with their deadly miniguns and rockets pouring down, then soldiers launched counter-attacked vehemently. A typical American way of fighting!

There now were only over eighty officers and soldiers in Quyet's company remaining. Many were dead and bloody wounded; their ammunition was almost exhausted. This made Quyet deeply regret the absence of the anti-aircraft missiles; they could turn the American helicopters into ashes. As he hid behind a rock, he nearly choked on his anger, watching helplessly as the surviving American soldiers rushed into the HU1E helicopters and took off with the dead and wounded ones with them. At the same time, the American soldiers gathered a few dozen of "Van Kieu" Montagnard people, all women, children, and elders, marching ahead of them as cannon fodder.

"Crazy" Quyet didn't know how to handle this situation, then Hao, the liaison agent came over and begs: Please

Commander..., assign me two soldiers. I would know how to relieve the siege for those people. Oh, yes, let me borrow your PRD as well."

Quyet had no time to think, he handed over the PRD and two big cartridge boxes to Hao, patting his shoulder, trustingly: "You have no choice now. Willing to save lives of the people, we have to accept the risk of a suicidal mission...your duty, I will give you two brave ones."

Just hearing that said, there were many arms raised to be volunteered in Hao's suicidal mission. Not to wait for Quyet's assignment, Hao glanced his eyes looking at the warriors raising their arms up and made signals to two of them to stand up. Hao asked them to load their AK 47's and each carried four American duckbill grenades and followed him.

All three quickly camouflaged as special commandos, slithered through the inching mounds forward. When Hao was about one hundred meters from the Van Kieu group, he found a high mound, raised the PRD ahead. The two others immersed themselves in the sand and slowly crawled in like sappers-style approaching the group of Van Kieu people, at close sight they jumped up, pointed the AK at the sky and shot a long volley of bullets, terrified the people as they ran away crying. The Americans were astounded, panicked, tried to cover their heads with their rucksacks, or threw their rucksacks away to escape.

Just then, the two soldiers fired another series of bullets into the sky to terrify them even more and shouted instructions for the Van Kieu people to run towards where their comrades were located. At the foot of the mountain,

Hao hid alone behind the mound, calmly firing long volleys of bullets towards the American soldiers. When realizing there was only one VC there, the Americans gathered, madly pouring all kinds of fire-powers…81mm. mortars, M79 grenade launcher, M60 machine guns, and AR15 rifles on Hao's spot. Though shrapnel fully stuck on his shoulder and back, bleeding profusely, Hao stood up, roaring "kill…kill them", echoing the whole corner of the jungle. He tried to put his strength on his feet and forcefully gritted the trigger angrily, kept shooting until there were no more bullets left, then threw the emptied gun away, dumped it like a banana tree being punished across its trunk.

In his position, taking the advantage of when the Americans busily focused on pouring heavy fire on Hao, Commander Quyet ordered four of his reinforced battalions to move forwards in formations at the flanks of the American troops, to pin them down on the open ground. 82 Mortar and 12.7 mm cannons from another North Vietnamese Army Force showered down. The Americans couldn't stand anymore. They screamed frantically, yelling at each other to carry the dead and the wounded to the helicopter's landing zone, get on the choppers and fly out.

Seizing the opportunity, Commander Quyet rushed to Hao's last location where he had just fallen, picked-up Hao on his back and ran to the rear. Hao's blood poured on his body and down to his feet, causing flies to fly everywhere and cover his face and scars injury on Hao's body.

At this time, Hao couldn't move, and couldn't recognize who was carrying him, just gasping: "Itching…so itching and hurt…Chase the flies away, chase them away…hurry up… chase them away…I am dying …those fucking flies…you fucking guys…who don't you chase the flies away, who do you let them bite me to death…Hurry up… kill them." At that time, Hao no longer had the strength to struggle and didn't siir anymore. Commander Quyet put Hao down on the ground, some soldiers quickly took off their shirts and smashed the swarm of black flies that bit into the bloodstained skin and all over Hao's wounds. Now that Hao's groans and curses became weakened. Suddenly Hao's tears ran out, he painfully cried: "Oh Mom, I am so much pain. Mom". They let go of his limbs, he hiccuped and stopped breathing.

Right then, incoming artillery guns and the roar of helicopters suddenly returned and appeared above the sky. Commander Quyet knew quite well that the next "act" of the enemy would be a "cleaning up" mission of the battlefield where lay dead American soldiers. This time, the American and the Saigonese soldiers fighting against the North Vietnamese ones from the air were pouring heavy artillery weapons pounding the battlefield all over the place…, all kinds of artillery that the US had given to South Vietnam, such as the 105, 155 mm, and the "King of the Battlefield" 175 mm…Soon after, here came the jet bombers…, diving low and dropping high explosive bombs: destructive bombs, drill bombs, napalm bombs, steel-pellet bombs, chemical bombs to erase the traces of a defeated battle.

Most often, this type of large-scale strategic raid they'd launched together with the Saigonese agents against the

Northern Vietnamese Army forces was from the military doctrine. Not wasting time, Quyet ordered every soldier in the platoons and squads to urgently deliver the wounded soldiers and the war martyrs back to the rear and clean up the battlefield, checking the headcount of troops, weapons, guns, ammo, and food. Everyone is very sad since the casualties were too high, the damage is too great. When fighting, the most important factors were weapons, now that there remained only a few grenades left; as for mortar 82, DKZ, and every machine guns and submachine guns as well as B40; B41 were almost out of ammo...the ammunition ration per soldier was down to about a half cartridge each.

Knowing that the American and the South Vietnamese will arrive soon by helicopters. Quyet gathered all the leaders of the Companies and Platoons for a consultation meeting. Most of them agreed that they couldn't stand when the enemy sent helicopters to land the American and Saigonese commandos back into the battlefield. Therefore, he radioed and asked for permission from the Headquarters to let everybody withdraw to the thick forest at the hill in the rear...He ordered his Company and Platoons Commanders to rearrange the battle formations, replenished weapons, then would secretly go back to take siege and counter-attack the enemy.

The radio operator hands the 2-Watt Radio over to Quyet...Quyet were asking eputy Division commander..., Quyet's voice turned into shouting match: "If you don't allow us to withdraw, I guarantee that my company would be wiped-out, whoever survives would be injured and be captured alive. I'll make it clear, Sir our company can't bestir and fight the enemy any longer while waiting for your reinforcements. We would all be eliminated, then only the dead ones would be there to welcome the arrival of reinforcements. I repeat, if you don't allow us to withdraw, I myself will give the order to withdraw. If I would be dismissed, or demoted to sergeant, I would still keep my decision!"

Quyet angrily threw down the radio and ordered his troops to fall back behind the combat zone. He assigned the Political Commissar to command of the troops' withdrawal, while he stayed with the reconnaissance group to keep track of the situation.

As he predicted, it took about five or seven minutes for the HU1E's's to lift off the defeated remnants of the American "Gray Wolf" Brigade, when groups of F4H and AC130 aircraft rushed in. The planes circled around the battlefield, howling in their fury, and then diving to release their ordnance. Explosions rumbled through and shook the unnamed hills. The whole sky was dark, punctuated with huge plumes of black smoke. Rocks and stones flew as if they had been sucked up into a whirlwind, the soldiers trying to huddle wherever they could to avoid the bombs and strafing.

Taking advantage of the black smoke covering the battlefield, Quyet grabbed the hand of the soldier assigned to be his aide and bodyguard and ran towards the place where the missile arrays had been set up. But when he got there, all he could do was shiver, cover his face, and burst into tears. Spread in front of him was a field of blood and charred burned human bones, burning trees, and the horrible odor of burned human flesh. The remnants of eight rocket launchers were scattered everywhere.

With their tears overflowing, Quyet and his aide clasped their hands and bowed to that ground covered with blood and bones, and then quickly left. Above them, the American airplanes were still roaring, bombs were still ripping through the air and falling wildly down on the unnamed hill.

The bombing got heavier, so bad that Quyet and his aide could not stand anymore and jumped into a trench, not knowing which side had dug it.

The trench was deep and wide, Quyet told his aide to stand guard and, exhausted, risked lying down and resting his legs on the smooth earth. He was very hungry. He sat up and took a bag of roasted rice from his rucksack, poured a handful for his aide, and ate some himself, along with a few sips of water from his canteen. "It would be nice to have a few sips of last night's wine," he sighed.

"Yes, it would, commander!" the aide replied.

Suddenly, the sky darkened and then it began to pour. Within minutes, the trench was flooded and from under the now soaked soil where Quyet had just laid down, he could see patches of human flesh and smell the horrible stench of decaying bodies.

"We're in the pit of the dead, commander," his aide cried out. The trench's sides were so steep that the aide could barely make it over the rim and Quyet had to push his ass up to help him. As he did, he slipped and fell back into the watery bottom, among the floating chunks of rotting corpses. Suffocated by the foul liquid and the poisonous gases released by the corpses that could have come from either side of the war, he fainted and could not rise. Quyet's aide, standing on the bank of the trench and trying in vain to get his commander out. Finally, all he could do was cry loudly like a child who was starved and had been beaten. He was assigned to protect his commander, but he failed and let his brave, steadfast commander die an ignoble, unjust, sorrowful death!

As the bombs started exploding around him again, this time he knew he had to get out and never again see his brave Commander again. With much sorrow, he bent down, and bowed three times, praying, and crying: "Oh our dearness Commander, please forgive me. I can't bring you back to our unit, to our comrades-in-arm anymore…My Heroes Commander, I pray for your sacred soul, please bless me to survive this war, and let me go back to my mother…I am her only son…uh huuh huuh hoo;" then he climbed out and frantically ran down the hill…

14

On the right flank of the unnamed hill, two Platoons of the 26th Reconnaissance Company, -the Beard continued to fight the Saigonese commandos after the American company from the "Gray Wolf" Brigade retreated. The North Vietnamese tactics switched from offensive to defensive and Tuan received a brief order from the Truong Son Corps' Battlefield Commander: "You are required to preserve our forces, and strengthen your trenches and other fortifications. Disperse our forces, set up observation posts, and stick close to the enemy. The goal is not to let the commandos go deeper into the area we are holding so that they cannot detect our newly opened roads. Keep on the defensive and hold against the enemy's attacks, forcing them to withdraw. Beware of B52 carpet bombing and other destructive air attacks from the Americans when they withdraw."

The guiding tactical philosophy of the Truong Son Corps Commander was clear. Tuan had only heard about the Commander, who was known both for his large size and for being present and finding solutions whenever traffic in the Truong Son roads—the Ho Chi Minh Trail—would clog up and many soldiers would die, whenever supplies and weapons could or could not get through to the battlefield. His mission was to fight and defend the Ho Chi Minh trail, the life-and-death road for victory against the Americans.

Understanding his own role, Tuan was not stressed, and in turn urged his troops to stay calm and relaxed. He had been fighting for nearly twenty years and the war had exhausted him. Countless times he had shed tears at the painful deaths of innocent people, of his comrades, of his soldiers. And he felt pain and sorrow at deaths of his enemies as well, since on whichever side they happened to be, every soldier had a home and family, every fighter wanted to live and enjoy happiness. Tuan had squeezed the trigger countless times, his hand firm and steady; he had fired with hatred, but he had shot and killed so much that he also felt fear and horror. He wished the war would end, wished to see the blood of both sides stop pouring out. But blood was spilled every day, and in the midst of this fierce battlefield of bombs and killings, whenever there was a day when they did not have to fight, to shoot at the enemy, when they could rest peacefully, it was a truly happy day.

So it was that his orders from headquarters to hold out and preserve his forces while letting the enemy withdraw made Tuan very happy. He understood that the Saigonese soldiers had not donned their uniforms and taken up weapons for the sake of noble and sacred ideals. What moved them were not dreams of the Fatherland but dreams of getting rich from the money they were paid. They surely understood that the Americans had no empathy for them; they, the South Vietnamese forces, were simply mercenaries. They went to war without caring about victory; all they wanted was to survive and to be back home. It broke Tuan's heart when he'd seen the frightened, pain-filled eyes of the Saigonese soldiers fighting against the Northern Vietnamese Armed Forces.

They shot and killed madly, drunk with blood-lust because no one who went to war wanted to lose and be defeated as well. The war forced people who had never known each other to become enemies and find ways to kill each other. Tuan felt sorry for the North Vietnamese soldiers, but also for the Saigonese soldiers for having to die in such a senseless way.

Now the strategy passed to him from the general commanding the Truong Son area of operations was to drive the enemy away from this area while keeping as much of the defending force as intact as possible, yet still chasing and terrifying the enemy, keeping them off-balance and defensive.

Tuan ordered B40 and B41 rockets and DKZ recoilless rifle rounds to be shot into suspected American and Saigonese positions every fifteen or twenty minutes. The North Vietnamese recon soldiers were ordered to crawl up close to the enemy and quickly fire into their positions and then quickly withdraw back to fortified bunkers. It was clear that the enemy could not bear these hit and run tactics, for on the 4th day, at about 5 AM, when the mountains and forests were covered with mist, the Americans suddenly landed HU1E helicopters in the fields where the

Tiger Spring

Saigonese commandos had secretly cleared locations at night. The enemy had been ordered to withdraw quickly, just carry their weapons and rush to the helicopters, leaving behind even their backpacks and their wounded.

Just as the helicopters took off, two B52s swooped in from the opposite direction to begin bombing, the terrifying sound of their explosions tearing the air, one after another. The whole vast area of the unnamed hill boiled up in huge columns of smoke and fire. Rocks and soil, trees and plants were mashed together, as in an earthquake.

Fortunately, the Truong Son Commander had warned the 759th Infantry Company and the 26th Reconnaissance Company to expect the carpet bombing, and so the two companies were not hit. The most painful loss for the Commander was of the two ground-based missile systems, sent from the Soviet Union, that had been destroyed right at the beginning of the battle. The detachment was spotted through the heat detectors on the American aircraft and both the missile arrays and the detachment of twelve gunners were annihilated, with not a single part of any of the men found; a fact that underscored the destructive power of the American weaponry.

Tuan mourned for these gunners, and sorely regretted the loss of the missile arrays. If they were still available, surely those helicopters would never have escaped. The missile squad commander's aggressiveness, impulsiveness, and subjectivity in focusing on victory but not caution, had cost too high a price.

Following the B52 carpet bombing came an all-out air raid by F4Hs and AC130s furiously dropping bombs and napalm all over the unnamed hill, with the Gatling guns of the AC130s "cleaning up" the battlefield. At the end, there were no more trees left to be burned; their trunks and branches of trees had turned into charcoal, and those only partially burned before burned again as smoke darkened the vast area.

As he waited for the American planes to finish their bombing and strafing runs, Company Commander Tuan commanded a platoon to take advantage of the huge black clouds providing cover and go back to the battlefield to collect whatever booty they could find, as well as any guns and ammunition left behind in the trenches and bunkers of the Americans and the Saigonese commandos.

Accompanying them were the two elephants given by the elder Ho Pung; both seemed to be familiar with the stench of spent explosives and the scenes of desolation after a battle and kept using their long trunks and front legs to push detritus to the side and clear the way for the soldiers. Huu and Hoan sat on their backs and controlled them like two skilled mahouts, only jumping down after the other soldiers finished loading sacks of booty and weapons onto the elephants' backs.

They collected numerous cans of meat, pate, dehydrated bread, sausages, and packs of cigarettes, including Rubies, Salems, and Winstons. They scrounged more than a dozen mortars, more than two dozen super-fast submachine guns and more than forty duck-billed grenades, left by the dead enemies in the tunnels.

Tuan, together with Huu, Hoan, and Platoon Leader The Cuong kept scouring the enemy trenches, foxholes, and bunkers in order to direct the gathering of booty. Approaching a half-flooded fox hole, they suddenly heard a cry of pain: "Oh...oh...I am in so much pain, Mom...Mom...oh my Mom! I am dead, mother! I am in so much pain..."

Tuan signaled to the others by waving his hand, and all four of them jumped into the pit, their gun barrels pointed straight down. A Saigonese commando, his entire uniform covered in blood, leaned his head against the side, panting heavily. He showed no fear of the gun barrels pointing at him, only stammered: "Water, water, please give me some water..."

Tuan told The Cuong and Hoan to bring the Saigonese soldier up. They laid him on the rim of the hole, and Tuan checked his wounds: his whole body had been torn up by shrapnel. The heaviest wounds were across his thighs; the blood gushing out of there was soaking his pants. Tuan asked The Cuong to wind tourniquets around both thighs and to stop the bleeding. The Saigonese commando waved his hand. He was barely breathing: "Well, I'm not going to make it. The bombs have killed me. Water...water please, I'm so thirsty..."

Huu, Hoan, and The Cuong all hurriedly checked their canteens. There was not a drop of water in any of them, and Tuan had lost his canteen somewhere. He made a sign to three others to go aside, opened the cap of the canteen and tried to spit some saliva into it. The Cuong, Hoan, and Huu did the same, trying to fill almost two thirds of the canteen with saliva. Then Tuan lifted the Saigonese commando's head up and slowly poured the saliva into his mouth. As he swallowed, the pain left his face and when he tilted his head to the side, it seemed there were drops of tears in his glazed eyes. Tuan closed his eyelids and said: "He's dead."

They put the Saigonese commando back down into the foxhole and used their entrenching shovels to turn it into a grave. As soon as they finished, they heard the bellow of the elephant: "Rak rakk…aya…oum."

"That's our male elephant, commander." Huu said. "Something must have happened to him to make him bellow so horribly."

The male elephant kept trumpeting, not only once but three times. Tuan, Huu, Hoan, and The Cuong understood that it was calling for help, Huu and Hoan had become very attached to the elephant couple since the day village elder Ho Pung offered them to the armed forces; they often fed them and played with them when they had some free time. Now all four men ran towards the place where they'd heard the elephant's cry, jumping over jagged mounds of rocks and logs still smoldering from the bombing. The smoke and dust sucked away their breaths. Huu, thin and small, found it difficult to run with his weapon and rucksack on his back. Tuan, The Cuong and Hoan, who were tall, with long legs, moved at twice his speed, Huu panting to keep up and resting every fifty or seventy meters. Tuan, feeling sorry for him, went back and without a word pulled Huu's rucksack off his back. "Commander, give it to me," The Cuong said.

"Do you think you're as strong as me? Go on!" Tuan strapped Huu's rucksack to his and continued to run ahead.

Finally, they reached the place where the male elephant

was bellowing. In front of them was a pit full of water, in it they could see Commander Quyet's corpse, floating among the chunks of rotting flesh. A dozen soldiers of the 759 Infantry Company were standing around the pit, all in tears. Seeing Huu and Hoan, the elephant couple exclaimed: " rrrak rrrak..." joyfully. The female elephant wagged her tail and approached Hoan. Hoan cupped his hands and patted the elephant's ear five times as she rubbed her head against his body. The male elephant came over to Huu and gently wrapped his long trunk around Huu's back, lifted him up, stomped on his four feet, circled around everyone, then put Huu down. "He greets everyone," Huu explained.

But Tuan was in mood to appreciate the elephant's greeting. He stood there unable to control the sobbing shaking his shoulder. A soldier tried to comfort him with a hug; he pushed Tuan back to where the elephants were standing. Overcoming his shock, Tuan quickly got himself back in control and wiped away his tears.

"What can we do to get Commander Quyet out of there? The pit is full of toxic gas..."

An officer of the 759th Company spoke up: "Sir, I'm Tan, Deputy Commander of 759th Company. Since you were not here, I borrowed the two elephants from Political Commissar Mao to try and find a way to retrieve Commander Quyet's corpse up, but I haven't been able to control them. It's fortunate that you are here now..."

"Huu, Hoan, my mahouts, which elephant do you think can pick Commander Quyet up," Tuan asked.

"Let me ask the elephants," Huu replied. He went up close to the male elephant's ear, stroked his head, and cupped his hands together to pat his ear. The male elephant raised his head to listen. Huu tapped his trunk and pointed to the pit, and said: Save...save..."

The male elephant's big ears flapped rapidly, as if he understood. "Commander, he agrees," Huu said and started to lead the elephant to the pit. Suddenly the female elephant scurried in front of her husband, blocking his way, her trunk sniffing and sneezing, her eyes red and watery.

"They are very smart and very sensitive," Huu said. "They can smell danger..."

"The animals' survival instinct is often better than ours," Tuan said. "Especially those that have lived through bombs and war...surely that the female elephant knew that her husband would be in danger, so she cried."

"Sure. That's why she tried to stop him."

"So, what shall we do now? No one can go down there. Just standing here is dangerous enough. We won't be killed here and now, but the poisonous gas from these corpses is contaminated with chemical toxins that would eventually cripple us and poison the next generation, if we survive, marry and have children. But if we let the elephant use his trunk, where all his organs of breathing, absorption, and digestion are located, he will be severely poisoned. These elephants have been helping us so much...oh, it's hard to decide!"

"Dear Commander," Huu said, "don't worry, the elephant's hearing and smell are very sensitive; he knows how much he can endure. You can see that the male elephant has already smelled the toxic gas from the corpses, but he knows he will be able to resist its affects and will be OK. Look, I take full responsibility for this."

Seemingly annoyed with his mate and unwilling to lose time, the male elephant didn't wait for his mahout Huu, but used his head to push his wife aside and slowly walked to the side of the pit, stomped on the rocky ground to take a firm stance, and plunged his trunk into the pit in the blink of an eye, He picked up Commander Quyet's corpse and shook the filthy water off it. Surprisingly, water from the commander's stomach also spewed out through his mouth. When the elephant seemed satisfied, he slowly turned back to the waiting soldiers and lay the corpse down on the ground.

Commander Quyet's corpse was wrapped in a poncho and then placed on a stretcher. An incense cluster was lit. Everybody took off their hats and quietly walked around the stretcher, saluting to say goodbye. The two elephants followed the men, and the male elephant again bellowed: "Rak rak oooou mmm." His low-pitched cry sounded like a lament.

On the way back, Commander Tuan and Huu rode on the back of the male elephant, The Cuong and Hoan on the back of the female. All four were haunted by Commander Quyet's death and remained silent. Again they had to pass through shattered rocks and boulders and burning tree trunks, which the elephants would kick out of the way. Both the men and the elephants were thirsty, their throats burning, but there was no water to be had. Even though hungry, thirsty, and sad about the death of Commander Quyet, still Huu took care with the elephant, signaling it to stop whenever he saw any surviving plants and jumping down to quickly pluck and feed them to both elephants. As they moved on, suddenly the male elephant stopped, raised his trunk high, turned around and trumpeted "Rak rak squeak...squek...rak" while flapping his ears.

"Water, there is water, commander!" Huu shouted.

"Where," Tuan asked, in surprise.

"The male elephant must have found a source of water somewhere, Commander."

The male elephant cried out again, and then took off, trotting, until they came upon a small stream of clear water gushing out of a ravine. Fully dressed, all four men ran to the water and jumped in, letting themselves sink to the bottom. The stream was wide but not deep, so the elephants couldn't immerse their whole bodies, but lay on their sides, swinging their trunks and spraying water into the air. Finally, the male elephant bellowed again and then used his trunk to push the female elephant ashore, slowly following her. On the bank, he started to shake off the water, but suddenly staggered, his front legs collapsing. The four men rushed ashore and ran to the elephant.

"Is he ill, Commander," Hoan wondered.

"Maybe he's been poisoned by the toxic gas from the pit..."

After a few minutes, the male elephant was able to stand up, but he kept sneezing nonstop and dripped drool onto the ground. Huu and Hoan had become familiar with the elephant temperament and conditions, so Huu quickly took a handful of salt from his backpack, put it in his canteen and mixed it with water for the male elephant to drink. Hoan also took a handful of B1 pills and gradually pushed them into his mouth. Afterward, Hoan fed him with dried rice porridge mixed with dried pork from the rations they'd scavenged from the Americans. After a while, the elephant seemed to recover. His ears, which had turned purple became pink again, and he was able to kneel on the ground so Tuan and Huu could mount him and continue their journey.

As they went on, they were lashed by rain, and saw lightening and black smoke. The flashes of lightning slashed across a sky darkened by the huge black clouds that swirled in the air like wandering souls. The terrible thunder made them cringe in fear since it reminded them of the sound of bombs. It rained nonstop, not heavily but enough to soak them, numbing their skin, causing them to shiver and clench their teeth. It took them almost a day to return to the Tiger Spring base. Welcoming them were the bodyguards, doctors, nurses, and medics, all of whom had been sleepless with anxiety. No one spoke, but all understood that the battle of the 26th Reconnaissance Company with the Americans had been terribly fierce and had cost great losses. Those who returned and those who had waited looked at each other in a painful silence, until suddenly one of the nurses, Lan, burst into tears and rushed, weeping, to the exhausted returnees. She hugged Hoan tightly, raising her tear-soaked face to him. Hoan let go of his AK and held her tightly in his arms, then released her.

"Why are there so many wounded? How many were killed?" Hoan slung his AK again and didn't answer her last question.

"It's the war, my dear. What can we do," he asked, and then burst into tears also, covering his face with both hands.

Someone grabbed his shoulders and squeezed them hard. "Comrade Hoan, stand up!" It was Political Commissar Mao.

Commander Tuan walked along the troops who'd remained on base, searching for Doctor Lien, feeling worried and bewildered. Where was she? Questions tumbled through his head. Lan, still standing next to Hoan, called out to him: "Hi, Commander Tuan."

"Where is Doctor Lien?" Tuan asked worriedly, scowling.

"Please go back and have a rest," Lan said, trying to calm him down. "I'll tell you about Lien tomorrow."

Tuan suddenly thought of the letter Lien had written to her boyfriend, Toan.

"She's gone, isn't she? Do you know where, Lan?"

"Yes, she had gone to the rear area; no one knows why."

But Tuan understood she had gone because of him. He sighed, feeling regret. He did not say goodbye to Lan, just waved at Huu and Hoan to return to their camp. Hoan secretly turned around and nodded to Lan as if he wanted to say something.

Back at headquarters of the Company, Tuan unfastened his K59 gun from his belt and hung it on a stake, then took off his high boots and threw them aside. Unconcerned about his stinking clothes that had been soaked with blood, he laid down on the bamboo mat and rested his head on his hands. Life was so sad when no one knew when the war would end, when the bloodshed would stop.

Tiger Spring

In four days and nights of one battle, twenty-five out of one hundred and twenty soldiers had been killed and more than a dozen were wounded. And his company had ended the lives of fifty or sixty enemy soldiers. Thinking back on it now, he was haunted by the painful, terrified screams of the American and ARVN soldiers fighting with the small, but fierce North Vietnamese soldiers who rushed into battle, shooting, bayoneting, engaging in hand-to-hand combat, regardless of bullets and bombs, regardless of how many enemy troops they were facing, regardless of whether they would win or lose.

The enemy had been terrified to fight face to face with the North Vietnamese troops, and the truth was not a small number of his own soldiers were terrified of American bombs, planes, and their artillery. Before battle, every soldier was eager to fire at the enemy, thrust a bayonet into the enemy's heart, even if it meant he would sacrifice himself, but when they were bombed, they felt like helpless victims of fate, bewildered and terrified that death could come at any moment.

Life on the battlefield consisted of surprise and heat. Eat quickly, drink quickly, sleep when possible, or don't sleep at all. Death came from all sides, not always from bullets or bombs, but from disease or poison snake bites. On the battlefield, even love was full of contradictions. He was deeply in love with Doctor Lien, but she had left without leaving any word, or a goodbye, only a grudge against him in her heart and sadness and pain in his.

Tuan skipped dinner. He wandered down to Tiger Spring and laid in the cold water until late at night to calm himself, and then went back. Huu made him a full bowl of milk from the can Lan had given them. Tuan asked for another bowl, then asked Huu to go the logistics department and fetch him a bottle of whiskey from the enemy booty they had taken. He finished off half of the bottle and passed out while Hoan and Huu had a delicious dinner.

Thanks to the booty from the American and ARVN that they had piled up on the backs of the elephants, Political Commissar Mao ordered everyone to enjoy a full meal. Each squad had two bottles of whiskey, and twelve packs of Salem or Ruby Queen cigarettes. When Tuan was fast asleep, Hoan asked Huu to go to his rendezvous place with Lan. But without Le, Huu felt lonely and sad.

"Lan is waiting for me," Hoan insisted. "If you don't come with me, it will be unsafe for us. Please help us, I beg you!"

"Alright, but this is the last time." Huu quietly slung his AK and hooked two grenades onto his cartridge belt. Hoan jumped up joyfully. "Thanks a lot, Huu. You're truly my best friend."

Meanwhile, Lan was trying to persuade Le to go with her to the clearing.

"Why do you want me to watch you making love," Le asked.

"I want you to go with Huu. You know he likes you a lot."

"But I don't like him. It's just embarrassing."

She was adamant. Lan hung a K59 pistol in her belt, put a US grenade into the pocket of her green uniform before leaving to their rendezvous place in the sparse forest, upstream of Tiger Spring. Under the sparkling moonlight, the water looked turbid because of the debris: rocks and soil, rotten branches and leaves torn up by the American bombs, still rushing down noisily, but somehow making the area seem less desolate.

Lan arrived before Hoan. She placed the pistol and the grenade discreetly behind one tree and then lay down on the soft grass under the canopy of a big Lythraceae tree. Above her a lonely male squirrel cried, "tock tock tock…" rhythmically but faintly. Far away, a bomb exploded and scared off the squirrel as well as some butterflies with black dotted yellow-brown wings black dots that had been sipping the sweetness of flowers and grass in front of Lan.

She lay quietly, enjoying the cool fresh air and the sounds of the forest. All the fresh fragrance of her youth, her eagerness to dedicate her life to the Fatherland had brought her here, to this medical station where she had been based for two years. Even though she had never had to face her own death by bombs, she had left her youth forever here. She became a woman before she had fallen in love. She had had many restless nights remembering the moment she dedicated her virginity to the suicide soldier. She did not regret the act, but still she felt sorry. Sorry for herself, sorry for the destiny of women during war, sorry for the soldiers who had never known love and before they had been killed.

Even the loss of her virginity was not as painful to her as the loss of her youth, gradually worn down by the extreme austerity of war. Every time she went down to the stream to wash her hair, Lan didn't dare to look at her face in the water. It seemed pitifully distorted. She kept trying to pretend that image was not her, that it was caused by the undulating water surface, titled by the waves that distorted her previously beautiful face. But washing her hair with a handful of hard, dry straws, looking at her hands in the sunlight, she was forced to realize that her youth had passed.

As she kept thinking such thoughts, suddenly two cold hands embraced her shoulders and she heard a familiar warm voice saying, "Hey! My love!"

Hoan released her thin shoulders, turned her face towards him, and kissed her passionately, revealing the fire of love that was burning in his heart. Lan drank in Hoan's burning eyes and sweaty face. "I missed you so much…Just a few days but it seemed like years," Hoan said breathlessly, hugging her, sniffing all over her neck, face, chin, and ears until his tongue found the salty tears on her eyelids.

"Why are you crying?" Now that Lan's heart was filled with the joy of loving and being loved, she hid her sorrowful thoughts about her lost youth. "I was afraid I wouldn't see you again…" she said sincerely.

"Were you afraid that I might die?" Hoan laughed merrily.

"Don't say stupid things like that…But who knows. You all go to the battle almost every day, and not all of you come back…I was so scared, my dear."

She tried to chase away her fear by hugging him tightly, still sobbing, kissing all over his face again and again, until Hoan could no longer bear his desire and slowly laid her down on the soft grass, gently unbuttoned her shirt, unfastened her belt, and then unbuttoned her trousers. As he was sliding them off, he suddenly stopped in surprise:

"Darling, where is your underwear?"

Lying on the grass in the beginning throes if ecstasy, Lan burst into laughter, spraying a little spittle onto his hair: "Don't you know how dirty the water in Tiger Spring is? It's itchy to take a bath. If you wash underwear and then put them on, the itching is unbearable. They stick to our skin, and we have to scratch all the time; it's quite embarrassing…"

"What a pity, I am sorry to hear there's such unimaginable suffering in our women's lives. Forget it. Keep on living, try your best, darling. Just enjoy love!"

Hoan moved onto her but did not undress. He knew that Huu was very close to them and would not be able to keep himself from watching them make love. They were both young men, he knew how tempting it would be.

He started making love to Lan anyway, slowly kissing her eyes, and then her mouth, and neck, and down to her belly. His moustache had grown thick and looked out of place on his round, pale face. But the way it touched her made Lan tremble; she arched, groaning, up to his well-proportioned body, making him even more excited, and he trailed caresses over her whole body. Lan struggled, squealing and giggling, tickling him so he would release her. They enjoyed each other's bodies to the utmost.

For poor Huu, without Le there to flirt and have fun with, the only way he could relieve his sadness would be by watching Hoan and Lan making love. Naked. But Hoan had remained fully dressed, so it was no fun at all. Angrily, he slung his AK back over his shoulder and walked towards the stream. The water trickled down from the high mountain as slowly as the sadness in his heart. He stood there for a long time, keeping his thoughts to himself, and then he wandered back to the camp.

By then, Hoan and Lan had fully satisfied each other. They lay on their backs on the cool grass, looking up at the moon shining with green light through the branches and leaves. Hoan reached over and covered her belly with her shirt. Lan heard a gurgling sound from his stomach, letting her know that he surely hadn't had his dinner.

"Your stomach is rumbling. Didn't you get dinner," she asked worriedly.

"My stomach is boiling, but I missed you so much, I just wanted to see you and I forgot to eat…"

And they wrapped themselves together again, like two pythons under the moonlight.

15

The coordinated effort, with the 759th Infantry Company of the Truong Son Corps, to drive out three companies of the Americans and Saigonese commandos and protect the newly opened, secret east to west roads in Quang Tri sector of the Truong Son Mountains, had left the 26th Reconnaissance Company badly tattered, with a serious loss of their fighting strength. A quarter of the officers and soldiers had been killed or wounded. Headquarters ordered the transfer of enough replacements to the company in order to keep it an effective fighting force.

As they waited, the troops studied political lessons, consolidated their fortifications and camps, and besides their military training, were allowed rest periods to improve their health.

With all their daily duties—rising at five, morning exercises, military training, the evenings spent studying politics and engaging in cultural activities—the only truly relaxing period was from half past five until eight p.m.

In the late afternoon in the Truong Son mountains, nature bestowed the most beautiful moments it possessed on humans and animals after sweltering hot days. There were still always bomb raids, and explosions were always there, but after the roar of the planes and the explosions died away, all kinds of birds and animals huddled in the hollows of trees, rocks, and groves, emerged again, chirping, dancing, singing the melodies of the forest.

Along the trails winding by the shallow section of Tiger Spring and very close to the mouth of "Gecko" cave, where the 26th Reconnaissance Company and the Medical Station staff used to bathe, butterflies and a scurry of light brown foxtail squirrels tended to gather. Among the dozen squirrels, one female was always bouncing around, her tail blooming out like a weasel's tail, beckoning the male squirrels who desperately followed her. Perhaps the butterflies, birds, and squirrels had grown familiar to the noise of human breathing and to the smell of hastily washed clothes drying on the rocks along the banks or cluttered in the middle of the spring. All felt free to sing, chirp, run, or dance close to the humans.

The squirrels were interested in the big tooth-brush trees scattered on both sides of the spring, their leaves and branches packed with small fruits that looked like ripe yellow corn kernels.

The male squirrels so enjoyed gnawing the ripe, fragrant, inviting little fruits that sometimes they almost forgot about chasing the erotic female squirrel, leaving her alone and a bit upset and angry, lounging by the spring, but still munching on the falling yellow fruits.

Tom, the American POW, was permitted to bathe with Commander Tuan, The Cuong, and Huu in the shallow water. He enjoyed the bathing immensely. Wearing a pair of loose trousers, he laid on his back on the jagged pebbles, letting the water run over his large, white body, covered with brown hair from his chest and abdomen to his limbs. He rested his head on a stone, his arms crossed behind him as a pillow, and closed his eyes to listen to the song of an oriole. It was as if the oriole's song made him forget all his pain, sadness, fear, and loneliness.

He told The Cuong that the song of the oriole, the bird with its red beak and a black circle around its neck, its golden feathers like sunlight, made him miss his mother, miss praying to God for blessings during Sunday mass…the bird's singing sounded like hymns. Even though he was in captivity, Tom had never loved life like he did then, when the song of the oriole was full of magic and charm, clear, high, and lovely in this place of bombs and fierce destruction. It was the song of the great forest, the mountain wind interspersed with whispers and rustling leaves and the sound of streams, murmuring day and night…the sounds of nature.

For Tom, the song of the oriole was soothing. The Cuong understood that the American was worn down and scared of the sound of bombs raids and explosions. He had not asked Tom how long he'd been in Vietnam, in how many battles he'd fought, how many VCs he'd killed. But every time he heard the roar of American planes, and especially the sound of exploding bombs, whether faraway or close, he searched for a tree stump or a rocky crevice, and slumped down in it, covering his ears with both hands and propping his butt up. Once The Cuong kicked Tom's ass, laughed, and said: "Your butt is as big as a bull's; if the bomb slides off a piece, would you survive?"

"I am afraid of American bombs, man," Tom said. "So many bombs and bullets! They terrify me!" And in this peaceful moment, lying under a cool stream, the water flowing sluggishly around him as he listened to the oriole singing, Tom was immersed in the wonderful fantasy world of the green forest. But the water coming from upstream was mixed with filthy soil, rocks, fragments of bombs, parts of trees, dead leaves, and even parts from human and animal corpses. Tom felt itchy, especially in his groin and his genitals, and had to scratch constantly. He asked The Cuong's permission to take off his baggy shorts, a request The Cuong translated to Commander Tuan. Tuan smiled and nodded.

Tom took off his shorts and happily jumped into the spring. Tom's scratched up penis was hairy and as big and long as a large cassava, making it funny looking to the three small Vietnamese men. Tom was not at all ashamed. He laughed innocently and said, "In my country, we bathe naked, not with clothes, you know." He laid on his back and let the thin water run over and caress his body as he closed his eyes and listened to the song of the oriole.

The last rays of a beautiful sunny day were glimmering on the water. Birds, squirrels, butterflies, and bees seemed to gather around the spring, clinging, hovering, and dancing on the rustling branches, and singing along with the cool breeze. Dusk was ecstatic with the scent of fragrant flowers and grass and the gentle breeze. The scurry of squirrels running after each other on the branches, the

Tiger Spring

males chasing after the female, so that flowers and fruits from the tooth brush trees from both sides of Tiger Stream kept falling into the drifting water. Tom fell asleep as the flowers and leaves sprinkled all over him and the thin water layer passed over him.

A group of about a dozen girls from the Tiger Spring Medical Station, carrying hoes, bags of cassava, and bamboo shoots came walking down on the trail across Tiger Spring. There was only a small dirt path to the right of some knee-high myrtle bushes. On the left side was the shallow stream where the American was laying with his eyes closed, his "big sweet potato" bouncing up and down with the rhythm of the stream flowing over him. Looking at it, the young girls screamed and ran away quickly. Their noises woke Tom up and he quickly covered himself with both hands. Tuan, Huu, and The Cuong burst into laughter. "It looks like Tom has cheered up some VC," Tuan said.

Tom was chuckling when suddenly old Ho Pung jumped into the stream and swung a machete straight at his head. The American, a skilled combat soldier, dodged Ho Phung's slash quickly, grabbed the old man's neck with his muscular hand, and lifted him out of the water.

"Tom, let the old man go," Tuan shouted.

Tom didn't understand what Tuan said but looking at his burning eyes and hearing his fierce and cold voice, he was scared to release old Ho Pung. Again, the old man waved his machete, ready to slash at Tom when The Cuong waded forward and stripped the bush-whacker from the old man's hand. "Old man, this isn't a cruel American. If he were, he would have shot me to death. He is my prisoner now, old man!"

The old man glared at the American and slid his weapon back into its wooden scabbard, then stepped out of the stream. "Is the male elephant poisoned," he asked Huu.

"Yes…he was infected with poisonous gas from the dead bodies. At first he wasn't too ill, but gradually he has weakened."

Old Ho Pung's eyes filled with tears: "I really want to see him, but I am afraid to see him cry. And I would cry as well. Well, you soldiers now have to release them back to their forest. These elephants know what kind of leaves can cure their illness. They are very smart. I've been raising them for ten years now, and I know them well."

Taking the old man's advice, the 26th Reconnaissance Company organized a farewell party to send the elephant couple back to the forest. All the doctors, nurses, and the medics of Tiger Spring Medical Station were there. Garlands of red flowers were draped around the elephant couple's necks, and everybody caressed and petted them. The elephants, understanding what was happening, bellowed sadly: "Aya oum…. rak rak…" Two big pots of hot porridge were served for their farewell party, but the couple ignored them. The male elephant moved forward leisurely, his wife following. After they'd gone about a hundred meters, they turned their heads, raised their long trunks, and swung them back and forth over their heads.

"They are saying goodbye to us! Let's hope that the male elephant will find the right wild herbs and recover, so they will come back to us," Tuan said. Such was his hope, but he had forgotten that just as the elephant couple returned to the forest, the Americans, after their failure to destroy the new road from East Truong Son to West Truong Son, had intensified their raiding fiercely. The Vietnamese soldiers could avoid facing the enemy and the wild beasts, but how could they avoid the toxic chemicals sprayed every day over the forest and fields of the ethnic minorities, and on the people themselves. Agent Orange fell like dusty rain, causing the leaves of the forest to wilt, the trees and plants to die. Wherever it fell, all that was left of the immense green forest were thin, dry, shriveled branches that released an unpleasantly fishy, bitter smell into the air. The two mahouts - Hoan and Huu—worried much about this, though they didn't dare talk to Commander Tuan about the fact that the elephant couple would be very susceptible to chemical poisoning. They had been feeling restless, worried, and uncomfortable, missing their elephants, constantly thinking about them as they wandered around aimlessly.

Two days later, a helicopter attacked the medical station's cassava field with rockets and machine gun fire. A few dozen military patients, some soldiers and all the medic cadres were out harvesting cassava. Huu and Hoan remembered that yesterday afternoon, an OV-10 reconnaissance plane had dropped "Tropical Plants" in this area; the aircraft may have reported the location of the field and now helicopters were swarming in to destroy the field.

Fortunately, the cassava field was very close to Tiger Spring Medical Station so that the 37mm and 12.7mm anti-aircraft guns of the Air Defense Troops on the neighboring mountain peaks were able to fire at the helicopters. In the middle of the cassava field though, the people working the harvest didn't know where to go to escape the attack until the elephant couple appeared, as if from nowhere, trumpeting "tuck…rattle" loudly, waving their trunks in one direction and running ahead, as if they were leading the way to safety.

All the harvesters abandoned their picks, knives, and baskets and hurriedly followed the elephants to a cave, where they would be safe. When the last person was in, the male elephant pushed the female in, and then followed her, stretching out his long trunk to sniff her ass.

In this way, more than three dozen people were saved, Huu and Hoan were elated when the elephant couple came back to the 26th Reconnaissance Company. The two of them hung around the elephants all day, and whenever they had free time, they went out to look for young banana trees for the elephant couple. Huu and Hoan both knew that the elephants were poisoned with dioxin, and the male elephant was also sickened by the contaminated gas in the pit from which he'd retrieved Commander Quyet's corpse. Gradually, as his health deteriorated, they could see his inherently majestic gait slowed down. People tried to show their love for the elephant couple by finding food and treats for them. Their care greatly confused Tom, the American, and he was even more surprised that once when the male elephant would not eat, Huu and Hoan ran inside the cave and brought out two golden medals, which they waved in front of the elephants. The male elephant trumpeted and stomped all his legs.

Tiger Spring

"How strange! Why does he jump up like that," Tom asked The Cuong.

"He knows that he's earned merit, so he feels honored and loves it," The Cuong explained. "Elephants are like humans; they like being flattered, rewarded, they sense it even without knowing what merit means. He's received the Victory Medal of the National Liberation Front of South Vietnam twice, with everyone applauding and a wreath and a medal draped around his neck. He ate well for a month; it made him so happy."

As they were talking about the elephants, suddenly an alarm went off. All the soldiers grabbed their weapons and rushed out, lining up and waiting for orders. Political Commissar Mao came rushing over, tripping as he ran, followed by Huu, who looked pale and breathless.

"Comrades! Hurry to save Commander Tuan. He's fighting with a tiger," Mao yelled and then called to Huu: "Huu, lead the way, quickly!"

In the thatched grass hill close to the deepest and widest section of Tiger Spring, Tuan was fighting with a black striped tiger, as big as a calf. Tuan's face and clothes were splattered all over with blood. He had stabbed the tiger with his dagger several times, but it was drunk with anger and the desire for human flesh. Each time the dagger hit, the beast thrust its horrid, fang-filled face forward and gouged at Tuan's face and body with its front claws. As the elephants bellowed and the entire company of more than a hundred men shouted and fired, the tiger panicked and jumped into the deep spring. A barrage of bullets chased after it, but the tiger kept diving into the deep water and bobbing up again on the surface. The male elephant angrily puffed out his stomach, blew air out of its trunk, and rushed into the water. Three strokes of its trunk left the tiger floating dead on the water, to the cheers of the soldiers.

From then on, whenever someone asked about that day, Tuan just laughed and said, "As a soldier of Uncle Ho, it's the same for me to fight the enemy or fight a tiger. It's no big deal. We have to fight almost every day…"

As for Huu, he often told that story passionately: "On the way to accompany Commander Tuan to have a meeting with the 759th Infantry Company of the Truong Son Corps, we had to go up a hill covered with thatch grass. All in a sudden the tiger sprang on us from the side next to the spring. I was so scared that I ran back to the unit and reported to Political Commissar Mao so he could mobilize everybody to come and rescue our commander. Since he was alone, Commander Tuan had no time to open his pistol holster; all he could do was pull out a dagger and fight the tiger until all of us and the elephant couple came to help."

"You had your AK, Huu; why didn't you shoot? Surely it would have been better if the tiger heard the gunfire, got scared and ran away?"

"If I could have handled it like that, what the fuck else is there to say," Huu swore angrily. But after thinking about it for a while, he calmed down. "OK, I was silly, cowardly, and scared, so my choice was to run back to ask for help. Luckily, our Commander was too brave! If he had been killed, I would regret it for the rest of my life."

The tiger was pulled out of the spring. But then, the

male elephant slowly staggered over, step by step, to the bank. He came to rest, lowering himself, sour-smelling blood mixed with gushing from his mouth and trunk. Tom, who had come with the soldiers to rescue Commander Tuan, watched as the elephant vomited the contents of its stomach, witnessing with his own eyes the way that American chemical poisons tragically killed this male elephant.

"Commander, please tell everyone to clear away from this place," Huu said. "The female elephant will call the herd to perform the burial ceremony for the male. Elephant funerals are done more carefully and more elaborately than those of human beings, Commander. And during the time they are burying their companion and planting trees for the grave, they won't cause trouble, won't disturb animals or anyone, as long as no one touches the new grave."

As soon as everybody had left, the female elephant sniffed the trunk, eyes and nose of the male elephant and then stood like a statue, fanning her ears into the face of the dead elephant, from time to time trumpeting out painful, pitiful cries.

16

Tom, back in the camp, didn't bother to take off his shoes and socks; he just lay on the ground, clutching his ears to block the lamentation of the female elephant. He wondered what the elephant's funeral would be like, but before he could put the question to The Cuong, his interpreter, he was suddenly struck with malaria. He sweated all over, his skin hot and feverish but feeling freezing cold. Commander Tuan and Political Commissar Mao were worried; they had been ordered to ensure Tom's good health while waiting for him to be transported by the Truong Son Corps to Hanoi.

Lan and Le had to give him three injections of Nivaquin in one day and forced him to swallow a gram of powdered Quinine. The injections gave him a very bad headache; he rolled around and screamed nonstop, refusing to swallow anything no matter how much everyone tried to convince him. Tuan, The Cuong, and even Hoan had to hold him tightly on a bamboo bed and force open his mouth to pour in a bowl of canned meat soup cooked with forest star fruit.

After three days, Tom's malaria abated; he stopped

vomiting, and started to regain his appetite. After a malaria attack, people always wanted to eat, though no matter how much they took in, their hunger could not be satisfied. On the battlefield, each soldier's rations were measured in grams, and Commander Tuan and Political Commissar Mao, unwillingly to take from their soldiers, donated half of their own food to Tom. Knowing nothing about that, Tom devoured his rations voraciously and still felt hungry. Seeking to reduce his hunger further, Political Commissar Mao gave him his box of condensed milk. Huu, witnessing this, felt uncomfortable. "Look, Huu I'm used to hunger and cold," Mao explained. "Our task is to ensure Tom's health to send him back to the US, where his speaking against the war will be invaluable."

With the special care he received, Tom recovered quickly, and was cured after only one week of severe malaria. Now he was well and could walk around. When the Russian Jeep came to pick Tom up and take him to Hanoi, everybody was informed, though no one knew how or when the American POW learned to say goodbye. As he slung his rucksack and climbed into the jeep, he waved to the soldiers who were looking at him and gave them a friendly smile. For the first time, he spoke in Vietnamese, in American accent:

"Goodbye! Thank you, good VC!"

Battalion Commander The Cuong had been assigned to interpret and to accompany the liaison officer from the Truong Son Corps bringing Tom back to Hanoi.

"How are you; do you feel you better," asked the Liaison Officer.

"I'm fine now. The thing that scared me the most was the malignant malaria, but thanks to your treatment and the good food you gave me, now I feel fine."

The Cuong laughed, "Did you know that when you were sick, my two officers each gave you half of their ration for a week, Tom?"

"Really? Well, now I know the truth about how nice you VC are. When I get back to the States, I will talk to the media…" Tom pondered for a while, then continued, "After almost six months living with you, I have come to understand what the VC are. You sacrifice your life for your country, you are truly brave, and you have compassion with each other. You have never really lived fully, so you do not know how much you are suffering, and you are not afraid of suffering. I really admire your endurance.

We Americans do not have that. It's right that we are defeated."

"What will you tell your people about the Vietnam war?" The liaison officer asked.

"I will condemn the war," Tom answered thoughtfully, "We Americans have been deceived by our President and our Government. We know nothing about Communists, and about Vietnamese people. American bombs are too fierce. Especially the destructive power of the B52s, it's really horrible. And the chemical poison; I am afraid that most of the American soldiers who have been fighting in the areas where Agent Orange and the luminescent agent were sprayed will probably be contaminated with poison…", he unbuttoned his shirt, exposing his bushy chest, "I always feel itchy and this part is reddened, so I must be contaminated as well with chemical toxins from our American planes. I'm so scared. When I get back home, I'll have to go for treatment before it is too late!"

Then he turned to The Cuong, "May I visit the elephant's grave, please?"

The Cuong briefed the liaison officer about the death of the male elephant, and the ceremonious way he was to be interred. His account roused the liaison officer's interest and he agreed to drive his jeep to the elephant's grave, which made The Cuong very happy.

He tried his best to explain the burial ceremony of the male elephant to Tom, "When the female elephant trumpeted, it was quite different than her usual call. About four or five hours later, a herd of nearly a dozen wild elephants rushed over. Seeing the female elephant using her ears to fan the dead male elephant as she trumpeted, the others trumpeted in unison, and then all of them gathered around the corpse, and using their tusks, one lifted the head and the others the legs, and in that way they carried the dead one to a high mound.

"Afterwards they pounded continuously on the ground with their four feet until they transformed the open space into a deep and wide pit. Using their trunks, they dragged the dead elephant into it and covered it up. Then, leaving the female prostrating herself next to the grave, the whole herd ran into the forest, and knocked over any trees with bright red flowers, and then used their trunks to drag them back to the new grave, dig holes around it, and re-planted the trees."

The two others did not believe what The Cuong said,

until they saw with their own eyes the elephant's huge grave mound surrounded by a forest of red flowers. Tom asked the liaison officer to take a photo of him and The Cuong standing by the elephant grave. The American stood there for a long while, then walked around, flipping through the fallen leaves scattered with dead petals, some of which he picked up and sniffed. Looking up at the tree trunks, he stared blankly at the dark gray mottled branches. Seeing his mood, the liaison officer told The Cuong to tell him to get back in the car. Sitting there, Tom turned into "the Quiet American."

He stopped asking questions or talking to the two others. It was very hot and the dry wind blowing from Laos brought with it the smell of fire. The driver, the liaison officer, The Cuong, and Tom were drenched in sweat, their clothes soggy for a while, though soon they dried as they rode along. Tom kept meditating, amazed at the devastation of war he saw along the two sides of the road, now and then shaking his head thoughtfully.

When the car had crossed the road from West Truong Son to East Truong Son, going through Ho village, of the Van Kieu ethnic group, and reached the Pha Ron - Quang Binh wharf, the liaison officer removed his Soviet-made Zennit camera from his chest, draped it on Tom and said, "From now on you play the role of an international journalist. You're French, OK? If you show up as an American, it would be hard for you to survive. You know why people hate Americans."

Tom nodded. He had witnessed the death, disaster, and catastrophic effects of the American bombing. He himself had been deathly afraid whenever he heard American warplanes rumbling in the distance. How much worse it was for those poor people who had to face being bombed daily by the Americans and the Saigonese. His days being treated in the Tiger Spring Medical Station had led him to understand why young Vietnamese of eighteen or twenty would calmly sign up to go to the battlefield, their hearts burning with love and patriotism, even if they had to sacrifice their lives. Tom had learned that the motto that the North Vietnamese learned from their Uncle Ho was, "Overcome any difficulty, defeat any enemy" and that they would never yield to the enemy's bombs. Losses and sacrifices happened every day on the battlefield, blood and tears overflowed daily, but they were proud and would never surrender. How could Americans ever understand this?

Tom remained immersed in such thoughts until the car was stopped by an old Van Kieu man and a child about ten years old. The old man was holding a boiled chicken and a handful of wild vegetable leaves on a banana leaf. Nearby, an old buffalo was chewing some green corn leaves half burned by the American bombs.

The old man waved his hand, his face brightening, "Soldiers, please trade this chicken for some rice."

Tom and The Cuong eyed the chicken hopefully. The liaison officer got out and approached the old man. "The enemy is bombing and strafing this place. Why are you bringing your kid and your buffalo here?"

"Our people have nothing to eat, only a few chickens like this one. We want to trade it for some rice we can bring back to share with the other villagers."

The Cuong had translated the old man's remarks to Tom. "Aren't these people afraid of death? This is a key target area for American aircraft."

The Cuong translated back to Tom. "We got used to bombs and bullets," the old man said, smiling. "If we survive, we survive; if we die, we die. Where else can we go?"

Tom shrugged, shaking his head.

They were carrying a few kilograms of rice in the car, which the liaison officer offered to the old man in exchange for half of the chicken. After the trade, he told the old man to get his grandson and the buffalo away from this dangerous area. Just at that moment, the air raid siren went off, and he ordered the driver to move the car, which was covered with camouflaging leaves, to a talus slope on the side of the mountain. All of them ran for cover, the buffalo leading them to a cave accessed through a ravine so narrow they had to enter one at a time. They all got in, but there was no space for the buffalo. Two AC130s and three helicopter gunships strafed the area at the cave entrance with machine gun fire and rockets. When the American aircraft had flown away, the old buffalo was lying dead in front of the ravine, its body shattered by rocket shrapnel and machine gun bullets.

The old man and his grandson hugged the neck of the dead buffalo, crying sorrowfully. The liaison officer and The Cuong tried to help them up and comfort them.

"If it wasn't for your buffalo leading the way into this ravine, we would all have been killed."

As The Cuong translated, Tom crossed himself. "What a country! Even the animals fight against the enemy. We

Americans didn't understand you and your culture, so we didn't know how great your courage and will to sacrifice are, nor the boldness and wisdom in your way of fighting. Now I understand why we are losing to the Vietnamese."

Having half a boiled chicken, but no more rice, the liaison officer told the driver to look for "State-owned Department Store No. 2" on the road. They would pick up some military rice vouchers.

It amazed Tom and The Cuong to hear that such a thing as a "State-owned Department Store" selling necessities and food to passing soldiers, existed in the middle of this fiercely contested area, blasted by bombs, and torn by bullets. They insisted on being allowed to go to it with the liaison agent.

To get to it, they had to go through a narrow, zing-zagging tunnel, crawling or bending over to fit. It was miserable for Tom, as was noted by the liaison officer. "It's good for him to see the reality of our lives, to know how bad our living conditions are, even as we fight against them," the liaison officer said to The Cuong.

After he'd passed through the tunnel, Tom had to lay down on the ground for a while, catching his breath before he stood up and entered the "Store"—which actually was built half-above ground, half underneath at the foot of a large mountain, the roof covered by large tree trunks. Inside, there were some shelves displaying a few dozen pairs of rubber-tire sandals, a few dozen hats, a few bars of soap, hair brushes, toothpaste, and toothbrushes, as well as a cast iron pan full of cooked rice. The staff were two young women about twenty-four or twenty-five years old, dressed like prehistoric people with only thin, tattered grass-colored T-shirts that came down over their thighs, and no underwear.

"Why are you dressed like this?" asked the liaison officer.

"What? Is there anything about us that scares you? You know very well how hot it is on the Truong Son trail, with no water and everybody always dirty and sweaty. Having to wear underwear is unbearable, dear!"

The Cuong translated to Tom, who was shocked, staring wide-eyed at the two women. The liaison officer opened his briefcase, took out a small pink piece of paper inscribed: "Truong Son Department Voucher" and gave it to one of the young women.

"I would like to get four rations of rice."

Tom quickly took pictures of the two young girls wrapping the packets of rice in torn off pages from old newspaper. He passed the camera to The Cuong.

"Could you take some pictures of me and these two young ladies?"

The Cuong told the women that the French journalist would like to have a photo with them. The elder one, with an austere face, stared at Tom. Her sharp, prying eyes looked at him from head to toe, at his clothes, which were hand-sewn from pieces of uniforms, and at his pale skin and belly bloated by living in the forest and being severely affected by malaria.

She shook her head. "He's not a French journalist! He's an American, an evil American! You captured him and now you're bringing him to Hanoi, to be returned to the

US to exchange him for dollars, right? I won't give him rice…I hate the invaders!"

As she spoke, she stomped her feet on the ground and grabbed a packet of rice from the liaison officer's hand. Suddenly a breeze blew through the ravine from behind, lifting up the women's loose, thin T shirts and revealing from their naked thighs up to their tanned bellies. Panicked, they shouted "Oh, oh" and hurriedly pulled the shirts down to cover their sore, red, ringworm-scarred legs. The liaison officer stood at attention, raised his hand, and saluted them and turned back to the tunnels, followed by Tom, The Cuong, and the driver.

They had exited the tunnel and the "State Department Store No 2" managed by the two young girls from Quang Binh province and were about two hundred meters away when they saw two groups of F4H and F105 attack aircraft rushing up from the South, circling twice around the tunnel area, howling as if to show their power and scare whoever was on the ground. Six of the planes dove down and dropped their bombs, as precisely as in a training exercise.

Suddenly, the second F4H was enveloped by salvos from 40mm, 37mm, and 12mm anti-aircraft guns and, unable to escape, crashed into a mountainside, where it burned brightly.

With one of the six fighters down, the other five swerved away from the area, fearing the anti-aircraft artillery positions located in the surrounding hills would shoot them down. Instead, they diverted to other parts of the road that the pilots had picked as secondary targets.

At that time, the liaison officer, The Cuong, Tom, and

the driver were crammed into a shelter carved into the mountainside near the road. The first salvo of bombs blew the car into the abyss, even though it was parked close to one side of the slope. Right after that came a series of deafening, terrifying explosions, with the dust from pulverized rocks darkening the sky. The four men had jammed into a very sturdy A-shaped shelter, reinforced by wooden beams, yet with every wave of bombs the walls around them shook and wobbled as if from an earthquake, Earth, shards of rocks, and the roar of the bombs rushed in through the entrance. All four men squatted and covered their ears with both hands, but it didn't keep their ears from ringing. The pressure swelled painfully in their chests and their bodies trembled violently.

Tom burst into tears, but no one cared, since they were all deafened, scared, and thinking they would die. In between the bomb runs, everybody felt frantically all over their bodies to see if they were wounded. Even The Cuong, who had experienced many battles, had never before had the feeling of waiting for the bombs to explode on him, for sudden death to come. It was no wonder that Tom was so terrified.

Fortunately, the attack aircraft only dropped bombs on the empty road for about fifteen minutes and then fled. All grew quiet again. The liaison officer ordered everybody to move the rocks and broken tree branches from in front of the tunnel in order to get out. Tom was still scared and hesitated, not daring to come out. The Cuong had to grab his hand and yank him to encourage him to get out.

Once outside, they looked in shock at the overlapping

bomb craters on the road they had just passed. Piles of red and black soil had been churned up on the surrounding mountains and hilltops, as if a terrible earthquake had just happened. Trees had been stripped of all their green leaves; their branches half-burned. The four men sat by a bomb crater permeated with the stink of explosives. The driver had yet to calm down, but even as he was trembling, he tried to pull the half chicken and the bottle of water out and gave them to the liaison officer, who divided the meat into four portions, with the three best going to The Cuong, Tom, and the driver, and only saving the bony part was for himself.

He tried to give half of his rice to Tom, but Tom refused. "That young girl hates us Americans so much, she didn't want me to eat rice, so I won't eat. I'd be ashamed to have it. Please go ahead, Officer!" As he tried to eat his portion of chicken, tears ran down his cheeks. "I wonder if they are still alive... the bombing was so fierce, no wonder why they hate us Americans so much. It's so bad for the American people..."

The liaison officer smiled. "Don't worry. They can't die. That "State Store" has been bombed every few days. They've been there for four years now. Whenever they hear the sound of the planes, they carry their goods into a deep, solid tunnel in the heart of the mountain. Nothing could penetrate there unless it was an atomic bomb." He handed Tom some rice and passed him the bottle of water. "Come on, don't save face that way. With the way bombs destroy their "store" like that, how can they not hate Americans?"

When he heard the translation by The Cuong, Tom took the rice.

"Just out of curiosity," he asked, "Does 'that part' of Vietnamese girls have no hair? When the two young girls' T-shirts were blown up, I could see those "parts" were smooth, without any hair, right?"

The Cuong couldn't help bursting into laughter as he ate. Wiping his mouth, he explained: "Vietnamese women are the same as all others. But because of constant attacks there is hardly enough water even to cook food, so where can these female soldiers get water to bathe? They may have some for cleaning every few days. But bathing is often a dry bath, meaning when it is so hot that they sweat all over, they go into a cellar, and one takes a towel to scrub the other until all the mud, bomb smoke, and sweat are gone. If they didn't shave their pubic hair, how could they avoid scabies, ringworm, and lice clinging to it?"

Tom shook his head. "Incredible! How could anyone ever understand such people, and even such animals in Vietnam! No one could imagine how they endured all these hardships, such suffering. I wonder if my fellow countrymen would ever believe the truth of it." His eyes still brimmed with tears.

At that moment, a convoy of trucks transporting wounded soldiers from the South passed by. All the drivers were young women in their late teens or twenties. The liaison officer stopped a GAT 63 truck and showed his Mission Order to a female driver. There were about twenty wounded soldiers in the rear of the truck. The female driver told him in Northern accent: "It's cramped, but you guys can get in. Be patient with the wounded ones' screams. It will take us five or six hours to reach the Headquarters of the Truong Son Corps where you can regroup. If the American planes spot us, you have to obey my orders, OK?"

Before they climbed into the truck, the liaison officer hung the camera back around Tom's neck and put his backpack on Tom's back. He asked The Cuong to tell Tom not to speak, not to ask questions, not to show emotion, and to keep taking pictures of the wounded soldiers, just as if Tom were a real international journalist; otherwise, knowing who Tom was, the wounded soldiers would be angry and might kill him. There was surely no way they could be stopped.

The GAT 63 maneuvered its way down a road plowed by bomb craters and blocked by piles of dirt and stones. While some of the less heavy wounded could sit, the rest lay on the floor. The two nurses kept injecting some soldiers and giving medication to the others. It was hot, the truck kept jolting them roughly, and everyone was soaked in sweat. Those in a coma, unconsciously called for their mothers. The word "Mom" spilling from their lips made those who were awake feel their hearts twist painfully; every soldier thought about and missed his mother. Tom felt the same: painfully sad, dead tired, home-sick, missing his mother, and feeling so sorry for the wounded young soldiers.

He agonized over the cruelty of the war, the damage rendered by the American bombs; he felt guilty about being one of those who had brought death and suffering to Vietnamese people. Never before in his military career had he felt that what he did was both meaningless and sinful. He wondered if he had not been taken prisoner, would he feel less tormented and regretful…When the truck reached the Truong Son Corps Military Infirmary Station and the wounded soldiers were unloaded, he couldn't hold back his tears.

He was handed over to the Policy Department of the Truong Son Corps. On behalf of the Unit to arrest and detain Tom, The Cuong signed the handover documents on behalf of the unit that captured him, including comments, evaluations, and suggestions:

> "Sergeant Thomas Kowalczyk, US Army, was captured in a battle with 759th Infantry Company of Truong Son Corps, and the 26th Reconnaissance Company at an unnamed hill on May 20, 1971. Sergeant Thomas McCain did not resist against the Liberation Army, and during his detention, he had no thoughts of escaping. He complied well with the regulations and discipline of the detention unit and was aware of the senseless war launched by the US Government. He wishes to come back to the United States soon and tell the truth about the crimes and mistakes of the US Government and President Nixon towards the Vietnamese people.
>
> His health status is poor, with severe malaria and suspected American chemical poisoning."
>
> Suggestion: Return Sergeant Thomas Kowalzcyk to the United States as soon as possible."

As The Cuong translated his comments to him, Tom was touched. Clasping his hands, he stammered: 'God will bless you and make your name famous. He will bless those who have true humanity, and He will curse whoever curses him, and all the people of the earth will be blessed through him.' Those are the words of the Creator, and I would like to use them to express my heart to the Liberation Army…Amen." then he turned to The Cuong, "You guys have been very good to me. Thank you, thank you, VC. One day I will come back here to see you and to apologize…but for now I can only say that in this war, your country is especially heroic. You Vietnamese know how to fight against fate…the war is unimaginably terrible for us Americans…"

17

After Tom, the POW, was on his way to Hanoi, Battalion Captain The Cuong asked the Commander of Truong Son Corps for some leave so he could track down Mai Nhung, his girlfriend from the Youth Volunteer Team 70 - 559 Corps that was responsible for repairing Road 20, the "Determined to Win" Road. The number 20 came from the fact that all the Youth Volunteers stationed there were in their twenties. The road stretched 125 kilometers from East to West Truong Son. Though Mai Nhung and The Cuong were at the same battlefield, he only heard from her occasionally, through crumpled, dust-covered letters, stained with her tears.

According to the regulations about confidentiality, only the name of her unit appeared on the envelope, with the day and month the letter was sent inside, so The Cuong could figure out that Mai Nhung was also in the East and West Truong Son. But looking for each other in that vast area was like looking for a needle in the jungle. Mai Nhung's unit was on the most difficult and fiercest section of Road 20, called the "Road Determined to Win." The road had three consecutive key points: the A-Shaped Curve, the Ta

Le Ravine, and the Phu La Nhich Pass, where Mai Nhung's unit was located. It was a difficult and dangerous journey; one had to face enemy artillery fire and bombs as well as gorges that dropped off deeply on each side of the road.

The Cuong's driver was afraid to take on the Ta Le Ravine, which was often flooded, and its approach continuously bombed or shelled by bombs and explosives. "You'd be better off catching a ride with one of the big-wheeled GAT trucks. Those drivers are experienced; if my jeep fell into a bomb crater we would just float away. You better stay here and find a ride; I'm going back to my unit now." Before The Cuong could say a word, the driver jumped into the jeep, handed Cuong his rucksack, and drove off.

It wasn't until late afternoon that The Cuong was able to stop a truck carrying a dozen soldiers through the 100 meters wide Ta Le Ravine. As the truck approached, he suddenly heard the sound of American aircraft. Clusters of bright flares followed by waves of bombs burst around the truck. The driver quickly swerved to the other side of the ravine, where two young volunteer girls wearing glittering reflective coats used flashlights to guide the truck to the entrance of a large tunnel carved into the side of the ravine. So they escaped death. But The Cuong kept thinking about his girlfriend and these young volunteer girls: how had they managed to survive at these three fiercest points for years? He wanted to get out and talk to the two volunteer girls since Mai Nhung had been here as well. But, in a short while they returned to their positions.

The bombardment ended, the American airplanes flew away, and the trucks started to flow again through the Ta Le

Ravine. The Cuong's truck merged with the flow of vehicles radiating off the main road from Ta Le to Phu La Nhich Pass near the border junction, towards Laos. This was an important and key road, the hub of the transport route from Road 20, the "Determined to Win" road, to the battlefields of South Vietnam, Laos, and Cambodia. That was why it was bombarded day and night, so much that it was impossible to even calculate the quantities of bombs that has fallen on it.

The convoys kept rushing forward, but the vehicles all came to a halt when one truck stalled in the middle of the road. All the drivers and their passengers were visibly worried and scared. Some started cursing nervously. A high-gloss, round bottomed Jeep tried to swerve past the convoys to reach the stalled GAT 63 truck. Three people got out, two of them holding AKs. The third was a tall, youthful looking officer in full uniform, including a helmet and high boots, a leather satchel on his shoulders, and a K59 pistol dangling from his waist. He stepped firmly up to the GAT 63.

"Whose truck is this?"

Silence. No answer. Only a clanking sound from under the truck.

"Where's the driver?" The man in the helmet asked, raising his voice.

The driver, wearing a broad brimmed hat, his face was covered with sweat and grease, crawled out from under the truck, gripping an AK. With a murderous expression, he slammed the butt of the weapon onto the ground.

"Here I am," he shouted. "What is it? Speak up, I'm listening!"

The man in the helmet glared at him.

"Hand me your weapon, comrade!"

The military driver snatched off his hat and threw it to the ground, staring at the man, his teeth clenched.

"Officer...Look at my face, Sir! I don't want to live anymore! Got it...Living in this miserable way, what for? I just want to die right away."

The two accompanying soldiers approached the driver. One grabbed the AK from his hand.

"Get in my car," the helmeted man said to the driver. "I'm the Front Commander. Your truck will be bulldozed off the cliff to clear the road. If we're stuck here when the American planes return, everybody will be killed. I'll assign you another truck...get in. We'll talk."

A bulldozer emerged from the "crab cave" in the gorge and quickly shoved the GAT 63 truck off the cliff.

As it did, the Commander took a closer look at the unruly driver. He was tall and thin, wearing tattered fatigues, and had an ass so flat as to be non-existent. His thin face was grayish, pale lips and two reddened eyes, dull with fatigue, vestige from acute malaria.

Seeing this pitiful image, the Commander lowered his gaze, his heart tightened. Trying to hide his emotion, he decided to reveal the truth from this miserable soldier. He drew closer to the driver, and put a warm hand on the man's thin, bony shoulder.

"Get in my car. I want to know more about the situation of you military drivers. Tell me the truth, tell me what life is really like for all of you, frankly."

Sensing the officer's sincerity, the driver got into the car and, as he sat, buried his face in his hands.

"Our life is too hard, Commander! We can endure the bombardment, but driving is tougher when we have to suffer from hunger and malaria. It is so miserable that sometimes I just want to die. But whenever I start thinking that way, I know I must wholeheartedly follow the call of the Party to struggle for the unification of the country, and even though I am suffering, I have to follow my ideology to the end. That's why we military drivers have to try to survive: to fulfill our duties, Commander!"

The Commander just let him cry, and then he put his arm around the driver's shoulder, trying to hold back his own emotions: "How long have you been driving in Truong Son?"

"Five years now, Commander!"

"And in those five years of driving in Truong Son, did you cry often?"

"To tell the truth, there were several times I was almost killed by bombs and never cried. But every time I have to bury my comrades-in-arms, I cry a lot…"

The Commander slapped the driver's skinny thigh. "Cry out all your tears today, but tomorrow, you will get a new truck and go back to your unit and then don't cry anymore. War is like that, what can we do? I will have a meeting with the High Command to reflect on what you told me and adjust the working conditions. What we have to do is to live and to fight…"

18

After the truck had passed through the Ta Le Ravine and climbed up the slope of the winding Phu La Nhich pass for about a kilometer, The Cuong got off and asked for directions to the 70th Youth Volunteer Team, which was stationed in the gorge in the middle of the pass.

The Cuong gave his official Truong Son introduction letter to a young volunteer carrying an AK, who was guarding the entrance to the command tunnel. He was very surprised to see that here in an area often the target of American bombs there was a series of tunnels carved deep in the middle of the long, wide, and gentle Phu La Nhich pass. The four sides of the entrance he came in were lined with sand bags, forming a solid wall, leaving only a very small passageway, just enough for one person to enter.

The Head of the 70th Youth Volunteer Team was Ms. Tan, from Nghe An province. She welcomed The Cuong but was very emotional knowing that he was Mai Nhung's boyfriend and also a soldier in Truong Son. She tried painfully to calm herself down by offering him some water in an iron bowl, her hand trembling.

Both became silent and contemplative. The Cuong now understood why he hadn't received a letter from Mai Nhung for six months. Ms. Tan quietly got up and went inside, and brought out an old, faded rucksack which she handed to The Cuong.

"These are some of Mai Nhung's things."

The Cuong tried to keep himself in control. "Where did she die, and where is she buried?"

"Mai Nhung died in Ta Le Ravine on February 15, seven months ago. That night, she was acting as a guidepost, one of the girls standing in the stream to guide a truck convoy through. She was exhausted, fell down, and was swept away by the current. We couldn't find her body because we were being bombed continuously. What she left was this rucksack with her diary in it. She wrote mostly about you in it. Reading it, I could feel your love was truly romantic, as beautiful as in a novel…It's so sad that both of you were based in the Truong Son for two years but could never meet each other."

The Cuong sighed. "Our love was truly pure and faithful. We were in love when we were at the university, and we promised to meet each other on the top of the Truong Son, and, after the reunification of the country, to return to Hanoi to be married. But now, I don't even know where her body is, and I can never know…oh Heaven!"

The Cuong said goodbye to Tan and made his way back to Tiger Spring Cave with his AK and two rucksacks slung on his shoulders, his and Mai Nhung's. For him, the road back was loaded with sadness: all his plans and dreams had ended with Mai Nhung's death. His memories of the days they were together in Hanoi tightened his heart.

He remembered the first time he had told Mai Nhung that he loved her; he remembered their first kiss, and the countless kisses that followed. The memories merged and swirled in his mind; they were young, they were in love, and love which once had been simple as an instinct, had now turned into a deep wound; he didn't think he could endure her loss. One moment he searched for and re-lived the memories of their beautiful youth together; the next, he struggled to forget, to forgo the pain that came when he evoked Mai Nhung's face and her voice.

In her rucksack he found only two sets of clothes, a few pairs of underwear, a bra, a mirror, a comb, a notebook, and letters, but still he felt he was carrying a great weight, the heavy burden of love, of loss, of memories that would cling in his mind and haunt him for the rest of his life. He wanted to hurry back to his unit so he could sit undistracted and read her diary about her days in Truong Son. Sure, she would have written about her love for him, about how much she missed him and longed to meet him on the top of Truong Son. But if he read all that, could he bear it? Their dream love, real and unreal and sacred, would never be again. Was it right that all those dreams and hopes of their youth would never come true? And he traveled, with all those thoughts, all those memories of youth without beginning or end, twisting and clinging in his mind all the way from Phu La Nhich pass until he returned to Tiger Spring.

19

When he got back, The Cuong was astonished at how devastated the landscape around Tiger Spring had become. It was hard to recognize any of the familiar streams and trails. The hills and mountains had almost been leveled by bombs: magnetic bombs, slow-timed bombs, cluster bombs. The whole area had been seeded with all kinds of mines. Electronic reconnaissance devices called "tropical trees," were dropped by American aircraft all over the secret roads and underground passages from Tiger Spring to the border junction and into Laos. The devices, hidden in the forest by leaves and other vegetation, would detect the sound of motor vehicles and passing soldiers, and then send signals for aircraft to attack.

For the most part, the Americans used AC130s to hunt for PAVN trucks, artillery positions, vehicle storage, and repair stations. Because of these new detection devices, for a long time, not a single convoy, not a single piece of anti-aircraft artillery moving along the Truong Son Trails could avoid being detected by AC130 aircraft and getting shot up by this "evil bird's: 40mm and 20 mm ordnance.

Tiger Spring

Day and night, the battlefield of the Truong Son mountain range was always a pan of fire. The United States had chosen it as a testing ground for the most advanced, most horrible scientific and technical achievements of 20th century America: a place to experiment with the use and effectiveness of modern killing weapons. The 26th Reconnaissance Company, encamped on the slope of the mountain, away from the safety of the Tiger Spring Cave, suffered in the midst of that situation, subjected to countless types of bombs from American aircraft, as well as the anti-personnel mines that were also dropped with the bombs. The mines encircled the garrison, entangled in the branches of trees, burrowed into mounds of earth, ready to explode with the slightest touch; they kept the company stuck where they were and vulnerable to the air attacks.

As a seasoned reconnaissance company, the 26th was skillful in combat, and understood how to overcome any of the many force majeure situations that occurred in war. But in this situation there was no enemy to fight face to face, and no place to which they could withdraw. The mines were all around them, and the planes kept coming, kept bombing and strafing. For the hundred soldiers of the company, there was only one possible way to create an escape route to the cave.

Six soldiers willing to martyr themselves formed into two teams. They cut branches to make long poles, and one by one advanced, poking the poles into the ground or brush until they hit a mine, which would immediately explode, killing the soldier. As each man died, he was replaced by the next, until a safe path for the company to withdraw to the cave was completed. All six volunteer martyrs died.

When the enemy discovered that the 26th Reconnaissance Company had begun withdrawing, three group of OV-10, OV-20 aircrafts and AC-130 fighters swarmed over the treetops and began bombing and strafing the length of the Tiger Spring.

The corpses of the six volunteer martyrs were wrapped in tarps and brought to the deepest part of the stream, where Company Commander Tuan himself weighed the corpses down under the water with rocks, as he wept. Before he left, still sobbing, he wiped away his tears and bowed deeply to the martyrs.

"Stay here for now, dear comrades. Later, we will come back and bury you on shore with a memorial service. But if we bury you now while the Americans are still bombing, we will lose your corpses, and I can't stand that...stay here, wait for us to come back..."

The thick black smoke from exploding bombs covered the whole area. Taking advantage of it, the nearly hundred surviving soldiers of the company secretly withdrew to Tiger Spring Cave along the path created for them by the six martyred soldiers.

The area in front of the entrance of the main cave was bombarded countless times, almost blocking it with huge slabs of stone, where before it had been wide and long enough for two trucks to come in and out. Fortunately, nature created Tiger Spring cave with many openings that allowed in light and air; the soldiers could live inside that immense cave, even if there had been a whole division of them. The Tiger Spring Medical Station had been situated in the best possible location to protect and care for wounded soldiers.

Once safely in the cave, Company Commander was tortured by the deaths of the six soldiers who had sacrificed themselves so heroically. Rather than wait for the bombing to cease, as he had told them, Tuan led a squad back to where the corpses were hidden and brought them back to the cave, to be commemorated properly in a memorial ceremony and buried in one of the cave's niches.

After days under attack, the company was finally able to rest in the quiet, cool cave, and eat well, after which both officers and soldiers started recovering quickly. There were many small pockets honeycombed off the main cavern, and The Cuong chose one small enough for him to be left alone. Everybody knew what happened to him and felt compassion and understanding about his deep grief when he brought back Mai Nhung's rucksack, filled with mementos of her life. Even though his most precious and closest treasure, his guitar, had been wrecked in the bombing, he did not care. At night, when all had slept, The Cuong silently sat up, lit a peanut oil lamp, and in its small circle of light read Mai Nhung's diary and tried to hold back his sobbing.

Next to The Cuong's niche, Hoan and Huu bunked together in another small niche hollowed in the stone. Hoan was happy to be close to the Medical Station; whenever he yearned to be with Lan, he would complain about a stomach ache or headache and go to Lan for some medicine. He would get to talk to her a little, and, when no one was looking, would touch her. Afterwards, he would go back and tell Huu what happened. Huu wanted to know all the details and was full of questions. How passionate was Lan when they made love in the hammock? Was it real love? What did Hoan feel? Was he really happy?

Hoan just chuckled and didn't reply, which made Huu furious. "OK, if you don't tell me anything, I'm not going to stand guard while you two fuck each other. I'll let Political Commissar Mao catch you ... and fuck both of you ..."

So it was that Hoan felt compelled to describe as poetically as he could the sweetness of his coupling with Huu: how strange and wonderful he had found the tastes and smells of her body, which were not like the perfumed scent of a flower, nor yet the pungent smell of a sweaty laborer, nor was the taste of it hot and salty, but it was rather like the faint fragrant of young rice wet with night dew, like the sweet taste of thousands of springs flowing from forests full of flowers and young grass. When they would start to make love, the first thing Hoan would do was lick Lan's body all over, loving that female taste. He described her hot, thick lips, so sexy, so fiery when he kissed her.

He described how ecstatic it made him feel to touch the tip of his tongue to her tender, round breasts. That was the way they always started their intercourse, as if guided by the instinct of a man and a woman who loved each other. In the hammock with her, madly in love, he still sometimes wondered if what he felt was the purest, utmost level of love. He only knew that his orgasm left him satisfied and happy, and his ultimate happiness occurred when he lost his inhibitions and cravings.

As for Lan, when they made love, she would keep her eyes closed as she panted and writhed, hugging him tightly, then releasing him and then tightly again as she moaned and when he asked her if she was satisfied, she nodded and tightened her arms around him again.

Hoan's voice rose and fell, sometimes low, sometimes lively and laughing as he described how he and Lan moved and felt as they made love. The way he went into all the details forced Huu to listen, to visualize their coupling vividly. It made him feel as uneasy as the time he and Hoan had spied on Tuan and Dr. Lien making love in the grove of banana bushes near Tiger Spring.

Finally, he interrupted Hoan. "I never tasted or smelled a young girl, so I don't quite understand. But I can't stand it anymore. Enough. You can write a love story later on...Hoan, the future love story writer..."

"Literature is your profession, not mine. Aren't you the one crazy about writing?"

"Yes, I loved literature since my childhood. If not for the war, I would have taken the entrance exam for the University of Literature..."

"But you have such bad handwriting, who can read your writing? If I were your teacher, I'd give you a zero..."

"It's true, I did get a bad grade when I was in high school, I always got four or five points off out of ten just because of my bad handwriting. Still I don't believe that I'm bad at literature..."

"You're lucky then the war took you before you had to take the high school final exams, otherwise you would have failed Literature."

"Probably." Huu laughed.

"Anyway, when you wrote the play *Iron Defense for the Border* for our unit to perform, who deciphered your handwriting?"

"After I finished writing, I read it to Van; he transcribed it."

"Well, if you become a leader, then you can always force your soldiers to translate your handwriting, right? Do you dream of being a leader?"

"I haven't thought about it much. Only when I looked at Commander Tuan and Political Commissar Mao, I think I'd really like to have rank like theirs. When do you think we can be promoted to lieutenant?"

"Never. Fucking hell, just to be promoted from private to sergeant takes a year and a half, never mind becoming a fucking second lieutenant…" Hoan sighed, "I don't know where this war will go and when it will end, so we can go back to university. When I'm demobilized, I'll take the entrance exam for the Music Art School. What about you?"

"Journalism and writing. That will be my career for the rest of my life…"

In the darkness, the night wind lightly swayed the hammock, as if sharing the yearning of the two young soldiers.

"If you stay in the army, what would you want to be," Hoan asked.

"A general. As a soldier, one must dream of becoming a general."

"And in journalism?"

"An editor-in-chief."

"And in literature?"

"A famous writer."

Hoan smiled.

"What if you are just a normal person?"

"Then I will try my best to be a mature person."

"What do you mean? I don't get it...that just sounds like rubbish..."

"You think being a mature person is easy? The day I went to the war, my father was busy mourning Uncle Ho. All he said to me was: "You have grown up, now you must try to live maturely."

"What did your father mean?"

"As far as I understand, he defined being mature as being decent, kind, and brave...something like that.."

Hoan smacked his lips. "Yes, you're right: it's not easy to be a kind, decent, and not cowardly person, especially when one is a soldier...how can one stop himself from thinking of food when he's starving? How can one be shelled or bombed, without being scared of death?"

"Everybody thinks about eating when they're hungry, but eating without becoming ashamed of yourself, that means you are mature. For example, when we were starving to death ourselves and dying to have some rice, we thought first of the Bong Va villagers who were suffering so much from starvation, we decided not to cook rice for ourselves. For me, I think that means we acted maturely."

"Your father was really an insightful person. Think simple, teach big! He is a true communist cadre. Like father, like son!"

"He's been District Chairman for nearly ten years now.

Because he is upright at work, besides those who like him, there are some who hate him, but no one has ever seen him act indecently or cowardly behavior in any circumstances. He is not corrupted, not greedy, not abusive in his position, and not reliant on power. He is a District Chairman, yet we still live in a thatch house. His bicycle has no brakes and no bells. For all of my three years in high school, I mostly ate sweet potatoes. Boiled, or dried sweet potatoes, or cooked with rice, with a few grains on each slice, until my stomach heaved, and I felt I was choking on sweet potatoes!" Huu shivered: "When I think back about how we had sweet potatoes all year round, it's really chilling!"

"Were you unhappy?"

"I've never been happy in my life, so I don't know whether I was unhappy…" Huu shook his head. "I really haven't seen anyone who's happy. Look at the class of revolutionary cadres who are "tough" like my father, or like Political Commissar Mao, those who have followed the revolution and this war all their lives. I have never seen them happy…"

"You sound pessimistic, Huu."

"No, I'm not. Once you acknowledge that life is like that, you must accept you need to continue to live, to exist, and to strive to move forward…"

"There you have what your future will be. Besides, you come from a privileged family, so whatever happens, you'll have a high position…"

"It's one's fate. Everybody has a fate that fits them. Like your shoe size…"

"What a philosophy. Anyway, it's nice chatting like this..."

And they kept speaking talking to each other, a conversation with no beginning and no end.

20

Huu and Hoan's rescue, by bringing food and the comfort of their presence to the Van Kieu in Bong Va village, had restored that small ethnic group's faith in the revolution, even in the midst of the continuous American bombing. The Van Kieu remained on the Truong Son Trail and even named all their children after President Ho Chi Minh. Because of their actions, Huu and Hoan were to be awarded the Victory Medal, third class, by the National Liberation Front of South Vietnam and admitted to the Communist Party of Vietnam.

They stood under the red flag with the yellow star, faded because of rain and sun, inside a hut in the middle of an old forest, in front of a line of troops, looking sharp and neat with their rucksacks on their backs, weapons on their shoulders, all raising their arms and reciting an oath from their hearts that they were ready "to sacrifice all their lives for the revolutionary cause of the Party and the people…", Huu was so touched he choked, trying to hold back his happy tears. His heart beat wildly and joyously inside his skinny chest. He thought of his father, wondering how he would feel when he learned that his youngest son had been admitted to the Party. He was certain that his father would be very happy and very proud, since he had striven all his life to devote himself to the Party, to sacrifice all for the Party and the revolution; the Party was in the blood running through his veins.

For Huu's father, the Party was the sun, the moon, his breath, his life. Because of that, even though he had fathered four children in the midst of the wars against the French and the Americans, he had no time to take care of them. They grew up in poverty, grateful still to have studied under the roof of a socialist school, where they learned to read and think as good Communists. For Huu's father, the purpose of human life was to march forward to Socialism, so that everybody would be equal, working according to their ability, paid according to their need, as they helped create a society without oppression and without injustice...

Even though Huu's grandfather had been a village and district chief during the French colonial period, to Huu's father's mind, he was only a slave and a henchman of the feudal colonialists; he bore the shame of people who had their country occupied. For Huu's father, not only must his life be linked closely to the Party, but also his sons, his grandchildren, and his great grandchildren must also follow his example and stand under the flag of the Party forever.

After forty long years of dedication to the revolution, Huu's father retired; he moved to a thatched-roof house and became a farmer, tilling a small plot, and raising pigs and chickens. However, he was proud that his four sons were in the ranks of the Party, and that all graduated from University. He never lost his trust in the Party, never doubted the immortality and permanence of the Party and the international communist movement, which for him could never be fractured and broken. That was why, years later, when the Socialist Republic of Soviet Union collapsed, he could not eat and suffered and cried for a week.

So it was that nothing made him more joyful and proud than knowing his youngest son, at the age of twenty, was admitted to the Party on a battlefield redolent with the smell of cordite from spent bullets. That very night, after they and their comrades in the squad had a small celebration, smoking a few cigarettes, and munching on a few hunks of dried meat and a bag of fried peanuts donated by Le and Lan, Hoan whispered to Huu that he missed Lan so much that they would go to their rendezvous place. Huu did not answer; he was still in the throes of excitement at the ecstasy of becoming a Party member and wanted to continue to enjoy that mood with his squad mates.

Hoan, on the contrary, felt there was a fire in his heart compelling him towards love with a force so strong that it seemed magical. He wished the party would end quickly so that he could go to Lan. "Enough, I want to leave, Huu," he whispered, sighing repeatedly while all around him people were singing and dancing until the whistle blew to signal bedtime and all parted to their different sleeping niches around the cave.

Huu and Hoan hooked up their mosquito-nets and laid down. All around them their comrades were quiet, fast asleep. Hoan gently rose and placed his rucksack inside the net and then covered it with a blanket, so that it looked like a person sleeping. He arranged his rubber-tire sandals on the ground, with their front turned outward, and went to Huu's bed. He pressed Huu's hand gently: their signal when they were going to sneak out and spend time with Le and Lan. Huu rose and motioned for Hoan to go outside.

It was a peaceful night, undisturbed by the sound of planes, gunfire, or explosions: a rare silent night on the battlefield. The two of them walked out of the cave and stood under the trees. The moon illuminated everything with a silver light, bright enough for Hoan to see Huu's tired face.

"I am so tired," Huu said, yawning. "I just want to sleep,"

"Please come with me. I miss Lan so much I'm going to die if I can't see her now. Have pity on me, Huu!'

"I don't think we should not go out tonight, Hoan. We just joined the Party this morning; it's not setting a good example if we immediately start breaking rules…"

"No problem. I'm sure. Mao is sleeping, he knew that we just had a party."

"But as Party members, we shouldn't act like that. We must not deceive the organization, deceive the Party…"

"The Party is in our heart, our mind. The Party does not forbid us falling in love. I am a Party member, but I don't accept that love is prohibited."

"But on the battlefield, if love is not accepted and recognized by the organization, it's a violation. We could be punished and kicked out of the Party,"

"Sure. But you know how much Mr. Mao and Commander Tuan sympathize with me."

"I know. We're their soldiers; we live and die with

them; how can they not sympathize with us. But discipline is discipline. Without iron discipline on the battlefield, it would be chaos. Don't make fun of Political Commissar Mao... He had forgiven us once, but he would not forgive being mocked..."

Dumbfounded, Hoan kept shuffling his feet on the soft ground. The moon was shining brightly on the peaceful forest emanating thousands of sparkling rays as if inviting couples to seek each other out. The breeze gently caressed the tops of the trees, sent clouds scudding playfully across the sky, making the landscape dreamy and fantastical.

Finally, Hoan couldn't stand it any longer. "OK, I'll go alone. I've already made an arrangement to meet Lan..."

He quickly ran off, disappearing under the forest canopy.

Huu snuck back to his niche, numbed with a certain sadness. He sighed, and quietly got inside the mosquito-net. He was very tired, but he couldn't sleep, worrying about Hoan being on his own. He kept tossing and turning on the bamboo bed, soaking the cover spread on it with sweat. He felt a premonition that Hoan and Lan were in danger, and staring blankly into the darkness, a vague sense of fear plagued him. He clasped his hands and prayed to Heaven and Buddha to keep Hoan safe, that nothing bad would happen...

Meanwhile Hoan was running bare-footed and eager along the familiar trail that led to his trysting place. For a long time, he had tried hard to suppress his feelings of love, knowing quite well that it had been created by the circumstances of war. In war, one had to be ready to sacrifice everything, even one's own life, and a love that came in the middle of the battlefield had no future. But love was forever love. They loved from the depths of their hearts. And now alone, running to his love on a beautiful moonlight night, in the middle of the jungle, he felt how noble their love was.

Lan came to him despite everything, knowing she was coming to happiness, coming to a sacred realm: a person who was longing to live, to give and to be given. She did not need to know what would come today or tomorrow, how her life would be…

The full moon shone brightly, hanging in the night sky as if watching the two lovers on the green grass. In the past, they had hidden themselves inside the hammock, despite the wind, the storms…because Huu was nearby. But this time, it seemed as if nature wanted to please them. The breeze was cool as Hoan helped Lan lay down and began kissing her all over her body. "Oh, wait, darling," she said, and Hoan realized how hard he had been pressing his strong body onto his slender, pale girlfriend. He was about to grab a shirt to put under Lan's back when suddenly there was a shout, "Comrade Hoan, stand up!"

It was Political Commissar Mao.

Three flashlights shone on Hoan who was still lying on top of Lan. One beam came from Mao, the other two from Tuan and a sentry, all shining on the two naked bodies. Hoan got shakily onto his feet, bewildered, panicked, still drunk with love. Then he saw Political Commissar Mao and Commander Tuan, both with murderous expressions on their faces. He turned and started to run away, but Mao rushed over, and elbowed him in the face, knocking him down on the grass.

Lan rushed to him, embracing him tightly with her thin, pale arms. She stood naked over Hoan, her long, silky black hair covering him, so she looked like a white statue of a mother protecting her son. She burst into tears, her body convulsing continuously. She let go of Hoan, bent down, and picked her shirt up from the grass to cover him, leaving her naked body exposed in the light of the flashlights.

Mao, Tuan, and the sentry all silently turned off their flashlights. The full moon suddenly hid in a passing cloud, as nature had taken pity on the young couple. It was dark and quiet, except for the sound of choked sobs from Lan.

"Let's go back, Mao…" Tuan said, and then gently turned to Hoan and Lan, "You two put your clothes on and get back to the unit. We'll figure out everything later."

Political Commissar Mao did not react. "Back…" he said shortly, as if ordering everyone, then turned the flashlight on to showing the way back, the light zigzagging, like Mao's state of mind. Tuan followed behind him, trembling. How strange that a brave man, not fazed by bullets or bombs, was now shivering as he listened to Lan's agonized sobs and Mao's dry voice barking "Back!" As he followed, he stumbled now and then, and the sentry had to grab him to keep him from falling down.

It was about half a kilometer from Hoan and Lan's trysting place back to the unit. A heavy atmosphere hung over the group. No one said a word. The beams from the three flashlights seemed to tremble. And then, as if he couldn't bear it anymore, Mao sat down on the grass and burst into tears.

Now the moon emerged from the passing cloud, its silver light shimmering on the treetops. The wind blew as if it was wiping away the tears of the old political officer, shed for the painful love of the young couple or for his own fate…

21

Before, only Huu, Heaven, the moon, and the wind knew about Hoan and Lan's secret love affair, but now everyone did. Battlefield discipline was like being run over by a train. Hoan was punished by being expelled from the Party and demoted from Private First Class to Private. Lan's case was handled by the commanding officer of the Tiger Spring Medical Station.

Being expelled from the Party was a horrible shock to Hoan. On the battlefield, sex was never to be confused with love. It was considered instead a degenerate, sinful act that demoralized soldiers. Hoan and Lan knew that well. The harsh life of soldiers on the battlefield was no place for romantic notions or soft hearts,

Painful as it was, Hoan and Lan accepted the decision of being expelled from the Party and the loss of rank. They met together again one late afternoon. This time, they didn't meet in their familiar place, but at a stream far away from the area that all the others from the Company or the Medical Station came to bathe.

It was dusk on the Truong Son Trail, the end of what

had been a sunny day, absent the usual sounds of bombs in the late afternoon. Tiger Spring had gone back to being gentle and poetic. Birds flocked overhead, singing and dozens of male and female squirrels chased after each other, and gleefully devoured the ripe fruits off the stamese-rough bushes alongside the stream.

Immersed in the stream, the couple hugged each other continuously, speechlessly, wanting to fill their sadness with the silence of love and just enjoy being together. Occasionally, Lan burst into laughter. They were in love and enjoyed being alone with each other, as if nothing else — sky, forest, stream, land, and water — were around them. Only two of them in the middle of nowhere.

After a while, Hoan carried Lan to the bank. When they reached it, he lay Lan on her back and peeled off her underwear, putting it to the side and then pressing on top of her, his legs still in the stream. As they made love, Lan put her hands behind his head and pressed her face against his.

"Darling," she gasped. "I'm with child. I feel it thrashing strongly inside me. Maybe it's a son!"

Hoan's thrusts increased as he frantically pushed into her. Then, suddenly, his hands fell from Lan and started sinking lifelessly into the stream. His head fell forward, against her face. His breathing grew faint. Feeling his weight pressing on her, Lan began waving her hands in the air and screaming: "Help…help…anyone there, help!"

Above her, she could see the round disc of the sun hanging on the trees, shining down on the stream bed, its rays growing weaker. Somehow it panicked Lan even more.

Huu was on the way down to the stream to bathe when he heard Lan's voice calling for help. Terrified, Huu ran as fast as he could towards the sound. The sun had almost set, and the shadows of the trees on both sides of the stream darkened the water, making it difficult to spot where Lan was calling from. Huu looked up at the sun, stretching out his arms nervously, and then jumped down to swim upstream, where he found Hoan and Lan lying on top of each other on the bank. As soon as she saw him Lan had time to call: "Huu…"and then fainted.

Huu stuck his hand under the collar of Hoan's T-shirt to feel his heart. It had stopped beating, and his body was cold. Pulling Hoan away from Lan, Huu opened his friend's mouth and blew a deep breath into his lungs, in vain. Hoan was dead.

Lan opened her eyes and sat up. She hugged Hoan's corpse, crying.

That night, after burying Hoan, Huu remained stunned. He could not eat dinner. He went back to his corner of the cave and covered himself with a blanket, his mind blank, his heart weighted with sadness. It was pouring outside, and cold air flowed into the murky, damp cave. To whom would he talk to from now on with Hoan gone? His two closest friends had been Hoan and The Cuong. But The Cuong stopped socializing with friends or playing music since the day he set up the altar with Mai Nhung's photo and her diary on it. Each evening, The Cuong would burn incense on it and whisper to her for a long time.

In his own corner, looking at the empty bamboo bed which used to be Hoan's, Huu felt so lonely and cold. Melancholy surrounded him, clinging to him all the time. He had lost his best friend.

He remained obsessed with the moment of that late afternoon when the sun had gone down hurriedly just as Hoan and Lan had come to lie on the bank of Tiger Spring. Huu loved poetry, though he had not written any of his own, but that night, thinking of the image of the sun, Huu woke up, noted down a poem composed by another soldier, Nguyen Thang:

The Sun In Me

Why did that afternoon end in such a hurry?
I raised my hands to keep it from sinking over the horizon
Hoping to keep the fragile remaining sunlight from
Sinking slowly into the surface of the water
Oh Sun, didn't you hear my appeal?
I kept appealing and the sun kept setting,
It let my friend become a soulless stone...
That afternoon became my last memory
Oh Sun, did you hear my appeal?
I kept appealing and the sun kept setting,
That afternoon, an afternoon of my dreadful pain...

The poem spoke to the sadness in his heart, Huu waited impatiently for the morning to come so he could bring the poem, and the sadness in his heart, to console and to share with Lan. At dawn, he asked Tuan's permission to skip morning exercises in order to go to the Tiger Spring Medical Station to see Lan and offer her the poem. He came at the right time: Lan was just finishing packing her personal belongings into a faded green rucksack, with holes on it. She was quietly arranging everything, her face calm and expressionless. Afterwards, she tore off a piece of red paper from a bag of incense-sticks, dipped it in a cup of water and applied it to her lips and cheeks to try to beautify herself after crying too much. Le, standing next to Lan, was crying.

Seeing Huu, Lan calmly said, "I'm putting on make-up so that in the other world, Hoan can still consider me beautiful, and he will be less sad. I'm glad you have come, so I can say goodbye to you and send my goodbyes to your comrades in the Company, including Political Commissar Mao and Commander Tuan. I wish you all return safely home!"

Huu passed her the poem. Lan read it silently, and pondered it for a while, thinking of that grim afternoon at Tiger Spring and the emptiness she felt now. Then she sighed and instinctively caressed her belly.

"Now let's go to see his grave…" she said to Huu.

She folded the copied poem and put it into the pocket of her proper new military uniform. Then she slung her backpack onto her shoulder, and holding a bunch of incense sticks, calmly proceeded to Hoan's grave.

It was located in a hidden niche of Tiger Spring Cave. The words carved in the stone above Hoan's grave were:

Private Ngo Khai Hoan
DoB: 20 February, 1952
Native land: Hanoi
Unit: 26th Reconnaissance Company – Armed Police

Tiger Spring

Died: 8 September, 1972
Place: Tiger Spring, Truong Son

Looking at the inscription, which was missing the words *"war martyr... sacrificed..."* Le and Lan burst into tears: tears of pain and sadness for the deceased, but also of frustration and disappointment for the callousness of the living, who had totally deleted from his life all that Hoan had contributed to the unit.

And that painful moment of farewell was so sacred; their tears delineating the eternal separation of those who were staying on the battlefield and the one who was returning to her birthplace. Lan lit the nine incense sticks, with each person holding three, according to tradition, and then burned the copied poem by the grave. *"Darling,"* she muttered, *"your name is Khai Hoan, which means Triumph, but your life was not triumphant. How bitter it is, darling. Please read this poem that Huu brought to pay tribute to you. I wish you holy living and holy dying, and please bless me and your baby and keep us safe as I return to my home. Please bless everybody in the Medical Station and the 26th Company and keep them safe and healthy and bring them back to their families; that is my prayer to you. Darling, don't be sad, you are the happiest person compared to your comrades-in-arm who have been forever on this Truong Son trail: you had me, and you have your son who will always think of you, and will burn incense sticks to commemorate you. I will go back home with your son, and on the day of reunification, I will come with your son to bring home your remains."*

When she was finished praying to Hoan, Lan felt relieved. She wiped her tears away, swung the two long braids of her hair behind her back, calmly nodded goodbye to Huu and Le, and began to run towards Tiger Spring.

Huu and Le wanted to run after her, to hold her back, or to share some words of comfort and encouragement in order to reduce her painful sadness. But then Huu stopped, realizing anything else then was superfluous. Trying to control his strong emotions, he held Le's hand and told her to go back to the Station.

It felt strange that at the moment Lan was leaving, the Truong Son Trail was blazing hot. The sun was like a blood-colored disk hanging halfway up the mountain. Lan calmly walked next to Tiger Spring to the place where she had bathed and made love with Hoan for the last time. Sitting on the stone slab, she put her feet, shoed in rubber sandals, into the water, and pulled a worn diary with yellowed pages from her first aid bag and sat there turning each page.

A breeze arrived from nowhere, scattering with it nineteen dried yellow leaves into the air. Nineteen leaves flying away, carrying with them nine years of her youthful spring. However, one had to accept there were no boundaries for suffering in life and one had to be ready to turn to another direction and nurture the future for future generations. With this thought, Lan stood up, looked ahead, and walked away.

But there in the heat of the Truong Son Trail, she felt a sudden chill. The war would end, but would anyone care about it? Was the baby in her belly the result of a burning, beautiful love in the most human sense or just a bitter, sinful wartime fling? Later, when their son grew up, what would she tell him about his father? Was his father a brave soldier, a hero, or just an alienated, lustful fuckup?

From the bottom of her heart, Lan could not find the answer. She slowly touched her face, where Hoan's lips had always hastily pressed against her skin each time they made love. Then she put her hand down on her belly and feeling the soft shifting of the baby, her heart warmed. She burst into tears. They rolled down her cheeks to her mouth, and she gnawed at them as if Hoan's love for her.

Above, the blood-red sun cast a hot light on a forest that was still buzzing with the sound of bombs.

22

The Truong Son battlefield had always been the site of fierce fighting, constantly attacked and bombarded by the Americans and the Saigonese forces in their attempt to destroy every road, unit, and troop transportation hub of the North Vietnamese Armed Forces, using all their most advanced weapons. There was not a place that had not been ravaged by bombs and mines.

By this time, even though the 26th Reconnaissance Company were not trained as combat engineers, their instinct to survive the fact they were surrounded by entangled or magnetic mines, made them tinker, research, and invent methods to protect themselves. The soldiers of the Company had become very good at clearing landmines. To explode magnetic bombs, they used a wire frame and pulled an iron block along the ground from afar; for entangled mines, sticks were used, and leaf mines were collected and burned. The company cleared minefields almost every day and night for other units, warehouses, docks, and base camps.

The Cuong was assigned a special mission to provide

security for a high-ranking delegation from the Ministry of Health led by Professor Doctor Dang Ngan. He came to Truong Son to do research and create antimalarial drugs. Accompanying the medical delegation were the poet Pham Tien, the painter Duc Du, the musician Tran Quang, and an artist of Truong Son group. The Cuong felt honored that he had been given the task of taking care of the logistical issues for the delegation, but he was very worried about their transportation, since American planes could appear and bomb at any time.

In the area where the delegation went to survey, the Saigonese commandos and scouts had planted all kinds of mines, especially anti-tank mines that had damaged many vehicles. Commander Tuan had asked for a Zin 157 truck from the Truong Son Corps to lead the way, protecting the delegation's vehicle coming behind. Assigned as the lead for the mission, Political Commissar Mao instructed, "Comrade The Cuong, at all costs, we must protect the delegation, especially Professor Doctor who is Head of our Medical Branch as well as the artists and writers ... they are national property, you know!"

"What we worry about are the American airplanes," The Cuong replied, "but as for defending the delegation, we will protect them with our own bodies, please don't worry."

Before continuing further on his mission, Professor Doctor Dang Ngan wanted to drop in at Tiger Spring Medical—a decision that brought great joy to everybody at the Station. They put on their best clothes to welcome the delegation. Standing in formation at the entrance of the Tiger Spring cave, five young nurses were chosen to hold five bouquets of wildflowers to offer the guests. Le was one among them.

The Cuong happily led the delegation in, greeted by applause from the soldiers and medical personnel. The five guests received flowers, shook hands, and embraced the medic soldiers. Painter Duc Du, a womanizer, took advantage when receiving flowers from a young girl to slip his hand behind her and pinch her butt. She stepped back, brushed his hand away, and glared: "You pervert! Get away!"

Standing near Huu, Le said: "It's nice for The Cuong to accompany this delegation instead of hanging around in the cave and mourning his girlfriend all the time. I am so sorry for him, Huu."

Huu glanced at her. "In the meanwhile, I'm thinking of you all the time and you don't feel sorry for me!"

Le pursed her lips. "I'm not crying any extra tears for a false person! You're always joking, running here and there, half the time acting like a teenager, half the time acting like an adult. How would it be worthy for a young girl to fall in love with such a person!"

Everyone was delighted by Professor Doctor Dang Ngan, since before coming from Hanoi to the Truong Son trail, he asked his staff to go to the big markets of Hanoi and buy two sacks of underwear made of thin cotton fabric—for women to use during their periods—as well as mirrors, combs, and a bag of soapberry fruits for them to use to wash their hair. Holding these things, some young girls burst into tears, causing the guests to try to control their emotions. Suddenly, some of the female medical staff, feeling ecstatic, burst into hysterical laughter, emitting ghostly yells. The five guests were bewildered; not knowing how to deal with the situation until the musician Tran Quang took up his guitar and sang the song: "East Truong Son, West Truong Son," and the crazy laughter stopped.

Anybody familiar with the people at Tiger Spring Medical Station would be familiar with the contagious disease of hysterical laughter. But the members of the delegation were really astounded.

"Dear Professor and comrades," Doctor Dat, Head of the Station explained, "most of these young girls are in their late teens and early twenties. Living conditions here are hard and unhygienic: the rainy season here lasts for six months, and there is continuous damp and wet. All these young girls try as much as they can to create laughter, so much that it becomes a 'laughing disease.' Once someone starts, everybody picks it up, and they can continue laughing all day…"

As they departed, Professor Doctor Dang Ngan and the others remained silent. No one dared to mention or joke about the laughter of the female medical staff. Instead, they were sorrowful, pained in their hearts about the condition of human lives in the war, with their numerous indescribable sufferings that turned even normal human laughter into a symptom of madness…

Their driver was used to driving many medical research scientists to the battlefield and was very good at telling humorous stories to prevent people from falling asleep and stressing out. But, after witnessing the laughing disease, he was silent and sometimes let his steering wheel skew off track. The Cuong, sitting next to him, had to remind him to follow the wheel tracks of the Zin 157 ahead…its wheels would crush any of the anti-tank mines the Saigonese commandos may have seeded on the trail.

Their first destination was Loong Luong village, in Lum Bum area of the Lao Thom people, near the border junction between road 20, road 128 and Phu La Nhich pass. The reason Professor Doctor Dang Ngan wanted to come here was that even though the village was located in the same bombed area and climate of the rest of the Truong Son, and the villagers had the same diet as other ethnic groups, no villager, from new born to adults ever had malaria, while 80% of the North Vietnamese troops had had the disease. If he could find the reason for their immunity, a preventive vaccine for the disease could be found.

Even though Loong Luong was called a village, in fact the people lived mainly in a large and deep cave in the heart of a large rocky mountain. Its entrance was wide at front and narrowed towards the back, so the cave was ventilated. Day and night it was filled with the scent of plants and with fresh air. Inside, there was a clear stream flowing through it, which was very convenient for the people. In the cave's niches and crannies, families were separated by wooden planks and woven bamboo screens made of dry forest leaves. There were three large caves used as the marketplace, and two others were used for the transit station to welcome special delegations coming in and out of the southern battlefield and the Laotian front, an area called Interchange Station No 5 Truong Son.

The marketplace was located next to the stream. The

sight of it in such an unusual location and all of the sounds — the murmuring of the water, the villagers and the soldiers calling to each other as they traded goods — created a strange but vibrant scene in the eyes of any visitors.

Professor Doctor Dang Ngan found the scenery and the living conditions of the Lao Thom ethnic people charming. Sitting by a fire burning with fresh logs, smelling the sweet scent of flowers, leaves, and the natural resin in the logs was very pleasant. His host, the village chief, was a man whose age was difficult to guess; he could have been as old as sixty or he could be younger. He was of medium size and had a plump, square face with red skin and curly gray hair that spilled loosely over his forehead. As he sat next to him, Professor Doctor Dang Ngan kept gently squeezing the elder man's shoulder and asking him questions about the way people ate, slept, and lived in this place. But when the doctor asked about his family, the elder man burst into tears.

"My wife and daughter," he said, in understandable Vietnamese, "have leprosy. There are sores all over their bodies, so they were forced to go into the forest...hou hou...I am the village head, and I must obey the village's rules, doctor, but I am suffering a lot. I miss my wife. I miss my daughter...I love them...doctor."

Dr. Dang Ngan was impressed by what the village chief had told him about their food and drink. Now, after hearing about the way the man's wife and daughter had been exiled into the forest, he stood up, Touched by his offer, the village chief and some others accompanied Dr. Dang Ngan to a hut that was half roofed with palm leaves, half-submerged on the bank of a shallow stream. Inside, a woman in rags was lying on her side on a bamboo mat, nursing a child about two years old. Next to the bamboo mat was a bamboo woven rice basket and a dry gourd containing water.

The elder man and his villagers stood about ten meters away from the hut. He lifted up the food basket, intending to throw it in, but Dr. Dang Ngan stopped him. He took the food basket and calmly entered the shack, calling out "hello." The leper woman looked confused and muttered in Laotian, "I don't…don't know."

The Doctor approached her, picked up the baby, took a handful of glutinous rice from the basket, kneaded it into a lump which he bit into and then spit it into the little girl's mouth. Then he tore off a piece of the fragrant grilled stream fish and fed the little girl. He broke the ball of sticky rice left in the basket into two pieces and gave half to the leper woman, while he sat next to her and ate the other half. When he was finished, he explained to the headman and the other people that leprosy was not contagious. It could be cured if people took the right medicine and treated the sores and kept the skin around them dry. Then he asked The Cuong and the security guards to take the leper woman and her daughter back to stay in a hut by the cave entrance. Every day, he gave her medicine and sprinkled powdered penicillin on the sores. The whole village was happy that the little girl was able to go back to the old village of Loong Luong and to her siblings.

The market in the middle of the cave was always cheerful, day and night. Buying and trading vegetables, fruits, meat, and fish of all kinds, the villagers set up five charcoal stoves and large cast iron pans in which they cooked the bones, meat, and intestines of wild boar, flavored with lemongrass, ginger, cardamom, and assorted bitter and sour leaves. The aroma from the cooking made everyone hungry. The delegation, The Cuong, and the security squad enjoyed a delicious pot as they recovered from their long trek. Dr. Dang Ngan enjoyed the food while recording the daily recipes of the Loong Luong villagers. The village chief gave him all the vegetables, tubers, and fruits available for his research on developing anti-malarial drugs, based on the diets of the ethnic people of Laos, who were not tormented by malaria.

The fact that the village chief's wife had been cured from leprosy moved through the area like the aftershock of an earthquake. The Vietnamese professor's reputation as "someone from Heaven" spread through the villages of Lao Thom in Lum Bum area, which was why the cave where the medical delegation stayed was always crowded with people of all types: villagers, soldiers, young volunteers, and special mission teams moving in and out from North Vietnam to South Vietnam who were resting at Interchange Station No 5 in the cave. Whoever had an unknown or hard to cure disease came to see the Doctor, asking for medicine or advice.

One evening, while drinking some bitter tea from Lao Thom, sitting by a fire emitting the sweet scent of the forest, Dr. Dang Ngan was approached by a group of seventeen kids, from the age of six to fourteen, accompanied by two young, skinny soldiers, both of whom were limping.

The kids were the children of the Central Highlands cadres who were being sent to study in North Vietnam. One of the soldiers, about twenty years old and looking very weary and tattered, was toting a woven black rattan basket, the type used by ethnic minorities, on his back. In it was the youngest boy in the group, his bandaged foot sticking out of the rattan.

After he took the basket off his back and placed it on the ground, the soldier pulled the boy out and introduced him to the Professor. "Dear Professor, we were so happy to hear about your research for antimalarial drugs; we hope you will be successful soon. These are the children of the key cadres in the Central Highlands; they are going to study in the North. This is Y Nghien Booc from the Bahnar. He fell and hurt his legs." He pointed at a soldier standing with the group, "This comrade has had to carry him all the way from the Central Highlands; it was really hard. Is there any medicine you can give him so he can walk by himself, please?"

A girl in ethnic minority clothes, who looked to be the eldest of the group, lifted the little boy up and placed him in the professor's lap. The little one had black eyes full of wit and the air of an old, experienced person. He put his arms on the professor's shoulders, "Professor, help me. My feet hurt a lot!"

"You're small as a piece of candy. How do you know I'm a professor?" The Doctor smiled. "These kids who have lived in the battlefield are smarter and more cunning than kids who are well cared for and pampered in the town, right?"

The boy interrupted him: "Oh, professor, these two soldiers love me very much and carried me all the time. My father is Bahnar, he's chairman of the district…"

"Which one?" The Professor asked.

"It's a military secret! I won't tell you…" The little boy laughed, then grimaced in pain as the doctor removed the bandage from his foot. At that moment, the Loong Luong village chief came over and lifted the boy's feet. Without a word, he took out a bottle of yellow forest honey from his shoulder bag, pasted the boy's foot with the honey and re-tied the bandages. "Have something to eat, then go to sleep. Tomorrow you will be fine and can walk by yourself!" He handed the little boy a grilled mountain frog.

"Thank you, old chief," the boy chirped. He sat on the professor's lap and ate the frog, his eyes shining, "Look, professor, I only pretended to fall so that these two soldiers had to carry me, but I feel really bad about it. The road was too long and steep and I couldn't walk… hee hee . But now I can walk tomorrow on my own. I won't ask them to carry me on their backs any more. I will walk so I can get exercise to fight against the Americans like my father."

The Cuong saw those two soldiers look at each other. As for the doctor, he was fond of the wise, honest way the little boy talked. He hugged him and patted his head, "What a clever boy! He'll be very tricky fighting against the Americans! Look how he deceived these two of our own soldiers!"

Doctor Dang Ngan asked his assistant to give the Central Highlands children a pack of all kinds of necessary medicines. The two soldiers and the eldest girl in the group said goodbye to the professor and the village chief as well as The Cuong, and then led all of them to the cave of the 5th Interchange Station to have dinner.

The dining area was in a small cave with bamboo dining tables big enough for six people. All ate standing up since there were no chairs or benches. Guests or passers-by would have whatever was being served. The kids were hungry and in this comfortable place were very excited, laughing happily to each other. The little boy with the bandaged foot was the youngest one and the only one given a wooden chair to sit on. His meal came in the kind of large iron bowl the soldiers used to call a B52 bowl, full of rice and cassava soup.

When he finished his food, he stroked his stomach. "May I have this iron bowl," he asked. "I'd love to have a bowl this big so that I can eat a lot, grow up quickly, and go back home to fight against the Americans like my father."

"I'll ask my commander's permission. Go to sleep now and tomorrow, before going North, you'll have a big iron bowl." The nurse smiled.

That night, while all the kids fell asleep, the two soldiers used a rucksack as a table to write a letter to Professor Doctor Dang Ngan, under the light of their flashlight. They didn't dare to go inside to give it to him, but instead left the letter at the entrance.

The next morning, The Cuong picked it up and gave it to the Professor. He read it while having his breakfast. As he did, tears streamed down his cheeks and the old Professor covered his face, his shoulders trembling. The Cuong picked the letter up:

Tiger Spring

Dear Professor, Doctor Dang Ngan,

We two soldiers would like to be anonymous, and not to mention our unit. This is the first time we met you. We know that you had been living a very nice, prestigious, and happy life in Japan, but you left all that and followed Uncle Ho's appeal to return to Vietnam and join the resistance against the French and now, against the Americans. Hearing that, at the age of seventy, you volunteered to go to the war in order to research malaria medicine for the soldiers, we were so touched. But we must tell you: we are deserters. We are afraid of the war!

Besides combat, and besides being bombed, we suffered a lot from malaria. We tried to eat but it was impossible to eat; we tried to sleep but it was impossible to sleep. Three injections every day, each painful down to the marrow of the bone. We sweated from every pore but were still cold as death. When we had the fever, we were lethargic and threw up everything we ate. When the fever stopped, we woke up, feeling like fakers, pretending to be sick; we felt like we were starving, but there was nothing to eat. Quinine soaked in our sweat, our tears, together with the rain water, our clothes were stinky, terrible like the smell of dead mice.

We feel it is necessary to describe the effects of malaria in detail so that you can imagine how hard it has been for us on the battlefield. We hope that your research will soon be successful, and our soldiers could soon have anti-malaria medicine.

Dear Professor, we were embarrassed to meet you and the children from the Central Highlands. The boy we carried on our back wishes to grow up quickly so he can return to fight America. But as for us, we can no longer stand the fierce and arduous life of the battlefield. We have no tomorrow; we don't know if we will live or die. We feel it is better to die, instead of suffering the fear of bombs and malaria.

We are truly sad and humiliated, but we will separate ourselves from the war. We don't know where we are going, to where we can return. We just know that we need to get away. But we wish you and the delegation every success, and we hope you will forgive us, the cowardly ones who'd had a chance to meet you..."

The Cuong passed the letter to the Professor to finish reading, then in anger, he crumpled it and threw it into the fire.

As he departed, the confidential confessions of the two young deserters made the Professor's heart ache. In the car, he remained silent as the car bounced over bumps. It was a different attitude for him; normally he liked to joke, tell humorous stories, and recite poems that he had just composed so that the driver and his companions would not fall asleep, and so they would be less scared when going along dangerous roads. His melancholy silence made the military driver feel anxious and insecure, and he loosened his grip on the steering wheel, enough to swerve a little from the track of the Zin 157 that was running ahead of them. At that, The Cuong had to persuade the Professor to move to the Zin 157 to ensure safety. That calmed down the military driver, and he kept on track, which helped the three romantic artists to be less stressed, less pale from fear.

In order to cross Road 128 where it was heavily mined from Lum Bum to Se Pon, they had to go underground. As they were turning, the Zin 157 was spotted by American aircraft which swooped down, dropping bombs and strafing. The Cuong pulled the Professor out of the Zin 157 and carried him to the side of the road. Just as he lay down on top of the professor, a piece of shrapnel hit his left thigh. At the same time, he suddenly felt the weight of another body pressing down on him, and then yet another pressing on the person above him.

The American planes finished their run and flew away. Everybody rushed out of the shelters by the side of the road to lift off the three people lying on top of the Professor. Crushed by them—there were two guards and The Cuong—it took a moment for the Professor to open his eyes. Meanwhile, The Cuong had fainted and was bleeding profusely. First aid was applied to stop the bleeding.

The delegation returned to Tiger Spring cave, where the Professor and his assistants brought The Cuong to the first aid station. Professor Doctor Dang Ngan operated on him. His leg was only attached by a piece of skin on his thigh, so the Professor had to amputate the leg. Afterward, the Professor sat aside and cried. Old people were like that, always apologetic and regretful, touched by sudden situations.

He knew that the cost of his own survival was borne by the three soldiers who were willing to die for him by covering him with their own bodies. He was very sorry for the one who lost a leg because of him, and he wept, touched by the comradeship of these comrades-in-arm, the humanity, and the noble sense of responsibility for him exhibited by the soldiers on the battlefield. Whether he wept tears of grief or tears of happiness, he didn't know.

Epilogue

It was during peacetime that the now General Huu returned to Tiger Spring to take part in a ceremony awarding the title of "Hero of the People's Armed Forces" to the Tiger Spring Medical Station. As he prepared for this trip, Huu was filled with different emotions. He was dying to meet Lan and Le. It had been more than forty years since they said farewell. Both happy and bitter memories played out like slow motion films right in front of his eyes. Their images, their voices, their embraces sometimes so warm, sometimes so cold, lingered The way he kept remembering and imagining them made this reunion in the fierce battleground of the old war seem to be something sacred and precious.

Then another mood emerged, giving Huu many sleepless nights before his departure to Tiger Spring. Secretly he hoped that Le and Lan would not attend the event. That way people would still remember them as two young girls in their late teens, slim and fair, with two long braids, and sweet voices speaking cheerfully in a Nghe An dialect. That way they would remain in the eyes of the veterans revisiting the battlefield as two sacred and immortal monuments to youth, purity, innocence, and indomitable and resilient heroism. Such a monument of youth would not be carved into the space of the mountains and forests, would not appear in heaven and earth, but would be carved forever into the minds of every person who had lived and fought there.

As it were, the reunion of the veterans at the Tiger Spring battlefield that day was held without the presence of Lan and Le. Like the wild flowers, like the birds flying somewhere in the sky, they had left no trace. No one, including Mr Dat, Head of the Tiger Spring Medical Station, had any news of them and somehow the atmosphere of the Heroic Award to Tiger Spring Medical Station seemed less cheerful.

That was the way Huu was feeling when suddenly a hand grabbed Huu's arm with a sold grip. He turned around to see the tanned face, tousled hair, and clear eyes of a person talked in a familiar low voice: "Cadre Huu! Have you forgotten the Bong Va villagers? But we and the other people in the region have not forgotten you…"

Huu was taken aback for a few seconds, and then he flashbacked… the dead forest, the mosquitoes, the flies, the slugs, and the wrasse… the dead bodies in the cave… the Bong Va village… the smell of frying buffalo meat of that meal, the eyes of the elder Huu quickly embraced the man, "I do remember. You are Ho Tech, you were the one who lit the torch to welcome us. I remember… I remember…" Huu choked, his sound muffled, a bit sad and ashamed.

"Cadre Huu, where is cadre Hoan?"

Ho Tech's question hit like a stone straight into Huu's

chest. Hoan, such a close friend through life and death, sharing all the sweet and bitter memories of fighting on the battlefield.

He was gone. Huu himself had carried his corpse into the cave, buried Hoan in a grave covered by the stones of Tiger Spring. But he had forgotten him. All the memories of him here, in the mountains and forests of Tiger Spring, in all the emotional turmoil of the Truong Son battlefield. Huu's mind raced from one memory to another, from this person to another person, this comrade-in-arm to another...this event, that story, a jumbled patchwork with no beginning and no ending, now crowded in his head.

He had to try to reimagine and remember Hoan's face. Hoan had looked like this, or like that. And thinking of their friendship now, Huu felt warm, less guilty, and regretful that he had not gone to guard Hoan and Lan during their rendezvous. He comforted himself that the important thing was that in his heart, Hoan was his closest friend. That was enough. Then he lied to Ho Tech, Pung appeared in his mind. "Ho Tech, is old Ho Pung still alive? I guess he is no more..."

"Our village chief passed away a long time ago..." Ho Tech had tears in his eyes, "when he was alive, he kept reminding us of cadre Huu and cadre Hoan...he talked about you and missed you a lot...poor old man..." Then, as if he just remembered something important, he hurriedly opened the canvas bag slung over his shoulder, rummaged through, and took out a piece of paper wrapped in several layers of plastic and handed it to Huu. "I knew that you would probably return for this big ceremony, so I come to wait for you. This is the receipt that cadre Huu wrote stating you took a buffalo from our village, and promised to pay five kilograms of rice, one kilogram of salt, and ten kilograms of glutamates to the villagers…"

Huu felt dazed. He turned pale, though not from fear or surprise. He trembled with immense sadness on receiving this note of debt and stood embarrassed facing this austere, small, and skinny old ethnic man. The debt was not about financial value. It was about a debt of gratitude to the ethnic people, to the old village chief of Bong Va village; not paying it was a huge mistake and he was the one who committed it. He was such an ingrate that when he was at the peak of glory, he had easily forgotten responsibility: forgotten memories, forgotten the painful imprints of the past, forgotten difficult days, forgotten the sharing of joy and sorrow of his comrades, his compatriots on the roads he had passed by. A quick thought appeared, very fast, but enough to leave a tormenting wound in his heart, a regret, guilt, and a pain…an insufferable pain.

He stared at the note for a while. The paper was yellowish, blackened and crumpled, then carefully folded. He inserted it into his wallet like a treasure. "Please help calculate for me," he said to Ho Tech, "how much would five kilograms of rice, one hundred kilograms of salt, and ten kilograms of glutamates cost now?"

Ho Tech raised a calloused, bony hand and pressed his knuckles to his forehead, mumbling calculations. "It must be thirty million dongs, including the transportation cost to the seller. I wonder if that is too expensive for you? Now a big buffalo costs only seven or eight million dong, cadre."

Ho Tech's honest words were like salt rubbed into the wound in Huu's aching heart. He took a roll of fifty million dongs from his bag and passed it to Ho Tech. "Take it and buy me everything you have told me, and for the rest, please buy gifts for Bong Va villagers from me. I apologize to the village chief and his relatives many, many times. I am sorry, I am sorry, Ho Tech, please tell the villagers to forgive me…"

That short meeting with Ho Tech was for Huu like the light of the sun shining and dispelling that easy human habit, shared by Huu himself, of easily forgetting the past, easily forgetting all the joys and sorrows during a historic period of life. His only comfort was the thought that human life passes quickly, and people worked hard at trying to only live in the present.

But memories still haunted him, left a lingering bitterness in his heart until the last day of his life.

* * *

It was another day of peace, when there was no more gunfire and bombs on the southern border nor the northern border of the country, that the veterans of the 26th Reconnaissance Company had a chance for a reunion. They were all a bit strange to each other at first glance, but then they recognized each other in their eyes, in which still burned the memory of the fire of the war years. They approached and hugged each other, smiling, tears streaming.

"Have all our old comrades-in-arms passed away? Out of more than one hundred, there are only a few dozen here,"

They were astounded, bewildered. They had no need to name the missing, but those still alive were tormented with the same question.

Former Political Commissar Mao dragged his weary feet over to each person, and his breath catching, asked, "Who are you? In which platoon, which battalion?"

His post-war life had been long and full of burdens. When asked about his family, he would just shake his head and say, "Just like everyone else, I am old now, I am going to meet my ancestors soon, it's over…"

Suddenly, someone dressed in an old, worn-out uniform, with ill-cut shaggy hair, an innocent face, white, crusty eyes, a crooked mouth, and trembling limbs, walked up to Mao. "Dad, I'm hungry," he stammered…"Dad."

All the veterans looked at this person who seemed neither an adult nor a child: it was hard to guess his age.

"This is my son," Mao said. "I was infected with Agent Orange on the battlefield, so he was born abnormal. Now he is forty years old, but clings to me all day, like a shadow."

"You were infected because you refused to drink the bulls' urine like us," Huu said. "Commander Tuan taught us to use the bulls' dung liquid, bison, and all kinds of insects to make our immune system stronger, and afterwards our children were normal. Anyway, dear Political Commissar…the war is long gone, Sir."

Tuan "the Beard" pensively said, "Listen! How can we say, "it's over". Mr. Mao has had three daughters…they are all infected by Agent Orange. The eldest and the second one could only lay in bed for more than thirty years now…live third one can walk, but she is deaf and dumb, with squishy, "Poor comrade Mao. After being suffered greatly through life and death a few times on the battlefield, demobilized and discharged after the war, then go back home to get married…only to give birth to Agent Orange infected children, one after another. Whomever is more unhappy than his wife or him?"

Former Political Commissar Mao blushed, trying to smile, "We have thought that Agent Orange had been heavily infected on our first child only, but it kept on going. My wife desperately wanted to have a son, and that's it." He slammed the table and said: "In reality, my wife and I never committed no sins…it's all because of the war."

Tuan went on insightfully, "Comrade Mao was honorably discharged as a ranked Captain, so with a modest pension, plus the war invalid allowance, and the Agent Orange compensation…raising four deformed children all of their life is not easy at all. Since mobilization, more than 100 comrades in our Company, many were killed during the war, and during the postwar time, some more have passed away for other reasons. Today, among some dozen left, most are not wealthy…but with our tradition of loving and caring for each other, sharing the difficulties during hard times, so on this special occasion of our reunion, I would like to suggest that our "Veterans Association" should raise a fund and name it "For our Comrades-in-Arm" to be used for—Funerals (coffins, ceremonials, paying tribute), Visitations with each other when someone is not well, and especially to support whoever in particularly needed situations. Right now, it's urgent to support comrade Mao's family and some other fellow comrades…"

At that moment, former Battalion Commander The Cuong walked out with the help of crutches and informed the survivors that he volunteered to be the Chairman of the Veterans Association of the 26th Reconnaissance Company and would like to organize a trip back to Truong Son trail and especially to Tiger Spring.

Everyone applauded. Then Tuan pronounced, as if giving an order, "Let's assign General Huu, my then liaison agent of mine, and the now General, to organize the trip to the rung Son and Tiger Spring." He laughed, "Since you're now a General, you have to take care of your soldiers, right?"

Everybody applauded again.

* * *

So it was that on the first day of Spring, General Huu ordered two buses transporting more than 40 veterans of the 26th Company to revisit their former battlefield. Together with them was Tom, their former POW. After the war, he had wanted to visit the place of his former captivity, but it was not until today the normalization agreement between the two countries was signed that he could fulfill his wish. Tom was now over seventy years old, but chemical exposure from the war had left red lumps, like small tumors all over him. When he flipped his shirt up, he revealed patches of brown, red, yellow, and black scales all over his body. All, Tom said, from dioxin contamination as well.

He had been granted a monthly veterans' disability payment, got married to his long time beautiful girlfriend who had been waiting for him. So, life seemed to be settled down with happiness, but the one who had been waiting for four years to be his wife had silently left him after some months living together. The reason was that Tom had horrible nightmares every night, he was delirious, scared, screaming, kicking, or tossed and turned until dawn, or he kept awake through the nights, wandering along the corridor of the apartment. The war syndrome that continued haunted him, loaded in his heart and mind...terrified her so horribly that she had to leave him.

Confiding about his life, Tom said, "Maybe it's good for her to leave, what if we might give birth to the Agent Orange infected children like Mr. Mao's?" Then he turned to be humorous..."And if our children are healthy, they might be sent to a certain country to fight, since the US government loves fighting, to show that America is always the Number One...Superpower of the world, right?"

Listening to his arguments, the veterans laughed. Now they were friends instead.

The Veterans' Delegation arrived at Tiger Spring cave, which had now become a tourist attraction for those who want to explore Truong Son and the legendary Ho Chi Minh Trail. The caves were still there, vast, desolate, and cold, but there were no traces of the war. No more days and nights lit by bombs and bullets, jammed with people sheltering inside. Instead, there were thousands and thousands of bats that returned every night. The war was over, the forest in Truong Son had revived itself. Tiger Spring itself was very clear, flowing and gently murmuring, rows of green trees along both sides. The dozen males and one female squirrel that had been there originally had expanded into hundreds of thousands, chasing each other along the rows of ripe red stamese-rough fruits. Tom insisted on revisiting the stream where he had bathed and shown his naked body to the young girls of the Tiger Spring Medical Station. But this time, Tom jumped into the stream fully clothed.

"Hey, why don't you strip down and show off your huge "potatoes" anymore," asked Tuan, and The Cuong, laughing, translated for Tom.

"No no, no, no…I'm old now, I don't like women anymore…" Tom answered, his face reddening so much he seemed to be choking, "To tell the truth to you Vietnamese veterans, 'that one' of mine was affected by toxic chemicals as well, and it atrophied a long time ago. Please don't talk about the pain of the war anymore; it's too sad. Thankfully, we are all veterans now."

Then Tom asked Tuan and Huu, as well as The Cuong, the now Chairman of their Veterans Association, to go back to the cave where he had been so scared of the geckos' cries. They went back to the huge Tiger Spring cave, with its many niches, moldy and cold, with no trace of the heat of war so many decades ago. Tom shivered. There was no sound of geckos during the day, and the bats only flew back at night time, so all they could only hear were the crows' cries "caw…caw…caw" from every corner.

The men's entry stirred up the crows, who flapped their wings and flew out like ghosts. These Trung Son crows had fed on so many corpses, human and animal, that they were as big as mallard ducks. Their dry, sharp cries chilled people. Thick layers of crow and bat guano covered everything, leaving a sour, rotten stink that so nauseated Tom that he vomited and rushed out. Only Tuan and General Huu continued on, straight to the niche where Hoan had lived.

The traces were still there, but as they moved the rocks apart, they could see no remains inside. Even the stele with Hoan's name and date of death on it had been taken away. "I am sure that Lan and Hoan's child brought his remains back to their hometown, Tuan," General Huu said.

Tuan was paralyzed with sadness. Silently looking at the trace of the grave, he turned to Huu, "As a General, you'd be able to look for Lan and her child in Ha Tinh province. When you know where they are, please tell me so that I can come and light some incense-sticks for Hoan…it is so sad that he is no more, but anyway, he has a child, and I hope that he has a son, to continue bearing his family name…"

* * *

Afterward, the delegation went to the Ta Le underground of the Determined to Win Road 20. The Cuong was very touched to be there. Even though he had only one good leg, the other a prosthesis, he determinedly led everyone underground, down to the big iron bars lined up next to the stream in the center of the Ta Le underground. The sound of the rushing stream so terrified Tom, the former American soldier, that he clung to the fence, afraid of being washed away. Tuan had to help him move on with a push. "Come on, don't be afraid."

It was here that The Cuong stopped and spoke to the

group, "Let's imagine our young girls in their teens and twenties, how whether day or night, when they heard the sound of the bombs from the American planes exploding, they would rush out here and stand in a line, acting as guideposts to indicate the way for our convoys to pass. Under the rain of bombs and rockets, in such a fast flowing stream, how did they manage to stay alive? Mai Nhung, my late girlfriend, was here for one year, four months, and twelve days. On the 15 February of 1973, Mai Nhung was standing as a guidepost and was swept away…There was no iron fence in those days…" The Cuong covered his face, unable to continue. It seemed that his tears had sunk into his heart.

Tuan lit a large bunch of incense-sticks, gave each man a stick, and then folded his hands and bowed in four directions as he prayed, "Dear comrade Mai Nhung and all our comrades in the army, dear young volunteers, and civilians who passed through this Ta Le underground, you lived and devoted your lives and sacrificed yourselves. Please accept the gratitude of those of us who survived, knowing that surely you are still living forever in our hearts."

The half-burned incense sticks were dropped into the fast-flowing stream of Ta Le underground. All felt sad, painful, and regretful. All felt guilty for neglecting what they should have done for the dead, for forgetting to make a wreath, even one of just wild flowers picked along the way to console the dead souls; all those who had poured out their blood and left their corpses here.

The Cuong, heavily supporting himself with his crutches, hobbled step by step onto the bank. He consoled himself that he had been able to come here before the end of his life to say farewell to his girlfriend. Death had taken the person most precious to him. War was so cruel, it took away so many things from human beings, like a fire burning through a green meadow, leaving only dark patches of soil.

* * *

The last mission of the Veterans of the 26th Reconnaissance Company In Truong Son was to look for the grave of Doctor Lien in the Truong Son Cemetery.

Among the thousands of graves lined up horizontally and vertically with steles with or without names in the immense cemetery located next to road 9, the bloody road of the Truong Son Trail, the grave of Doctor Hoang Thi Lien was located among the graves of martyrs of the 70th Youth Volunteer Team who died on Determined to Win Road 20 of Truong Son Trail.

The veterans covered Doctor Lien's grave with flowers. Among the wreaths placed, one was from Tom, the POW who had been given first aid and taken care of by Doctor Lien in Tiger Spring Medical Station.

As for Tuan, he placed a wreath of white flowers on Lien's grave, burned three incense-sticks, and prayed: "Dear Lien, it's you who has taught me how to live happily. My wish to come and light the incense-sticks, to lay a white flower wreath for you is now fulfilled. You'd lost your virginity not for love. I beg your pardon one more time. Please forgive me, please forgive those who are living, dear Lien. It was all because of war, dear."

Huu Uoc

That night, all the veterans, together with Tom, stayed in the guesthouse of Truong Son Corps, quite close to the Truong Son Cemetery. It seemed that no one slept that whole night. Their hearts were loaded with melancholy and haunting memories of the pain and the sorrow of war. The sky was dark, with heavy clouds and cold wind blowing through the mountain sides at night, which made them feel colder.

Near dawn, when the whole mountainous area of Truong Son was covered by a thin, pale mist, there suddenly appeared a pink cloud shining between them and the Truong Son cemetery. And the pounding footsteps of an invisible army echoed all around them…

August 19, 2021
—HUU UOC

About the Author

Huu Uoc was born in 1953 in Phu Cu District, Hung Yên Province. Vietnam. In 1970, he enlisted in the Army of North Vietnam and was based, until 1974, in the Vietnam-Laos war theatres (east and west of Truong Son mountain range). When the war ended in 1975, he studied in Mass Media at the University of Vietnam. In 1980, he was assigned as Head of the Newsroom Department of the People's Police—Vietnam.

In July 1985, he was imprisoned by the Vietnam Government for publishing an article against the People Police on a negative issue. From 1986–1988, Huu Uoc was put on trial three times by the government.

On 17 May 1988, thanks to the change of the Communist Party of Vietnam's "Reform Policies or Doi-Moi", he was declared "Not Guilty and Presumed Innocent." The Government restored his standing as a Party Member, and he returned to his position with the newspaper where his career flourished.

In 1996, he was promoted as Editor-in-chief of the World Security Newspaper; in 2003, he was assigned as Editor-in-chief of People's Police and People's Police Television National Network; in 2006, he was promoted as Brigadier General of the People's Police VN; in 2008, he was awarded the National Medal – Labour Hero of Vietnam; in 2009, he was assigned as Deputy General, Department of the Political Department of the People's Police; and in 2010, he was promoted as Lieutenant General of the People Police and Honorable Chairman of the Police Writers' Affiliation.

In addition to his successful career, Lieutenant General Huu Uoc spent his personal time as a writer and artist. Among his literary works and arts, he has created:
- 6 Collections of Poems
- 4 Reportages and Short Stories
- Two novels: *Destiny* (three volumes) and *Tiger Spring*
- 19 film scripts and stage scripts
- 27 songs
- 500 lacquered and oil paintings.